THE
GIRL
IN
THE
GROUND

BOOKS BY STACY GREEN

THE GIRL IN THE GROUND

STACY GREEN

bookouture

Published by Bookouture in 2021

An imprint of Storyfire Ltd.
Carmelite House
50 Victoria Embankment
London EC4Y 0DZ

www.bookouture.com

ISBN: 978-1-80314-095-7
eBook ISBN: 978-1-80314-094-0

PROLOGUE

The little girl played in the sand, looking for the small, shiny river rocks that always washed up on the shore. She loved all the different colors, but today she had a mission. She wanted to find gold, just like Laura Ingalls had done on an episode of *Little House on the Prairie*. That had been right here in Minnesota, and the little girl was certain that she could find some too. She just needed to be patient and keep her eyes open. She brushed her hands against her swimming suit. Sand caked her hands and fingernails; Mommy would make her do the dishes tonight if she didn't get the dirt out from under them.

"Come here."

She shaded her eyes so she could see her older sister better. "Why?" Petunia had spent all morning bragging that she got to wear a pretty, yellow two-piece swimsuit, and the little girl had to wear her sister's old baby swimming suit. She didn't want to hear about how pretty the yellow looked against Petunia's brown skin or how the ruffles bounced when she walked. She just wanted to find gold.

"Because I said so," Petunia huffed, hands on her hips. The little girl knew she might as well go see what she wanted. Petunia was three years older and bossy, but she still loved her big sister. She walked barefoot over to where Petunia stood.

Petunia put her finger on her lips. The little girl knew that meant "be quiet," so she tiptoed the rest of the way. Her sister motioned for her to come closer, so she did, peering over the big, fallen log. "Is that a nest?"

"Yup," Petunia said. "See that black and white duck over there? Pretty sure she's the mama. She looks like she wants to protect her family. That's why I said be quiet."

She eyed the duck floating along the water, her little feet flapping beneath the surface. Her black feathers gleamed under the sun. The little girl inched forward. "Do ducks attack people?"

"No, dummy. But I don't want to stress her out anymore." Petunia grabbed her hand. "Mom said to come back at two and it's"—Petunia looked at her Mickey Mouse watch—"and it's two thirty. We have to go."

Petunia grabbed her hand and tried to drag her away, but the little girl couldn't move.

"Tunie," she whispered. "There's a man watching us."

ONE

Endless water was all around her. Nikki was sinking down, pulled by the weight of her clothes. The cold water felt like a million knives slicing into her exposed skin. She flailed her arms only to sink farther. Her body felt like lead, as it slowly dropped to the bottom of the lake. All she could think was what would happen to Lacey now?

"Nicole?"

Nikki shook her head, yanked back into the present by her therapist's voice. "I'm sorry. What did you say?"

The older woman crossed her legs and leaned back in her chair. "We've talked at length about how Lacey feels about tomorrow. But how do you feel?"

Nikki didn't know what to say. Three months ago, a serial killer had killed Nikki's ex-husband and kidnapped her five-year-old daughter. She'd nearly died saving Lacey's life. With her boyfriend Rory's encouragement, she'd taken a leave of absence from the FBI, and she and Lacey had spent the last few months trying to heal. But Nikki had to go back to work tomorrow. As much as she loved her job, it was going to be hard.

"I'm okay," Nikki finally answered. "Lacey has bonded with my boyfriend's parents, so she'll be staying with them during the

day while Rory and I work. I know she'll be safe." Rory's parents
had been a godsend since Tyler's death. Nikki hadn't been sure she
would ever have the chance to start over with the Todds, but death
and tragedy often brought people together.

"Have you and the Todds actually talked about the past?"

Nikki wanted to tell her that it was okay to say it: the murder of
her parents. Rory's older brother Mark had spent twenty years
wrongly imprisoned for their murders; DNA evidence had finally
exonerated him earlier this year. Nikki had spoken on Mark's
behalf, and he'd been released with a clean record. He'd also
received a very lucrative monetary settlement from the state of
Minnesota, which he used to buy his parents a new house on five
acres.

Both Rory and Mark had long forgiven Nikki. It was her testimony that had sent Mark to jail, but they both understood that she
was just a child. Their parents, however, had refused to speak to
her, until they'd met and fallen in love with Lacey. They might
have struggled to understand her and Rory's relationship, but they
could accept it if it meant they got a sweet little five-year-old to
spoil.

"Some," Nikki answered. "There's not a lot more to say.
They've been so kind since everything happened, and I don't feel
like I have the right to push them to talk about the past."

The therapist smiled faintly. "And how are you doing? Are you
looking after yourself?"

"I'm trying to eat right and sleep. I exercise as much as I can."
Nikki shrugged. "What else am I supposed to do?"

"Keep doing those things," the therapist said. "Especially since
you're going back to work. Your job is demanding, but you still
have to find time to rest and keep an eye on your health."

On her way out, Nikki stopped at the front desk to schedule
her next few appointments. The worst part about therapy was the
way she felt afterwards. Absolutely wrung out. She wanted
nothing more than to go home and take a nap, but if she did she

wouldn't be able to sleep tonight, and nights were already hard enough.

As she waited for the patient in front of her to finish, she dug around in her bag for her phone. Going back to work meant a full schedule, and she wasn't sure when she could come in next. It would be a risk to schedule too many appointments in advance. She decided to make an appointment for the end of next week. That would give her almost two weeks to settle back in at work.

Nikki's heart lurched into her throat when she saw three missed calls in the last thirty minutes, all from Rory, and a fourth missed call from Lakeview Hospital in Stillwater.

Hands shaking, she hit the redial button and prayed Rory would answer. Had something happened to Rory or Lacey? Nausea rolled through Nikki.

"Hey, baby." Rory's voice sounded strained. "You get my message?"

"I didn't even take the time to listen to it. What's wrong? Is Lacey okay?"

"Shit, yes, she's fine. Sorry, I didn't think you might see my calls and think something was wrong with her. Yes, she's with Mom. I just had a little accident at work."

Nikki sagged against the wall, her knees still weak at the idea of Lacey being injured. "What sort of accident?"

Rory owned a successful construction company, and recently, over a thousand acres of farmland and tree groves had been sold to a developer, and he'd been lucky enough to land the project to work on the site. He'd spent the last three months working with the developer to design a new bedroom community of high-end homes, and construction had started two weeks ago. Rory had been excited because the deal was lucrative—it was so expansive that all three of his crews would be working at the Heights, as they'd called it, for the next eighteen months—assuming everything went according to schedule.

"A stupid one, but I'll be fine. Just a few stitches. I'm trying to get discharged but it's taking forever. Can you do me a huge favor?"

"First tell me what happened," Nikki demanded. "You dodged that question."

He sighed. "I had a run-in with the jackhammer, and it took a chunk out of my leg. I'm getting stitches and then I'll head back out to the site. I need you to go meet Miller out there."

Rory was talking so fast and quietly that Nikki could barely understand him. "Why is the sheriff out at your construction site?"

"All I know is that after I left, my guys kept working. I got a text from my foreman that they found bones and that Miller's on the way out there."

"Bones? As in human remains?" Nikki asked; her shocked voice was louder than she intended, and the woman in front of her turned around and shook her head. The receptionist put a finger over her lips in a shushing motion.

"I don't know for sure, but my foreman's pretty freaked and nothing shakes him."

Forgoing the line and curious looks, Nikki headed outside, her phone cradled against her ear. "If Miller's headed out to the site, why do you need me to be there?"

"You're headed back from therapy, right? It's on your way. If you could just stop and see what the hell's going on, I'd just really appreciate it. God knows when I'll get out of here, and I can't have any more delays on this project."

Nikki knew that the rain had already delayed the ground-breaking by a week, and now Rory wouldn't be able to work on the area until the bones were collected. If the medical examiner decided the remains might be Native American, the entire project could come to a grinding halt. The McFarland family had owned the land for years, but multiple tribes had lived there long before that, and Rory had told her just the other day that the crew had found arrowheads at the edge of the site. "Let's hope they aren't human," she said, and reminded him about the complications if they'd uncovered a piece of Native American history.

"That would be even worse," Rory said. "They might not let me dig until I can prove that the site isn't a sacred burial ground."

Rory's mother had Apache heritage, and Rory had been brought up to respect the culture's customs. Even if the state allowed him to keep going, Nikki knew his conscience wouldn't if there were chances other remains might be found.

Thanks to the hot, wet air, Nikki was already sweating by the time she reached the jeep. She started the engine and turned up the air. "Well, try not to stress too much yet. They might not even be human."

Rory grunted. "Not with my luck." He paused. "Listen, I have to go. I'll see you over there as soon as I get discharged," he said and ended the call. Nikki was worried about him—he hadn't said "I love you," something he'd said to her every time they got off the phone since they'd found Lacey. Nikki felt silly, but she hadn't realized how much she was comforted by those words.

She'd only been to the Heights once, but Nikki remembered exactly how to get to the McFarland farm. It was one of those places ingrained in her memory from childhood. Every year, Nikki and her parents went to the McFarlands' pumpkin patch. After she and her father had picked out the perfect pumpkin to carve, they would get homemade apple cider and visit the animals. The McFarlands farmed corn and soybeans, but they kept several dairy cows in a large pen near the house, so the cows were used to people coming and going. One of Nikki's earliest memories was standing on the middle rung of the white fence, with her father behind her, trying to get the cows to moo back at her. Instead, the curious cow strolled up to the fence and licked Nikki in the face, sending her scrambling off.

Her father had belly laughed and nearly dropped Nikki while her mother frantically dug in her purse for something to clean Nikki's face. Tyler had loved that story when she told it on their first date. He'd grown up in the city, and he'd been fascinated by Nikki's stories of rural Minnesota.

Nikki bit her lip, fighting back her emotions. While her

marriage with Tyler just hadn't worked out, they'd remained friends and co-parents. He was a good man, an excellent FBI agent. Tyler had deserved so much better than to lose his life at the hands of a deranged killer. At least, she thought to herself, she'd put his killer in prison where he belonged.

TWO

As happy as she was for Rory to get the project, Nikki hated seeing the clearing where the McFarlands' rambling farmhouse had been. Stillwater had exploded in size since she was a kid, and while progress might be crucial to a town's survival, it was also a stark reminder of how quickly timed passed. It didn't seem all that long ago that Nikki had stood on the fence, getting licked by the cow. She drove past that clearing toward the back of the property, where Rory had first broken ground.

Work trucks lined part of the road, along with a couple of Washington County cruisers. She didn't see Rory's truck anywhere, so he must have driven himself to the hospital.

"Fantastic," Nikki muttered. She could see Ricky Fillenger standing in the shade of a big maple, looking at his phone. Ricky was a small-time drug dealer Rory had laid off last year for dealing at one of his construction sites. But the current project was so large that he'd needed every capable worker, and Ricky had sworn to Rory that he wasn't dealing anymore. Nikki had been wary, but Rory always saw the best in people. That was one of the things she loved most about him.

Nikki parked behind the sheriff's cruiser. She opened the door and immediately wished she had a hair tie. June in Minnesota was usually near-perfect weather, but humidity had set in this morning, and according to the weather forecast, the misery would last for several days. She locked the jeep and started toward the large white tent that had been set up near the back of the property line. It looked like they'd managed to dig out the hole for the foundation, but as far as she could tell, the crew hadn't gotten much farther. She kept her head down, hoping to slip by Ricky without having to deal with him.

"Hey, Agent Hunt, hold up," she heard him say.

Nikki bit the inside of her cheek to keep from giving Ricky a dirty look. He strode over to her, a smirk playing at the corners of his mouth. Nikki had had several other run-ins with Ricky: she'd considered him a suspect in in the murder of two girls several months ago and besides his drug dealing, he had several other misdemeanors.

"Rory ain't here," Ricky said. "He got hurt and had to go get stitches."

"I know." Nikki enjoyed a beat of satisfaction at the disappointment on Ricky's face. "He called and told me about the remains and asked me to come out. Any word on whether or not they're human?"

"They're human." Ricky stuck a wad of chew beneath his tongue. "I'm the one who found them. Foreman would have crushed 'em with the excavator, but I saw the slab and stopped him." He dabbed at his sunburned face with a dingy, red handkerchief. "Rory got the jackhammer and was trying to break up the cement. I told him just to bust it up with the excavator, but he wanted to know what was underneath the concrete. Good thing he kept going, I guess."

Nikki wasn't following. She shaded her eyes and looked up at Ricky. "You're saying the bones were under a slab of concrete? Was it an old headstone or something?"

"Honestly, it looked to me like someone mixed a bag of cement and poured it on top." He eyed her, his gaze lingering on her chest a beat too long.

"How did you see the actual remains?" Nikki asked, irritated with his cryptic words. "If someone poured cement on top of them, the body would have fused with it." She pointed toward the tent, where she could see someone from the medical examiner's office working. "She's digging over there, so I'm guessing that didn't happen."

"Nope," he said. "The cement was poured on top of a few inches of dirt. And the bones are in a big trunk."

So much for the remains being Native American, or even just an old grave. If Ricky was right, they'd likely found a murder victim. As much as Nikki wanted to argue that didn't necessarily mean the remains were human, the odds weren't sounding good. Despite the delay it would mean for Rory, the investigator in Nikki seemed to spark back to life. This was what she knew, what she was good at. As important as the past three months had been in Lacey's healing process, Nikki had felt like a caged animal at times, trapped with her guilt. "I'll go talk to the sheriff and see what I can find out."

Nikki headed toward the white tent. Sheriff Kent Miller stood beneath it, the back of his uniform damp with sweat. A woman from the medical examiner's office knelt on top of a blue tarp, examining a small bone.

"Hey, Sheriff." Nikki made sure to stay on the outside of the yellow tape. She'd come here as a favor for Rory, and she wasn't going to get involved unless Miller asked for the FBI's help. Nikki and Miller had attended the same high school; she hadn't known him well back then, but they'd worked a few cases together in Still-water over the last few months. "Got a minute?"

Miller looked back her, half grinning. "I appreciate the respect but ignore that tape and come look at this. I still can't believe it."

Nikki ducked under the tape and walked over to join him. "The remains were in a trunk?" she asked.

"Still are," he corrected her. "They'll go to the medical examiner's office. I've already talked to Blanchard, and she's going to bring in the bone doctor too."

Blanchard was the chief medical examiner for Washington County and one of the best pathologists Nikki had worked with, but given the skeletal remains, they'd need a forensic anthropologist if they had any hope of figuring out how the victim had died.

The inside of the trunk appeared to be in good condition, although it definitely didn't appear to be an antique. "Kent, feel free to send the trunk to the FBI lab. Courtney can try to find fingerprints or trace evidence." It was a long shot, given the cement had been poured over the top and down the sides. Washington County had a good forensics team, but they didn't have Courtney, who was one of Nikki's team. She could extract tangible evidence from just about anything.

Wishing she'd grabbed a pair of latex gloves, Nikki knelt to get a better look at the remains. Collecting bones was a painstaking process, as each piece had to be labeled and bagged as evidence, so most of the skeleton was still in the trunk. The lack of flesh and biological materials cut down on the smell, but a foul odor of general rot permeated the air.

"The body was left in the fetal position," the death investigator said. "Given the fusing in the growth plates, I think we're probably looking at a teenager or a young adult."

The top of the trunk had been removed and lay on the tarp next to the hole. "This is leather, and not particularly old," Nikki said. "No scratch marks on the inside. Victim was either already dead or unconscious when they were put into this thing."

"Whoever put the body here was smart to choose this area," Miller said. "It's far enough back from where the original farmhouse was that no one would have seen, and before the reservoir was created, anybody could access the property from this end. I don't remember if McFarland had fences, but anyone who thinks of covering the trunk with cement and then dirt is probably going to know how to get around the fence. I assume you're here because Rory called you. Any idea when he'll be back?"

"He said he was getting stitches and the hospital was busy."

She touched the death investigator's shoulder. "Do you have any idea of how old the bones are?"

"It's hard to tell since it was in the trunk and somewhat protected from the elements. There doesn't appear to be any biological material left, so it's been here for a good while, I think." The death investigator held up a dirt-crusted locket. She wiped off the dirt with her gloved hand and then slipped the locket into a plastic evidence bag and handed it to Nikki. "This looks like the lockets we all had in high school."

"It does," Nikki said, trying to make out the details on the locket. It looked like sterling silver, the small clasp caked with dirt. "So there's a good chance the victim is female."

"I'm not authorized to make that determination. But in my professional opinion, yes, this is a female." The investigator's expression turned grim as she held up an evidence bag containing tiny, fragile bones. "These are fetal bones."

Nikki stared at the tiny fragments in the bag, fresh sadness washing through her. The woman who had been murdered had been pregnant. Nikki's mind raced with questions. Had this woman wanted her baby? Had she tried for years to get pregnant? She immediately thought about the victim's family—they had lost a daughter and a grandchild. How long had they been wondering what happened to them? If they were still alive, bringing the family closure was an absolute necessity. If Nikki had to go decades without knowing what had happened to Lacey... Her throat constricted, and she forced the thought out of her head. She reminded herself that Lacey was safe.

Nikki had seen plenty of horrific things in her law enforcement career but killing a pregnant woman and stuffing her in a trunk ranked among the cruelest.

"Good news is the jaw is pretty intact," Miller said, interrupting Nikki's thoughts. "Hopefully we can match the teeth to dental records."

"Call Courtney, she'll put you in contact with our forensic odontologist. If there's a missing persons report with dental records, he'll find it faster than anyone. The lab is at your disposal, and Liam and I will help in any way we can."

"Thanks." Concern flickered in Miller's dark eyes. "Tomorrow's the big day, right?"

Nikki tried to smile. "I decided starting back on a Monday was just bad luck."

"You sure you're ready?"

"I think so. I'm more worried about Lacey."

Her nearly six-year-old daughter had rebounded from her ordeal better than Nikki expected, but she also understood that her father had been murdered by one of the bad men that Nikki hunted down. She wasn't sure how Lacey was going to respond to Nikki going back to work.

"She doesn't understand why I'd go back to the same job that got her daddy killed, and she's afraid the same thing will happen to me."

Miller squeezed her shoulder. He had two daughters of his own and would do anything for them. "Your job did not get Tyler killed. It still would have happened," he said quietly.

"Still my fault," she said tightly. She shook her head, refusing to break down. "But that's a conversation for my therapist."

"What's Lacey going to do while you're at work?" Miller asked. Tyler's job in white-collar crimes had meant his schedule was more flexible than Nikki's, and he'd been more understanding with it than most would have been.

"She's grown pretty attached to Rory's parents," Nikki said. "She'll stay there during the day for now. I'm still trying to decide what to do about school." Lacey had attended kindergarten before Tyler's murder, and the school was close to Nikki's house. But without Tyler to pick her up after school, Nikki wasn't sure what to do. Lacey had always been a happy, social child who loved meeting new people. Before the murder, she would have adjusted to a new school just fine. But Nikki hated the idea of yet another major change in Lacey's life.

"By the way, Sheriff, I see that your nose is peeling," she said teasingly. "It only takes one good burn to get skin cancer."

Miller rolled his eyes. "You sound like my wife. Listen, tell Rory I'm sorry but this place is going to be shut down for a day or two until we're certain everything's processed." He looked down at the remains and sighed. "I have a feeling this one is going to be next to impossible to solve. We don't have funding for a cold case department."

"Liam and I will help in any way we can," Nikki said. "I fully expect to be stuck behind my desk for the next couple of days, dealing with paperwork and phone calls, but if I can't come out, I'll make sure he does. At the very least, we can get this person identified and give the family closure, assuming they're still around."

Nikki left Miller and his team to their miserable task and headed to the Todds'. She called Rory from the jeep and left a voicemail letting him know that Miller had things under control, but the site was definitely going to be shut down for a few days. She took the long way, skipping the busy interstate for the scenic two-lane roads. Her mind wandered on the drive. She hoped Rory's injury was as minor as he'd said. He was already going to be stressed about getting behind schedule, but an injury would add to the stress, and they'd all had enough to last a lifetime.

When Nikki was growing up, her family's farm had bordered the Todds', so it was still strange to see them living in a gated community. Mark had used some of his wrongful imprisonment settlement from the state to buy the brand new, single-story open-concept home for his parents. The home sat on almost an acre, and the sprawling yard had enough room for Ruth's flower garden and a swimming pool, along with the huge playhouse Rory and Mark had constructed for Lacey.

Nikki found Lacey and Rory's mother in the backyard, planting.

"Mommy." Lacey made a beeline toward her, still in her swimsuit and pool floaties. "Granny Ruth is putting in a butterfly bush. Do you know what that is? It's a big tree that butterflies like. It makes them come to the yard. Isn't that cool?"

Nikki forced a smile, barely managing to control her emotions. Lacey had come a long way in three months, and Rory's parents had a great deal to do with her progress. Despite Nikki's help in clearing Mark's name, they'd rightfully resented her and refused to be in the same room with her when she started seeing Rory. But when Lacey had gone missing, Ruth had helped Nikki—she'd seen that Nikki was a good person, far removed from the young girl she once was. She was a mother now, just like Ruth.

Ruth and Larry had offered to babysit Lacey while Nikki had her first therapy session. Nikki was certain her daughter wouldn't have done so well the past three months without them. "That's very cool. I'm sure it will attract all sorts of butterflies."

Lacey wrapped her arms around Nikki's waist and squeezed hard. "Where's Rory?"

Nikki wiped the smudge of dirt off her daughter's face. "Working, silly. It's the middle of the afternoon."

"But he called Granny and said that shit had hit the fan. What does that mean?"

Rory's mother tossed her gardening gloves on the ground and stood, stretching her back. "It just means that Rory's work is super busy right now, honey. Why don't you go in and get us some water while I talk to your mom?"

"Okey dokey." Lacey loved using the old-fashioned term she'd picked up from Rory's father. She ran into the house.

As soon as she was out of earshot, Ruth dropped her trowel. "Rory said something about finding bones?"

"Beneath concrete, in a trunk," Nikki replied. She decided not to mention the fetal bones. Ricky would ensure the entire town knew about the remains before the day was over, but only she, Miller, and the death investigator knew about the baby.

Ruth pressed her hand over her heart. "My word. Are you taking the case?"

"I told the sheriff we'll help in any way we can, but it's a cold case. They're very hard to solve. I just hope we can find out who she is."

Nikki spent the next couple of hours with Lacey and Ruth, helping pot her annuals.

When she first started spending time with Ruth, things had still been awkward between them. As a kid, Nikki had a good relationship with Ruth, who didn't mind having teenagers running in and out of her house at all hours. Larry didn't seem to mind either as long as they hung out in the basement rec room, but he was so quiet Nikki often had a hard time reading him. Before Mark's incarceration, it wasn't out of the norm for Nikki to go to Ruth for advice on things she didn't want to talk to her own mother about. They'd been slowly getting back to that point the past few weeks, chatting over afternoon coffee or in the garden. But today they were both quiet as they worked, letting Lacey do the talking.

Nikki knew Ruth was likely more worried about her son's injury than about what had been found on the site, but Nikki couldn't stop worrying about the victims. Things had just begun to feel somewhat normal, but she was afraid the girl in the ground would change everything.

"Like this, sweet pea." Ruth showed Lacey how to loosen the petunia's roots so they did better in the pots. "Pour a little water in before we put the flower inside."

Watching Lacey with Ruth always felt bittersweet to Nikki. The only grandparents she'd known were Tyler's, and while they loved her dearly, neither had the energy to keep up with her. Ruth was always on the go, just like Lacey, and teaching her how to garden had not only been a good way for them to bond, but it was a useful way to keep Lacey's mind off darker things.

"Rory's here." Lacey jumped up from her spot on the deck and raced out the front door. She'd always greeted her father this way, but this was the first time she'd actually run out to meet Rory.

The two of them had been worried that Lacey's grief over her father would lead her to feel resentment towards Rory—that he was trying to take Tyler's place. Instead, she'd grown more attached to Rory.

Nikki headed outside to find Lacey examining Rory's left leg. His jeans had been partially shredded below the knee, and the bandage stretched down his entire calf. "That looks like more than a few stitches."

"Eighteen," Lacey said, wide-eyed. "I'm going to count them when he takes the bandage off to clean it."

"Granny said dinner's almost ready." Nikki ruffled her daughter's hair. "Run in and help her set the table."

Lacey raced back into the house, and Rory leaned against the truck, taking the weight off his injured leg. He pushed his sunglasses on top of his head, and a bolt of worry went through Nikki.

Rory's face was pale, but his eyes were bloodshot, almost wild. "They're still getting her out of the trunk." His voice was hoarse, like he'd been crying.

"Skeletal remains take a while," Nikki said. "But there's a good chance we'll at least be able to identify her by dental records."

His green eyes met hers as he spoke sadly. "I already know who she is."

THREE

Nikki stared at Rory. "What are you talking about?" she asked.

"I knew it as soon as I saw the trunk," he said, his entire body tense. "The locket just confirmed it. I bought it for her."

"Who?"

"My high school girlfriend, Becky Anderson. I bought her that trunk because she needed it and didn't have the money. The locket was a Christmas gift."

Nikki's head spun, but she tried to think rationally. "Did you have her locket inscribed?"

Rory nodded. "On the inside. Did you look at it?"

"Not yet," Nikki said. "As for the trunk, it's a pretty basic leather trunk. I saw plenty of them in college. I think I even had one. Those things are more common than you realize. The trunk certainly doesn't mean it's her, and until we confirm that it's her locket, neither does it. Tons of women wear lockets and it looked pretty nondescript."

She fanned her shirt collar, hoping a tiny wisp of air would help ease the anxiety working its way through her. Rory was probably overreacting, but if he happened to be right about the bones, they were going to have a mess on their hands. "When was the last time you saw Becky?"

"Summer after graduation, 1997. We'd broken up, but she came back to town to see friends. I ran into her at the bowling alley." Rory looked up at the sky, his jaw tight. "I don't know if she came back to town or not after that, but I never saw her again."

"I think you're jumping to conclusions," Nikki said gently.

"But what if it's her, Nik?"

"Then her family will have closure," Nikki said softly. "That's the only way to look at it and not go crazy."

"Hardin asked me about her that fall," Rory said. "He said her family hadn't heard from her in a few weeks." He stared up at the hazy sky, worrying his lower lip. "He said they were probably over-reacting, but all I could think about was that Hardin put my brother in prison and he wanted to do the same thing to me. I blew him off, and then never heard any more about it. I just assumed she'd been found." He rubbed his watery eyes. "She deserved better than being dumped in a trunk in a shallow hole at the back of the cornfield."

Hardin had been the first deputy on the scene the night Nikki's parents had been murdered. Hardin's grudge against Rory's brother had led to Mark's wrongful imprisonment. Nikki couldn't blame Rory for his reaction to the man. "Then I'm sure it's not her. It's not like Hardin would have just backed off. And Miller will run her name and be able to rule her out pretty quickly." Nikki studied him. "You did tell Miller you believed it could be Becky, right?"

"Right."

Lacey appeared on the front porch. "Granny says come eat."

Nikki rubbed his back. "Try not to worry too much. I told Miller to call Courtney to fast track the investigation, but I'll call her myself too. She should be able to find out who the victim is from dental records."

"Don't mention Becky," Rory said. "If you really think there's a good chance it's not her, I mean." He jammed his hands in his pockets and stared at the ground. "People in this town know enough of my family's business already."

"I won't," she said and stood on her tiptoes to kiss Rory. She wanted to reassure him, but his half-hearted kiss sent a chill of foreboding down her back. Nikki wasn't sure she could handle another major catastrophe in their lives.

Rory had been quiet for much of dinner, along with Nikki. She was still processing what he'd told her. She should have told him about the fetal bones, but after what he'd said, she didn't see the point in further upsetting him.

It was late by the time they got home, and Lacey needed a bath. She'd scrubbed most of the dirt out of her fingernails before dinner, but her knees and arms were dirty. By the time she brushed her teeth, Lacey was so tired she fell right to sleep without remembering she wanted to count Rory's stitches.

Coming down the stairs, Nikki found Rory sitting at the kitchen table, staring at his beer. "She passed out," she said.

Rory took a long swig of beer. "Wish I could. My mind won't stop replaying the last time I saw Becky."

Nikki stood behind him, rubbing his broad shoulders. "Why don't you call Miller and see if he's found anything yet?"

He didn't respond, and Nikki could feel his muscles tense. "No."

Nikki dropped her hands and sat down across from him. "Why on earth not?"

"You really have to ask that?"

It took Nikki a few seconds to figure out what he meant. As an agent, she knew that Rory would be a person of interest if it turned out to be Becky.

"I found her. I'm the one who started with the jackhammer. I'm the one who bid for this project. They'll say I was trying to destroy evidence or something."

She understood his distrust given everything that had happened to his older brother. Mark spent twenty years declaring his innocence, and their family had nearly been destroyed. If she were in his shoes, Nikki would probably have the same misgivings.

She reached across the table and grabbed his hands. "Listen to me. Miller is trustworthy. He's not a bad cop like the one who ruined Mark's life," she said, referring to the man who'd essentially railroaded Rory's brother. "There is just no way he would do something like that. And my team will help as much as we can too."

"And you will, right?"

Nikki had been dreading this moment. She'd always walked a fine line at work—she'd been involved in more than one case that had become personal—but her boss hadn't been pleased with some of her decisions. He had more empathy than anyone else she'd worked with, including her mentor at the Behavioral Analysis Unit at Quantico, but she wasn't sure she could get away with working another personal case. "If the remains turn out to be hers, I won't be able to help very much. Not because you're going to be a real suspect, but because they'll have to rule you out. If I help and we actually find out who did this, we would run the real risk of a defense attorney getting the case thrown out because of my involvement."

Rory scowled. "Yet I'm not supposed to be worried about being screwed over like Mark?"

"No, you're not," Nikki said. "The two cases are entirely different, with entirely different investigators. But if it is Becky, don't you want her to get justice?"

He drained the last of his beer. "If it's Becky, it's too late for justice. I'm going to bed." He kissed her on the cheek and left the room, leaving Nikki on edge. She tried to remind herself that he'd had an extremely rough day and he had to be exhausted, but his overall attitude made her uneasy.

Nikki grabbed her laptop off the counter, her worry about returning to work nagging at her. She felt ready to go back and knew that even though she and Lacey had an uphill battle, they'd be all right because of their support system. But the idea of walking into the big FBI building in St. Paul amid the whispers and knowing looks made her skin crawl. The attention wouldn't be malicious, but the pity and assumptions made Nikki uncomfortable. It was a lot easier to deal with a straightforward jerk than a well-meaning colleague.

Resigned, she checked her work emails, something she hadn't done in a couple of weeks. Most people knew she'd gone on leave, but there were always requests for profiling assistance and appearances in her inbox.

She scanned the messages, making sure nothing urgent had come through. A familiar name caught her eye. Why in the world was Justin Nash emailing her?

Nash was a year ahead of her, but he was already a legend at Quantico by the time Nikki had arrived, since his grandfather had been among the first black FBI agents, and both his parents were civil rights lawyers. His sharp cheekbones and sculpted lips had also made him strikingly attractive to almost everyone at the academy.

The last Nikki had heard, Nash landed a coveted job at the Maryland office after graduation. New agents rarely had their choice of location, but apparently being a legend made a difference.

Nicole,

First off, please accept my condolences about Tyler. I'm sorry you have had to endure such a tragedy. I realize this is a terrible time to ask for a favor, but I've heard you will be back to the office this coming Tuesday. I'm working on a sex trafficking task force and could really use your help. I'll explain more in person, but I'd love a chance to sit down with you when I get into town next week and pick your brain about a couple of things. Work related only, I promise.

Nash had emailed late last week, but he'd likely called the office first. Nikki couldn't think of any other way he would have found out her return date. She couldn't help but roll her eyes at his last sentence. Nikki and Nash had begun flirting the day she'd walked into her first class at Quantico; they'd gone out a few times and had fun, but the relationship hadn't been serious. Once Nikki met Tyler, she hadn't given Nash a second thought. Tyler hadn't been as exciting as Nash, but he was trustworthy and loyal, and he and Nikki had bonded quickly. Even after the divorce, Tyler had remained her best friend.

She leaned back in the chair, rubbing her temples. Dealing with Nash was the last thing she wanted to do her first week back, but she remembered how relentless he'd been during their time at the FBI Academy and her curiosity was piqued. What business would a Maryland agent have in Minnesota?

She couldn't remember him mentioning any family in the area, but she'd only been half listening most of the time.

"May as well just deal with him and get it over with," Nikki mumbled to herself. She fired off a quick reply, letting him know she would be in the office by nine a.m. tomorrow. She planned on arriving earlier to get settled back in. The office was usually pretty sparse before nine in the morning, and Nikki hoped she could sneak back into the fray without too much fuss being made.

Had she made a mistake by not pushing Rory to tell the police about Becky and the locket? That information might help identify the remains, or at least ease Rory's worries. He'd already searched various social media sites looking for any sign of her, but so far hadn't found any. Nikki had assured him she might not be on social media or even on the grid, but it was odd not to find her anywhere. There were dozens of Becky Andersons, but so far none of them had belonged to the right Becky.

Nikki logged into the state's missing and unidentified remains database. Even if the remains belonged to Becky, a missing persons report may not have been filed, especially since she'd been a foster kid who'd moved away from her hometown. If she didn't see anything in the missing persons database, Nikki would check the various FBI databases for any records of Becky.

A big yawn made her eyes water. Should she really look for these answers? So far, she wasn't doing anything to jeopardize a case, but if she did find a missing persons report, did she pass the information on to Miller so he could expedite things? Should she tell Rory if she found something?

The professional answer was no, because if it turned out to be Becky, the best thing Nikki could do for Rory was to stay out of it and let Miller and Liam work the case. She didn't want to do anything to compromise Miller's reputation or his ability to put the right person away for the crime.

It was time to let someone else handle things. Tomorrow was a big day, and Nikki had to get some rest.

FOUR

She knew it was silly, but Nikki felt like she'd stepped into a spotlight as soon as she entered the FBI building. Every person in the building knew who she was, either because of the media circus around Tyler or her parents' murders or because she'd worked with them on prior cases. She knew that every single person in this building knew why she'd taken leave, and most probably knew she was coming back today. She'd arrived early this morning to avoid talking to very many people, so she waved to the security guard and practically ran to the elevator.

Major crimes occupied the entire top floor, and Nikki watched the buttons light up as the elevator ascended, sweat dampening the back of her neck. The doors opened and she stepped out, her cheeks heating. She scanned the sea of cubicles, relieved to see most people hadn't arrived for work yet. Her heart hammered against her ribcage as she walked slowly to her boss's office, dreading the awkward exchange. It was the first time she'd seen Special Agent in Charge Hernandez face to face since Tyler's funeral.

Hernandez's door was open; Nikki knocked and entered her boss's office. Hernandez smiled and gestured for her to sit. "Agent Hunt. It's good to see you. How are you and your daughter doing?"

Special Agent in Charge Victor Hernandez was Nikki's bureau chief, and he was probably the most even-keeled person Nikki had ever met. He was a perfect choice to handle the bureaucracy of the FBI, and Nikki had been lucky he trusted her enough to run her unit with little interference. Hernandez hadn't been happy with all of her decisions during the capture of Tyler's killer, and Nikki knew she was lucky that he had more patience than a lot of other supervisory agents.

"We're doing fine," Nikki said. "Just taking everything day by day." She felt too wired for small talk, and she needed to keep her mind occupied. "I'd like to start catching up on work if that's okay."

Hernandez eyed her. "You told me last week that you planned to ease back into things."

"I am," Nikki said. "I've got a ton of paperwork to do, and I want to get up to speed on cases."

"You don't have to rush back into the field," Hernandez said. "You went through a terrible trauma."

"I know. That's why I'm focusing on paperwork... for today at least," Nikki said. "My therapist thinks I'm ready, sir."

He sighed. "Agent Hunt, in the past, your personal history—while tragic—proved to be a valuable asset. You're able to identify with victims and their families on a level that many agents can't, and I believe that's essential to solving crimes. That's one of the reasons I wanted you to head the profiling unit, and it's also why I've let you work on some cases that many others wouldn't. I believed you could handle any situation."

Nikki balked. "You think that's changed?"

"I don't know," Hernandez said. "You had years to work through what happened to your parents. It's only been three months since you almost lost your child and... well, you know. I don't have to say it. My point is, no one is going to judge you if you need more time before getting back into the field. You're not going to be penalized or pushed out. I fought to get you here, and I certainly don't want to lose you. But I have to protect this office and the cases we work, and I'm sure you know what a defense attorney might do if there's any hint you weren't ready to be back on the job."

"That's why we have psychologists to evaluate us before we're allowed to come back to work," Nikki said dryly. She knew he was in her corner, but he was also in a tough spot. "I promise you that I'm ready, but if something changes, I'll step back."

"That's all I'm asking." Hernandez checked his watch. "Your return is well timed. An agent working on a trafficking case has asked for your expertise, and I think it's a great way for you to ease back into everything. He's probably waiting outside your office."

Nikki tried not to scowl. "Let me guess. Justin Nash?" Her email had explicitly said after nine a.m. Leave it to Nash to waltz in and demand her time. That attitude was part of the reason Nikki had never been serious about dating him at the academy. It was nothing more than good sex and the occasional real conversation.

So much for having time to settle in, she thought. "I better not keep him waiting, then," she told Hernandez and strode off.

Nikki headed for her corner office at the opposite side of the building and sure enough, Nash waited, leaning against the wall. "Good morning, Justin."

He turned and smiled, and for a minute Nikki felt like a brand-new recruit at the FBI Academy again. It was easy to develop a crush on Nash. "Nikki. I was starting to worry you'd changed your mind about returning today," he said with a smile that quickly faded. "I'm truly sorry about what happened to Tyler. How are you doing?"

"Fine," Nikki said, unlocking her office door.

Nash looked sheepish. "I was afraid you wouldn't want to see me."

"Because I was a notch for your bedpost forever ago?" Nikki laughed. "I was a willing participant." She hesitated, not wanting to appear rude. "Would you mind giving me a few minutes? This is the first I've seen my office in a while. I just want to get settled."

"No problem. Where's your break room? I'll grab us coffees. You still take too much cream and sugar?"

"Always," Nikki replied, and she watched him walk off. The pressure in her chest eased. She just needed a few minutes to decompress.

Nikki gestured for Nash to take a seat in front of her desk. She'd cleared it of mail, logged into the computer and set her phone on the wireless charger she kept in the office. She was surprised at how at ease she felt after so many months. "Your email mentioned you were working on a sex trafficking case."

Nodding, he sat down. "Yes, I partnered with the DOJ. Four years ago, the Department of Justice put together a task force consisting of various law enforcement specialists, with the goal of infiltrating sex traffickers—preferably the large networks operating throughout the country. A credible informant says a major player is operating out of the Twin Cities area. I'd like you to assist me with an interview and create a profile for the suspect."

"Who is the interview with?"

"A limo service owner. We believe he is using his business to transport trafficking victims."

Nikki wasn't sure if that meant he was taking girls to buyers, customers, or moving them from state to state. "It's going to be hard to profile someone from a single interview," she told Nash. "You mentioned an informant. Can I have access to her?"

Nash shook his head. "That's out of the question. She's in protective custody. I just need your help profiling this one guy."

Normally Nikki would insist on face-to-face interviews with everyone involved, because body language was crucial to reading between the lines and creating a profile, but she understood Nash was at the mercy of the DOJ and the task force.

"And you believe your informant's information is accurate?" Nikki asked.

"Absolutely," Nash said. "I'd like to talk to the driver this afternoon. Are you free for lunch?"

Nikki had hoped to spend the day in the office, but she might as well get back on the horse. "Text me the time and where to meet."

"Great." He stood to leave, looking awkwardly between her and the door. "You're not familiar with the case, and I know it makes it tough when I can't give you more details. But I just need you to observe him."

Someone knocked sharply, and then the door flew open. "Welcome back." Courtney strolled in carrying a large coffee and a box of pastries from Black Sheep Coffee in St. Paul, Nikki's favorite place. She stopped short, staring at Nash. "Is this a bad time?"

Courtney had been one of the first people Nikki brought on when she was asked to head up the criminal profiling unit several years ago. They'd bonded quickly, and Courtney had been one of the only people to know about Nikki's past for a long time. As the head of forensics, she was a jack of all trades most days, and she was a vital part of Nikki's team.

"I need to run anyway," Nash said. "I'll email that information to you, and you can let me know about this afternoon." He hesitated. "It's really good to see you, Nicole."

Nikki flushed, knowing Courtney was going to pounce the second the door shut. "You too."

He nodded at Courtney. "Agent Justin Nash."

Courtney's eyes widened, and Nikki inwardly groaned. No one had a worse poker face than Court. "Courtney. Forensics. At your service."

"Good to know." Nash grinned and then headed out the door.

Courtney waited all of two seconds to shut the door and then whirled on Nikki. "As in *the* Justin Nash?"

Nikki nodded. "The one and only. He's working on a task force and wants help profiling a suspect. Hernandez said I'd be happy to assist him."

"Makes sense." Courtney handed her the warm cup. "Caramel macchiato, extra caramel."

"Thanks." Nikki sipped the coffee, enjoying the sugary sweetness.

Courtney plopped down in the seat Nash had vacated. "So I have remains in the lab that Rory's crew found."

"I know," Nikki said. "I was there yesterday. Did you get anything from the trunk?"

"Not yet," Courtney said. "The cement ruined the top, obviously. It even leaked inside a little bit, but there's a serial number I'm trying to salvage. If I can figure it out, we can at least get a possible time frame. Blanchard called the forensic anthropologist, but he's at a conference for the next week."

Miller wouldn't be allowed to dip into his budget to bring in another forensic anthropologist for a cold case, Nikki knew. The odds of solving cases like this were slim, and, as sheriff, Miller had to account for every dime spent.

"I put him in touch with our forensic odontologist," Courtney said. "Miller's compiling a list of missing women in the area over the last couple of decades and sending it over. The skull and teeth are in pretty good condition. If we can find records to compare them with, I think we can identify her."

"What about DNA from her bones and the fetus?"

"I've got my assistant working on the adult female DNA." Courtney pursed her lips, trying and failing to hide her emotions. "I'm working on extracting a sample from the fetal bones. They're so fragile."

"You'll get it," Nikki said. "I have faith in you."

"Oh, I know I'll get the sample," Courtney said. "It just makes me so angry. And the chances of finding the person who killed them is miniscule."

Nikki agreed, but she hated seeing her normally bubbly friend upset. "Stranger things have happened, you know," she said.

"True." Courtney stood and stretched. "And karma does have a way of making things right, eventually."

Nikki's computer chimed. "Dang. He must have had that file ready to go."

"Who? Nash?"

Nikki nodded, cherry-picking the key points of the email for her friend. "Nash just sent me everything he has on his case. He has a list of a dozen girls between the ages of eleven and sixteen who are believed to have been trafficked by a network of individuals right here in the Twin Cities."

Courtney scowled. "Does he know if any of the girls on it are still alive?"

"A few are marked as deceased," Nikki said. "This list goes back to the late nineties."

"I remember how exciting it was to get internet in our college dorms," Courtney said. "It was life changing for students. Figures the slimeballs out there immediately started using it to buy and sell kids."

"Yep," Nikki said. "And even with all the developments in technology, we still have a hard time catching these guys because they're always a step ahead of us. Instead of snatching kids like they did in the nineties, they're luring them in online. They switch servers all the time—always hosted in another country where we have no jurisdiction—ensuring that we're always two steps behind. It's maddening."

"I assume they've gone through NamUs thoroughly?" Courtney asked. NamUs was the national databank for missing and unidentified persons.

"He didn't say," Nikki said. "But it's a federal task force, so I'm sure they have."

"Well, if you need any help, let me know. You know I'm a junkie."

Everyone had their way of coping with the demands of the job, like reading or biking or something relatively normal, but Courtney usually spent her small window of free time on the internet, combing through missing persons files and trying to match them with unclaimed remains across the country. The database was a great tool, but it was time-consuming with debatable payoff, so Nikki doubted the task force had spent much time on it, especially Nash. He never liked doing the tedious stuff that actually helped catch bad guys.

Courtney finished her own coffee and dropped the cup into the recycling bin Nikki kept in her office. "I better get to the lab. We're still testing the trunk for biological samples, and I don't want anyone touching it when I'm not there."

"Call me if you get something," Nikki said. "Thanks again for the coffee."

"No problem." Courtney hesitated at the door. "You're okay, right?"

"Work has always been a sanctuary for me," Nikki said. "I'm glad to be back."

"How's Lacey?"

"Better than I expected, honestly. Having Rory's family around has been a godsend."

"Good," Courtney said. "Hopefully I can get this cold case identified so he can get back to work."

After Courtney left for the lab, Nikki checked her email and responded to the pertinent ones. At least the past few months had been relatively quiet after a string of high-profile cases.

"It's good to see you behind the desk again." Liam Wilson, her partner, stood in the doorway. His navy dress pants and light blue shirt looked professional, but Liam's height and red hair still made him stick out in a crowd. He held up a paper bag and grinned. "I stopped at the bakery near my place and snagged some croissants. Pretty sure I got the last chocolate."

The croissants from a Vietnamese bakery in St. Paul were out of this world, and they sold out quickly. "You are awesome."

He laughed. "Well, there were three. I ate two."

Liam ate like he had a hollow leg, so Nikki wasn't surprised. "I can only eat one anyway or I'll be walking around with a stomachache. Guess who you missed this morning?" She opened the plastic container and inhaled the delicious scent.

"Courtney?" He pointed to the now empty coffee cup. "I picked up a couple almond ones for her."

"She'll be happy since she's stuck in the lab working on the fetal bones found in that suitcase where Rory's working." Nikki slathered butter on the croissant and took a bite. "God, I haven't had these in forever. So good."

"I know," Liam said. "Thankfully they're busy so I don't stop very often, or I might actually start gaining weight."

"Shut up," Nikki said between bites. "No woman wants to hear that, especially while she's stuffing her face."

Liam laughed. "By the way, Miller called me this morning and wanted to know if I'd be able to help out once the bones are identified. He said you guys had already spoken about it."

"Yeah." Nikki tried not to show her surprise at Miller calling Liam directly. She'd offered the team, but he knew she was back to work today. Unless the remains turned out to be tied to Rory, there was no reason Nikki couldn't have assisted as well. "Do they have an ID on the adult female yet?"

"They're comparing dental records of missing persons this morning. How's Rory doing?"

"Frustrated," Nikki said. "He wants to find out who the remains are, but it's also stressful from a business standpoint. He's already behind on the job. By the way, I wasn't talking about Courtney earlier. You remember me talking about Justin Nash from the academy?"

Liam's eyes lit up. He was an FBI history junkie, and she knew the Adam Walsh case had been one of the driving forces behind his decision to go into law enforcement. "He's here?"

"He wants my help on a profile," Nikki said. "And don't get too excited. He doesn't have the résumé that his parents do."

"I'd still love to pick his brain some time. He's had to have learned a lot from them."

Nikki told him about the interview she'd agreed to help with later today, along with what Nash had told her about the traffick-ers. "I'm not sure there's enough information for a profile, but I'm going to see what I can do."

"Good luck," he said. "I'll let you know if I hear from Miller. I've got a pile of reports to catch up."

She nodded, her mouth full of croissant. Nikki was lucky to work with people like Liam and Courtney. She'd have to take them both out for drinks when they all had time.

Rory's number flashed on her phone. Nikki licked her fingers and answered. "Hey. I just inhaled a gooey chocolate croissant. How's your morning going?"

"It's her." Rory's voice shook. "Miller said she's been missing since 1997, probably since that same night. I always wondered why she never came back to see her friends, but I forced myself to forget about her." He drew a shuddering sob. "Her brother and I lost touch after we broke up. Why didn't he tell me she was missing?"

"I don't know," Nikki said softly. "But, Rory, this isn't a positive identification. She could still be alive, it might not be her—"

"Miller said he'd have an official ID soon, but the locket they found has her initials on it." He drew a shuddering breath. "He also said she was pregnant. The baby could be mine." Pressure dug into Nikki's sternum. She could hear Rory breathing hard, but she couldn't tell if he was crying or having a panic attack. "Did you know?"

"Yes. The death investigator told us about the fetal bones yesterday."

"Why didn't you say anything?" Rory demanded.

"Because it didn't matter until she was identified," Nikki said soothingly. She felt terrible, but she was only trying to protect Rory. "If I had told you about the fetal bones yesterday, how much worse would you have felt?"

Rory didn't answer right away, but she could tell that he was crying. "I haven't thought about her in forever. She wanted to be a nurse. She talked about enrolling in a part-time program in the city. She would have been a great nurse, Nik."

"I'm sure she would have. I wish there was something I could say to take your pain away, but, Rory, you're jumping to conclusions—"

"I shouldn't be throwing this at you on your first day back," Rory said. "Not after everything you went through with Tyler."

"Of course you should talk to me," Nikki said. "We can't compare our situations. Loss is loss, and grief is grief. You have every right to be this upset, and you need to talk about it. Bottling things up is the worst thing to do. I speak from experience," she said, trying to lighten the mood.

"Miller wants me to come down and make a statement," he said. "I really don't want to go alone."

"When are you going?" Nikki wasn't surprised that Miller had asked him to come in to talk. The circumstantial evidence was enough to warrant talking to Rory since he'd likely known Becky better than most people.

"I told him later this afternoon," he said. "Mom and Dad are busy until then, and I promised Lacey we'd go to the park."

Nikki wished she could articulate how much Rory's love for Lacey meant to her. "I have a lunch meeting, but I should be able to meet you there. How's Lacey doing?"

"Good, I think," he said. "We watched cartoons and had Cinnamon Toast Crunch for breakfast."

Nikki rolled her eyes. She tried not to let Lacey eat a lot of sugary cereals, but Rory had a hard time saying no, and Lacey knew it.

"She's in the kitchen doing a puzzle." Rory's voice had steadied some. Hopefully having Lacey to focus on would help him get through the day.

"Tell her I'll see her tonight," Nikki said. "I love you. We'll get through this."

"Yeah, I hope so," he said. "I love you too."

Unease rippled through Nikki as she logged into the FBI's

missing persons database and retrieved the report on Becky. The girl had been beautiful: shiny blonde hair, crystal blue eyes and the widest smile Nikki had ever seen. She thought back to the decaying skeleton she'd seen in the ground yesterday, dirt caking the white bones. Was the silver locket all that remained of Becky now?

FIVE

Nikki didn't need her GPS to find the place Nash had selected for lunch. As part of the prestigious Minnesota Club, Herbie's on the Park was a popular place for business lunches because of its unrivaled happy hour. Its location near the Science Museum made parking difficult, but Nikki managed to find a place in the parking garage. She shut off the engine, glanced in the rearview mirror and smoothed her hair. She'd worn a little makeup today for the first time in a while, but she'd probably end up sweating it off on the walk to Herbie's.

The sun beat down on her dark blue blouse, and Nikki could feel the back of her neck getting damp with sweat. She hadn't planned on leaving the office today, or she would have dressed accordingly. Nikki hadn't been to Herbie's for a long time, mostly because its location at the ancient and sometimes-uppity Minnesota Club had always turned her off.

A young hostess dressed in a black and white uniform led her to Nash's table.

"Sorry I'm late." Nikki sat down, hoping she didn't look too melted and unprofessional.

"Right on time," Nash said. "What are you drinking these

days?" A sly grin played at the corner of his mouth. "If I remember correctly, you liked Coors Lite back at the academy."

"Thankfully, my taste buds have matured." Nikki spread the black napkin over her lap, trying to hide her reaction. Tyler had been a Coors Lite guy, and back then, she'd been happy to drink whatever he was willing to buy. "But I don't drink on the job."

Nash held up his glass. "Heavy on Coke, very light on whiskey. Just a splash to add flavor."

"You don't have to justify anything to me. I'm not your supervisory officer." Nikki ordered a Coke and decided to change the subject before things continued down nostalgia road. "I had a chance to read everything you sent to me. I didn't expect the list to go back to 1999. How did the task force determine these missing girls were victims of trafficking?"

Nash pushed his glass aside and leaned forward, his forearms on the table. "I haven't tracked down all of their next of kin yet, but I have spoken to a couple of family members whose girls both disappeared from Shingle Creek Crossing, a shopping center, two years apart, both fourteen." He sipped his drink.

"Every parent's nightmare." The paralyzing panic that had gripped her when she'd lost sight of Lacey at the Mall of America a few months ago was burned into Nikki's brain. She'd worked countless missing kid cases, but that was the first time her own child had been in harm's way. "Malls and department stores are still prime hunting grounds for people looking to kidnap children—they can watch the kids who come to the mall, figure out which one is in the most vulnerable position. Then they make their move. But sex traffickers don't usually snatch girls outright. A lot of them, as I'm sure you know, spend time grooming so they can make the victims dependent on them. They've even been known to infiltrate families."

Nash sipped his drink. "Yep. My parents spent all their time talking about all that."

Nikki knew Nash was talking about the kidnapping of little Adam Walsh. Nash's father had been part of the investigation into the kidnapping that had changed the way police approach missing children cases. It was one of the first missing children cases the FBI assisted on, and Adam's kidnapping and subsequent death spawned an entire generation of change in law enforcement. In the years following Adam's death, statistics about stranger abduction had been inflated in some cases where there were runaways and other mitigating circumstances, and the public started to forget that most abductions are committed by someone the child knew.

"My mom used the 'little Adam Walsh' warning for years, especially since we had the same last name." As a little kid, shopping with her mother had been boring. Every time Nikki tried to escape to play in the clothes rack, her mother reminded her of little Adam Walsh, whose 'mommy just turned her head for a second.'

"Mine too," Nash said dryly.

Nikki decided to steer him back on track. "These two were taken in the nineties, right? How do you know they were part of a trafficking ring?"

"Testimony from our informant," Nash said. "Along with evidence I'm not allowed to share with you."

Nikki could tell by the set of his jaw that he wasn't going to divulge any more. "All right, then. Who are we interviewing today?"

"Gordon Kendrick. He owns a limousine and party service that's used by the professional sports teams and visiting celebrities. He's a favorite of the politicians too."

She knew there was more to the interview and that Nash's involvement with the DOJ task force limited the amount of information he could share, so she didn't press him. She was here only to observe Kendrick and give her opinion on a potential criminal profile. Normally, she'd already know the basics on Kendrick: his age, background, and anything else she could drum up from public records and the FBI's various databases. Figuring out how a person operated within his social and work circles was the first step in a profile, but Nikki would have to rely on Kendrick's body language and answers to Nash's questions.

Nash checked his watch. "He should be here any minute." His gaze was on the entrance and he fiddled with his tie, trying to loosen it. Nikki noted the bead of sweat across his brow.

"That suit jacket looks pretty warm," Nikki said. "I'm sure Kendrick won't care if you greet him in your dress shirt and tie."

Pink spread over Nash's cheeks. "Is it that obvious?"

"You look nervous as hell," Nikki said bluntly. "Like, rookie nervous. Should we be afraid of this guy?"

"No, of course not," Nash said. "I just want to get this interview right the first time. We only have one shot. If he is involved in trafficking, he could be connected to an entire organization who will be on alert after I question him."

"He knows he's meeting an FBI agent, right?" Nikki said. "He's the one who should be nervous, not you."

"I know," Nash said without looking at her.

"He does know you're an agent, right?" Nikki asked, growing irritated.

"Just follow my lead and give me your observations on him. You don't need to know more than that."

Nikki glared at him. "I'm not taking part in an interview that is done unethically or illegally. So if we're supposed to pretend this is some kind of business meeting to trick him into talking, I'm not interested."

Nash turned to look Nikki straight in the eye. "Can you just trust me?" he said sternly.

Nikki wasn't certain that she could, but it was probably too late to back out now. And if she could help take down traffickers by giving her opinion, she had to take the risk. Walking away now wouldn't do anyone any good.

"By the way," Nash continued. "What do you know about those remains found in Washington County yesterday?" he asked.

Nikki wondered why in the world would Nash be asking about a cold case. Was he trying to distract her? Change the subject? "Remains were found in a trunk, buried and covered with cement and dirt," she said quickly.

"God," Nash said. "Talk about overkill, pardon the pun. I heard you were out at the scene."

"How in the world did you know that?" Nikki said, growing increasingly irritated.

Nash laughed. "You know you're kind of a celebrity, especially among law enforcement. I always knew you were going to be an incredible agent, but I have to hand it to you, Nicole, you've caught some of the worst killers in modern history. It's almost as if you're a real mind reader."

"Rest assured, I'm not," Nikki said. "I'm a trained behavioralist."

"What does that mean?"

"It means I know when someone's lying," she said, done with his line of questioning. "Why are you asking about the remains?"

Nash looked toward the door and sighed. "Now he's late."

"Justin," Nikki said. "Why do you want to know about the remains?"

He studied her for a moment. "This stays between us, right?"

"Of course," Nikki said.

He took another drink of his whiskey and Coke. "Was she pregnant?"

Nikki hadn't expected that question. She knew that Miller had deliberately kept that information out of the news. "That's an oddly specific guess."

"Not really," he said. "About eighteen months ago, we nailed a guy from Ohio downloading some of the sickest shit I've seen in my life. We searched his computer and found videos with him and minors. He immediately begs for a deal in exchange for information. He led us to three girls who'd been trafficked and a house mother charged with their daily care."

Nikki's mind was racing. What did this have to do with the remains? "Did you get anything out of this house mother?" she asked.

"Before she took her own life, yeah," Nash said. "She left a note and hand-drawn map, which led to graves. Two seventeen-year-old girls both killed while pregnant." Nash had turned a little green. "Their remains weren't fully decomposed, but their faces were so badly beaten—pulverized—that facial reconstruction wasn't possible. We have DNA from both the girls and the unborn babies, but they haven't matched anyone in CODIS."

"Sadly, that doesn't surprise me. The number of predators like that walking around is a lot higher than we imagine." She still didn't see the connection to Minnesota. "These were in Ohio, right?"

"Their holding place was, yes," Nash said. "But the bodies were buried in northern Washington County. That sheriff was miserable to work with. I believe you have personal experience with him as well."

"Hardin?" He'd been a lieutenant when Nikki's parents had been murdered and one of the first ones at the crime scene. Hardin had recently been forced to retire. "Is there any chance one of those girls could have been the two you mentioned earlier?"

"Fortunately, we have DNA from both of them and no, it didn't match," Nash said. "We don't even know the definitive number of girls taken by these guys."

"These guys?" Nikki pressed. "The DOJ thinks they've all been taken by the same traffickers? That's a stretch, because these victims are passed around and moved so much it's entirely possible they were initially taken from another part of the country."

"I know," Nash said. "But between the two bodies in Washington County uncovered last year and now a third, I think we might be zeroing in on something."

"That makes no sense," Nikki said. "You don't have any real evidence linking—"

"Just because I can't share it with you doesn't mean it doesn't exist," Nash said testily. "Listen, you know the new sheriff out in Washington County, right?"

"Miller," Nikki said. "I've worked with him on a few cases now. He's one of the best. Our lab is assisting his investigation to identify the remains quickly, but right now, we don't know how old the bones are or how the victim died. We only know she was female."

Nikki still wasn't sure if she could trust Nash, but she did want to help the victims in his case. "After we finish up here, I can introduce you to Sheriff Miller. We aren't far from Stillwater. I was planning on stopping by the station, anyway."

"Great." Nash's eyes widened. "Shit, there he is." Nash stood and waved, making sure to smooth his tie. "By the way, he thinks you and I are investigating him for tax fraud."

A casually dressed man in dark-wash jeans and a buttoned-down shirt headed toward them. Petite and slim, Gordon Kendrick always joked about being better suited for race cars than limos in his commercials. He appeared even smaller in person, but he walked with the swagger of a confident businessman.

"Mr. Kendrick," Nash said. "Thank you for meeting with me on such short notice."

"Anything for our law enforcement personnel." Kendrick stopped short, his eyes on Nikki. "Is this Agent Hunt?"

Nikki was still trying to comprehend what Nash had mumbled about tax fraud. How could he wait until the last minute to tell her Kendrick thought this was about taxes? She offered her hand. "Special Agent Hunt." Nikki gestured for him to take the empty seat at the table. "I'm actually here in an unofficial capacity, right, Justin?"

"Agent Hunt is simply here to observe," Nash said, bypassing her question.

Kendrick sat down, still staring at her. "Sorry, I'm a little confused. I thought Agent Hunt was assigned my case? That's what the email said when you first contacted me."

It took Nikki a second to realize that he was referring to Tyler, not her. He was responsible for tax investigations—this was his area of expertise. Her gaze slid to Justin, who refused to look at her. "Remind me when you received the original communication, Mr. Kendrick," Nikki said.

"Three, maybe four months ago," Kendrick said. "You wrote to me saying you wanted to discuss the investigation and that if I wanted to get out of this without doing time, I'd be working with you. I admit, it took me a while to respond, and then when I didn't hear from you, I started hoping I'd slipped through the cracks."

"I see," Nikki said, gathering her things. "If you'll excuse me." She directed her next words at Nash. "Good luck." She turned on her heel and headed for the door before she did something she'd end up regretting.

"Nicole, wait." Nash had caught up with her by the time she reached the lobby. "I should have told you that Tyler had been investigating him for tax fraud. But I thought that if I did, you wouldn't help. It was a mistake and I'm sorry."

She still didn't buy it. "You used me so that Kendrick would agree to meet you. Why didn't you just pretend to be Tyler instead of dragging me here?"

"Because I don't run my investigations like that," he hissed. "And I do need your help, Nicole."

"I don't care," Nikki said flatly. "Frankly, I'm starting to wonder how much time you've had in the field and exactly how you got this assignment, because from where I'm sitting, you're a train wreck."

"Then help me," Nash pleaded. "Please come back to the table. Kendrick is suspicious now, and we can't lose him."

She hugged her chest. "If Kendrick's being investigated for tax evasion, what has he got to do with your case?"

"Maybe nothing," he said. "I'm not here because of the tax investigation. My informant gave me Kendrick's name. I brought you here because Kendrick only knows that Agent Hunt was assigned his case." Nash glanced behind him. "I promise to tell you everything after this meeting. But please stay."

"Not until you admit that part of the reason you wanted my help is because I'm Tyler's wife. Ex-wife," she quickly corrected herself. She'd been dealing with Tyler's will and legal issues and had gotten too used to being called "spouse."

"I asked you to come here because of that, yes," Nash said. "I was stupid not to warn you and think you would play along, but I swear to God this is a real case, and I do need your help."

"Fine," Nikki said. "But if I catch you in any more lies, I'm out. I'm not risking my career for you because of a hunch."

"It's more than a hunch, I promise," Nash said. "And it's not even my hunch. It was your husband's instincts that brought me here. Do you trust him?"

"Ex-husband," Nikki said curtly. "Don't ask me anything personal about Tyler again. You've forfeited that right."

She headed back to the table without saying another word. Hell would freeze over before she'd let Nash ruin Tyler's reputation as an agent.

SIX

"I'm glad you came back," Kendrick said, holding up a glass of wine. "I was afraid I'd offended you."

"No, I apologize," Nikki said. "I thought I had to get to another meeting, but it's been rescheduled."

Nash flashed a gleaming, fake smile as he explained what he dubbed a mishap. "I thought Agent Hunt had been briefed about our interview, but I was mistaken. Your tax case has been reassigned."

Nikki knew she was supposed to watch Kendrick, but she was caught up in Nash's ability to lie by omission. He delivered his lines with such confidence Kendrick didn't ask who'd been assigned the case.

"I'm innocent," Kendrick said emphatically. "My soon-to-be ex-wife is behind the tax stuff."

"Your ex-wife is the crook, then?" Nash asked.

Kendrick nodded. "She handled the books. Turned out she cooked them too. I'm not going to jail for that woman. Pretty sure she's using my cars to run prostitutes."

Nash leaned back in his chair, his eyebrows raised. "Really? You have any evidence to back up that accusation?"

"After I found out about the tax investigation, I started looking into things. I found information in my wife's personal calendar about a room in a shitty motel. When I first saw it, I figured she was cheating again. I followed her and waited. We have a prenup. If she cheats on me, she gets nothing."

"You set out to get the proof." Nikki spoke without thinking. She was so used to leading interviews that staying quiet was difficult.

"Sure did," Kendrick huffed. "She used a company car to drive to the hotel and then went in alone for about twenty minutes. She came back out with two teenaged girls dressed very suggestively. They looked underage to me. I tried to follow and see where she went, but I screwed up and lost her in traffic."

"How did you get into her personal calendar?" Nash asked. "Assuming you're referring to something digital?"

Kendrick snickered. "She's irritatingly old-school, walks around with a little planner. After I found out about the tax evasion charges, I searched her things after she passed out drunk one night."

"Have you found out anything more since you last spoke to Mr. Hunt?" Nash asked.

"Nope," he said. "I walked out on her and haven't seen her since, either. Let her have my damn house. I bought myself a penthouse down here. It's different, but I'm enjoying it."

"Do you believe she has any idea what you saw?"

Kendrick shook his head. "She's too busy thinking about herself."

Nikki rubbed her temples. She couldn't tell if Nash was naive or if he was just playing along with Kendrick. The man stood to lose a lot of money in the divorce if he couldn't prove his wife had been cheating, and Nikki didn't believe for a second that he'd allegedly stumbled across the note about the hotel meeting on his wife's calendar. She glanced at Nash, debating whether questioning Kendrick was worth pissing Nash off. Considering the trick he'd played to get her here, Nikki decided she didn't care.

"Mr. Kendrick, can I ask you something?"

"Of course," Kendrick said. "I'm an open book. I'm not going to jail for her."

"That's good to hear," Nikki said. "Agent Nash will need all of the surveillance footage you have of your wife. You've had her tailed for a while, I assume?"

Nash looked at her in confusion, but Kendrick didn't flinch.

"I just have the one from when I followed her," he said.

"Agent Hunt, we have no reason to think he has additional—"

She kept her eyes locked on Kendrick's. "Mr. Kendrick, we both know you're lying."

Kendrick's expression was carefully blank. "How you figure, young lady?"

"Common sense and years of experience"—she emphasized the word for Nash's benefit—"tell me there's no way a man of your financial means isn't going to have his wife investigated if he thinks she's doing something that could cost him money."

Nash cleared his throat, obviously trying to take control of the conversation, but Nikki ignored him. Kendrick hadn't moved, but his left eye twitched and that's all Nikki needed. Adrenaline pumped through her veins, and a familiar rush had started to take over. "I get the impression you've been unhappy with your wife for a while. You started thinking about a divorce, but you knew that it would cost you half unless she was cheating. So you had her tailed."

Kendrick's broad shoulders slumped. "Fine. I was having her tailed, okay?"

"For leverage in the divorce," Nikki said. "That makes more sense. Do you have copies of any of the videos?" She assumed Nash would want to see the videos.

"My private investigator does." Kendrick's face turned pink with anger. He patted his chest. "I wasn't aware of any of her illegal shit, and I'm not going down with her."

"Fair enough." Her phone vibrated with a text from Sheriff Miller.

Rory said you were coming for his statement. He refuses to talk
until you get here. ETA?

All the air in her lungs seemed to evaporate. She knew Rory
had trust issues with the police, but why was he being difficult with
Miller? She was reading too much into it, Nikki told herself. Miller
asking for her ETA made her think he didn't have much patience
for Rory, but again maybe she was just reading into things.

"Mr. Kendrick, I suggest turning over everything you have to
Agent Nash. He'll get the applicable information to white-collar
crimes, and a new agent will reach out to you."

She looked at Nash. "If there's anything else I need to work on
the profile, please email it to me. I'm sure I'll hear from you soon."
She stood up for the second time. "I really do need to leave, unfortunately. Good luck to you, Mr. Kendrick."

"You as well, Agent Hunt."

"Agent Hunt," Nash said as she turned to leave. "Will I see you
in Washington County later?"

"Most likely," Nikki said without looking back at him. She
needed to get to Rory as soon as she could.

SEVEN

Nikki found Rory in the front lobby of the Washington County police station. He was sitting on the lone visitor's bench, tapping his right foot and chewing on his fingernails. She sat down next to him. "You okay?"

He shook his head. "Miller heard from the medical examiner. Dental records officially identified her as Becky." Rory's jaw tightened as he struggled to rein in his emotions.

Nikki rubbed his back. "I'm so sorry."

"I told Miller and Liam that I wanted to wait to give my statement until you were here. Pretty sure they're pissed off at me."

"Don't worry about it," Nikki said. "This is just procedure. You guys dated, and you unfortunately found the remains. Miller and Liam have to talk to you so they can eliminate you, find out anything you might remember from back then to help with the investigation and move on. You might be able to help them find Becky's killer."

"I can't stop thinking about the baby. What if it's mine?"

"We'll work through that if it happens," Nikki said, trying to think like an investigator and not a worried girlfriend. "When was the last time you were... intimate?"

"Day we graduated," he answered. "We'd broken up a month earlier, but everyone was partying. One thing led to another."

"Did she look pregnant when you saw her that fall?"

He shrugged, looking down at the floor. "She wore a baggy sweatshirt. I thought she'd put on a little weight. It never crossed my mind..."

The secure door next to the front counter buzzed and opened. Miller emerged, followed by Liam. Both looked grim enough to send her stomach into fresh somersaults. "Thanks for coming, Nicole," Miller said. "Rory is understandably nervous given his family's history with the department."

"Let's get this over with now that she's here." Rory stood and held his hand out for Nikki to take.

She stared up at him in surprise. "I can't sit in the room with you."

The little color that he had drained from his face. "Why not?"

"Because it's not my case, and until Miller officially clears you, they have to consider you a suspect. My direct involvement at any level could jeopardize convicting the real killer." She squeezed his hand. "But this is Miller and Liam. You can trust them."

"Can she listen on the other side of the glass? You guys have those two-way deals, right? And it's all recorded," Rory said. "I'm going to tell her everything the minute I leave anyway."

Miller glanced at Liam, who shrugged. "He's right. I don't see the problem given her clearance and their personal relationship."

"Fine." Miller led the way through the security doors and the others followed. "Nikki, the audio/visual room is down the hall. The cameras start recording as soon as the door opens. Code is 5870."

"Thanks." She gave Rory a final reassuring smile and then left him in Miller and Liam's hands.

The room at the end of the hall housed more than a dozen video cameras from the sheriff's office, including the interview rooms, entrance and exit, parking lot and lobby.

Nikki sat down in front of the monitor showing Rory and turned up the volume.

Miller joined Rory and Liam, closing the door. Armed with a legal pad and pencil, he sat down next to Liam and began.

"How did you meet Becky Anderson?" he asked Rory.

"I hung out with her older brother," Rory replied quickly.

Miller checked his notebook. "Jay Briggs, right? You still keep in touch with him?"

"No." Nikki could tell by the set of his jaw that Rory wasn't going to offer any information unless he was asked. He seemed determined to make things as difficult for himself as possible.

"According to the report filed by her friend in Minneapolis, Becky never returned from a visit back to Stillwater in 1997."

Her friend had filed the report? What about Becky's family? Nikki thought. Rory seemed to be thinking the same thing. "Why didn't her dad and brother file it?"

"I can't divulge that information," Miller said.

"Why did you and Becky break up, and when?" Liam asked.

Rory sighed. "Before graduation, right after her birthday. April 1997."

A few beats of silence followed, and then Liam seemed to realize he was going to have to push Rory through the interview to get the answers he needed. "Why did you break up?"

"She wanted to move to the Cities, and I didn't. My life was here."

"Did you see her when she came home that following September?"

"Ran into her at the bowling alley," he said. "Exchanged greetings and then avoided her."

"That was a Saturday, right?" Liam was flipping through his own little notebook.

Rory shrugged. "Probably."

Miller dragged his hands down his face. "Rory, this doesn't have to be hard. We're asking everyone who knew Becky about the last time they saw her."

Rory's jaw twitched, and Nikki could tell he was fighting back emotion. He drew a ragged breath. "Was she really pregnant?"

"It appears so," Miller said. "But the medical examiner will make that determination based on DNA matching."

"It's not mine." Rory sounded like he was trying to convince himself too. "We were careful. Kids were the last thing I needed back then." He picked at a small crack in the table. "How did she die?"

Liam and Miller glanced at each other. Nikki's stomach somersaulted as she watched their silent exchange. They'd clearly had a plan for questioning Rory, which was normal procedure, but watching things like this was unnerving, especially since she could read both so well.

"We're still waiting on the autopsy report," Miller said. "The FBI lab is rushing DNA on the fetal bones."

"Good," Rory said.

"What happened the last night that you saw her?" Liam asked.

Rory looked at him impatiently. "I told you."

"Elaborate." Liam's voice had an edge of warning to it. Nikki knew he would get enough of Rory's attitude soon.

"I ran into her at the bowling alley," Rory said. "I remember thinking she looked like she gained a little weight, which was a good thing. She was always really thin. Guess we know why now."

"What did you guys talk about?" Liam asked.

"Dude, that was twenty years ago, and I'd been drinking. I barely remember that night."

Miller jotted something down in his notebook. "You remember how long you two spoke for?"

"Few minutes at most. You want the name of the bowling alley?"

"Johnson Lanes, right?" Liam's tone was light, but the involuntary glance at the camera was impossible to miss.

Knowing the name of the bowling alley meant they'd already talked to someone in Becky's life, and given the line of questioning, Nikki was starting to think that person had a much better memory than Rory. And what were Miller and Liam holding back? Did they know something about the family that Rory didn't?

If she asked Liam, he'd probably tell her. But then she'd have to keep it from Rory, and this wasn't her case. If she expected Rory to trust Miller and Liam, then she had to do the same.

Nikki settled back into the chair and pulled out her laptop, hoping that working would distract her from analyzing every word they asked Rory. She logged into the FBI's private server, hoping to look at Kendrick's file, but since she wasn't in white-collar crimes, she didn't have the clearance to access it. She thought about calling Tyler's former boss, but he was even more by the book than Tyler had been. The conversation would be a waste of time. Fortunately, she'd put everything of Tyler's in storage, except for the items his parents asked for. She'd stacked at least six boxes of work items in the storage unit, and she was fairly certain he'd organized them alphabetically.

During their marriage, Nikki had teased him about being a hoarder since he never threw away anything related to a case, no matter how old it might have been.

Grief welled up inside of her, but Nikki shoved it down as deep as she could. She didn't want to feel anything right now. Rory needed her to be strong for him. If Becky's baby turned out to be his, he would be devastated.

Her phone started to ring, and Justin Nash's number flashed on the screen. Nikki rolled her eyes and sent him to voicemail. She wasn't interested in working with him any more than necessary.

Nikki went back to his email and studied the contents again, trying to listen to the interview as well. Miller and Liam had asked about Rory's relationship with Becky.

"On and off," Rory said. "It was high school. Not serious."

Nikki wondered if Becky had felt the same way. Rory had said she'd wanted him to move with her after graduation, but he'd refused. That sounded serious enough for a high school romance.

She winced when Liam asked that exact question.

"She knew we wouldn't last," Rory said. "She just didn't want to be alone in the city. But I couldn't leave my parents..."

Nikki read everything Nash had sent again and made a few notes about what she'd observed with Kendrick. "There isn't even enough for a profile," she muttered.

Miller and Liam continued asking about the nature of their relationship. Rory still gave one-word answers for the most part, but he answered the questions with a little less attitude.

"Can you write down and sign what you just told us?" Miller asked, sliding a legal notebook over to Rory. "I can type it up for you, but I'm slow. I don't want you to make an unnecessary trip back here."

Rory was visibly relieved, and Nikki felt some of her own anxiety fading. Her gaze drifted to the clock. Had she really been sitting here for forty-five minutes? Her stomach growled, so Nikki gathered her things and walked down to the break room in search of sustenance.

"I think he did it." A bubbly female voice came from the break room. "My brother went to high school with them, and let's just say the Rory Todd we know now isn't the same person he was back then." Nikki backed against the wall, hoping to stay out of sight.

"Yeah, but is anyone?" Nikki recognized the voice she heard as belonging to Deputy Reynolds, one of Miller's most experienced investigators. "That doesn't mean that he did it."

"No, but plenty of people knew how crazy their relationship was back then. My brother said Rory left town about a week after Becky visited and didn't come back for a few months. He came back a changed man, supposedly."

"That doesn't mean anything, Britney. I think you watch too many crime shows."

She giggled. "Probably, but they're addictive. Did you know that Rory worked at McFarland farms back then?"

"So did half the people around here," Reynolds said.

"Whatever," Britney snickered. "He's dating a big-time FBI

agent. I'm sure he won't do any time, anyway. Agent Hunt will see to that."

Nikki had heard enough. She strolled into the break room, a fake smile plastered on her face. "What about Agent Hunt?"

A petite girl in her twenties looked terrified. Reynolds grinned, clearly enjoying Britney's discomfort. He winked at Nikki. "Welcome back."

"Thanks."

Liam rounded the corner, nearly running into Nikki. "Sorry, boss. Rory's just writing up his statement."

"I heard," she said. "I had to get something to eat since I skipped lunch."

"I thought you had a lunch meeting with Justin Nash." Liam grinned down at her.

"I did, and let's just say, his greatest skill is still nepotism." She glanced around his tall frame to make sure they were alone. "Can I ask a question about the interview?"

Liam nodded and then leaned against the wall, hands in his pockets. Even slouching, his lean frame still had several inches on Nikki. "You want to know why her family didn't file a missing persons report?"

She laughed despite herself. "You know me better than I give you credit for. Why didn't they?"

"Miller talked to the dad and the brother yesterday. They weren't speaking with Becky when she disappeared, but they had reason to think she was alive."

She knew he wouldn't elaborate further without Miller's permission, but something else had been nagging at Nikki. "Hardin was sheriff back then. Rory said Hardin asked him about Becky, but the sheriff gave the impression that he thought the family was overreacting. And he never talked to Rory about it again?"

"That's in the file," Liam said. "Rory's parents alibied him. And Hardin noted that Becky had a history of disappearing for a while, even in high school."

"So he did think the family was overreacting," Nikki said, relieved to hear Rory had been right about the previous sheriff. "But when she still didn't show up, didn't her family eventually wonder where she was? Did they go back to the police?"

"Apparently she sent postcards every once in a while," Liam said. "Obviously we know it wasn't her, but someone kept that up for several years."

"Did they write her back? What was the return address?"

Liam shrugged. "You'd have to ask Miller that."

Nikki couldn't put Miller in that position right now. Rory was innocent and Miller would determine that. The less Nikki knew, the better. "I'm just worried about Rory, especially if it turns out that the baby was his. Does the math even work out?"

"Yes," Liam said. "Blanchard put the fetus at around five months gestation. But that doesn't mean it is his. He just needs to focus on what's going on right now and make sure he tells us everything."

Uneasiness washed over Nikki. "Why don't you think he's telling you everything?"

"I'm not saying he isn't," Liam quickly backpedaled, but Nikki couldn't shake the look in his eyes. What else did Liam know that he couldn't tell her?

"He would never hurt anyone." Nikki shook her head, half numb. "He doesn't have it in him." Still, she understood that Miller needed answers to these questions, and they were the same ones she would have asked. "You're swabbing for paternity before he leaves?"

"Miller is, yeah." Liam glanced over his shoulder. "He's probably done now."

A familiar voice floated down the hall from Miller's office. Nikki groaned. "Here comes Nash." She quickly explained how Nash had wanted her at the meeting because she was Tyler's ex-wife. "Nash's informant named Kendrick's company as involved in trafficking. Nash found out that Tyler had been investigating

Kendrick for tax fraud and used Tyler's name to set up the interview."

"He follow you here or something?"

"I wouldn't be this calm if he had," Nikki said. "Nash thinks two bodies found in Washington County might be tied to his trafficking case."

Liam glanced down the hall toward Miller's open office door. "I should stop by and see what Miller's next steps are."

"Have at it," Nikki said. "I've seen enough of Justin Nash today."

She found Rory pacing in the lobby.

"Hey." Nikki squeezed his shoulder. "You did great. Don't you feel better now that you've gotten this over with?"

"Sure." Rory was already halfway out the door. "Did you talk to Liam and Miller before you left?"

"Liam," Nikki said. "Why?"

Rory dragged his hands through his wavy hair. "It bugs me that her dad and brother didn't file the report. Did Miller check them out?"

"I'm sure he has or will," Nikki said evasively.

Rory stopped walking to look down at her. "Did Liam tell you anything? There's got to be a reason her father did nothing."

"There is," Nikki said. "But I can't tell you any more than that."

The muscle in Rory's jaw worked, and she could see the tension in his muscular, tanned arms. "Yeah, I know. I shouldn't have asked."

"Nicole."

"Damn." Nikki stopped walking and turned around to see Nash jogging toward them.

"I didn't get a chance to thank you for helping me at lunch today."

"No problem. I have my doubts on being able to provide a decent profile with the little information I have, but I'll try."

Nash nodded, his gaze shifting to Rory. "Justin Nash."

Rory shook his outstretched hand, but Nikki could see the wariness in his eyes. Nash was exceptionally handsome and still possessed the same swagger she'd remembered from the academy. "Rory Todd."

"Sorry for the hold-up," Nash said. "I just wanted to go over a few things with Nicole on a case she's helping out on."

"No problem." Rory leaned down and kissed her harder than usual. "Thanks for coming. I'll see you at home."

Nikki was surprised at his quick escape, but she didn't have time to think about it. "What, Justin?"

"I'm sorry for today," Nash said. "I should have been totally honest."

"Yes, you should have. What did Miller say about your suggestion that Becky's case could be connected to the old cases from Washington County?"

"He's going to look into them," Nash said. "Seems like a good guy."

"He is."

"What did you think of Kendrick?" Nash asked.

Nikki shrugged. "At this point, it's hard to say. Did he give you contact information for his private investigator?"

"I made an appointment with him for tomorrow around eleven. If I send you the details, is there any chance you'd meet me there?"

Nikki wanted to say no, but she was too curious about Kendrick's story. And if Nash was right about a trafficking ring in the area, Nikki wanted to get to the bottom of it before more victims were taken.

EIGHT

Nikki was jarred out of a deep sleep by her ringing cell.

"Hello?" she answered groggily, debating on how she would hurt whoever was calling at six thirty a.m. She'd struggled to get to sleep, the events of the day whirling around in her brain. She couldn't get Rory's devastated face out of her mind and found herself awake during the night checking that he was still asleep next to her. As she turned towards him now to make sure she hadn't woken him, she saw that he wasn't beside her in the bed.

"Agent Hunt, this is Hernandez. I'm sorry to call you so damn early, but I need a favor." Nikki sat up, surprised at the agitation in her boss's voice.

"Sir, are you all right?" she said.

"I'm fine, but a friend of mine's surrogate has gone missing. The surrogate's due in a couple of weeks, and the biological parents specifically asked for you to help find the woman and their unborn son. The mother is certain they've been kidnapped." He paused for a second and then continued. "I know that you just got back and this is a missing child, so if you need to say no, I promise you I'll respect that."

Nikki never wanted to say no to something so much in her life. The hours that Nikki had gone without her own daughter, not knowing if she were safe, were the worst of her life. It was the worst thing that any parent could go through and despite all her instincts driving her to help another mother, the thought of going through such an intense experience so soon after Lacey's kidnapping terrified Nikki. But she had a job to do.

"I can handle it," Nikki said. "Can you text me the address? I'm in Stillwater, but I'll get there as fast as I can."

She ended the call and found Rory in the kitchen, still in his boxer briefs, leaning against the counter and watching the coffee brew.

"I just got called into a kidnapping case." Nikki tried not to let her anxiety show. "A missing surrogate. I'm not sure when the baby is due, but she's pretty far along."

Rory turned and looked at her with worried, tired eyes. "Seriously?"

"My boss called me himself. I've got to get to St. Paul. I'm sorry to dump this on you, but if you're stuck home waiting for Miller to clear the area where you found the remains, could you hang out with Lacey? Or take her to your parents if you end up working?"

"Of course," he said. "But I think you should talk to her before you leave."

"I will." She could tell he hadn't slept much. "Those are some dark circles under your eyes."

Rory dragged his hand through his curls, making his hair stand on end. "I can't stop thinking about her being stuffed in that trunk. And the baby never had a chance."

"Miller will do everything he can to find her killer."

"That's what I'm afraid of."

Nikki told herself the butterflies in her stomach had nothing to do with Rory's strange words. "I'm not following you."

"It's selfish, but I don't want to relive those days," he said. "High school was rough. I got bullied for being Mark's brother until I stood up for myself. Then I just got into fights."

"I know how you feel," Nikki said, remembering the gossip

she'd overheard yesterday. "And I'll be there for you as much as I can. But for now, let's just try to hope for the best."

Lacey used to be a deep sleeper, but since Tyler's death, she seemed to be resting with one ear open. In the initial weeks after the murder, Lacey slept with Nikki, clinging to her in her sleep. She'd gradually improved over the past few months, but noises she'd never noticed before, like the ice maker, still woke her up, so it was no surprise that she'd woken when Nikki tried to sneak in and kiss her goodbye.

Her curls a mess, Lacey sat up and rubbed her eyes. "Mommy, why are you dressed in the middle of the night?" she mumbled.

"Lace, you know I'm back at work now," Nikki started.

Lacey pointed at the clock radio that Rory had given her to listen to when she was scared at night. "You said you wouldn't leave until after breakfast. It's not even time for the sun to wake up."

Nikki sat down beside her and tried to smooth some of the tangles in her thick, dark hair. She'd inherited the dark hair and blue eyes from Nikki, but her personality was a lot more like her father's. "I know, and I wasn't going to go in until after breakfast, but my boss called, and he needs my help. We don't have much time, either." She didn't want to say the words "missing" and put Lacey's ordeal at the forefront of her mind.

"I guess it's okay if you're going with your boss. He can take care of you, right?" Her little voice cracked.

Nikki gathered her in a tight hug. "I promise you I'll be safe." She pulled her old phone out of her pocket and handed it to Lacey. "This doesn't have games or the internet, but you can text me any time you want. Remember how Rory taught you?"

Lacey's eyes widened and she grabbed the phone. "Really? Can I call you?"

"I'll be working, honey. But how about this? You can text me every couple of hours and ask if I'm okay. I'll make sure to check my phone so I can reply back. How's that sound?"

Lacey nodded, cradling the phone as if it were gold. "Is it charged?"

"Yep, and since it doesn't have that extra stuff, the battery should last a few days." She motioned for Lacey to lie back down. "Rory knows what's going on, so you'll probably hang out with him or Granny Ruth today." And, most likely, the next several days. Missing persons cases were rarely solved in a day.

"I should go to Granny's cause we have to finish planting." Lacey pulled the blanket to her chin. "I promised her I'd help."

"Good girl." Nikki kissed her on the forehead. "Now go back to sleep, and don't worry about me." She tapped the phone still clutched in her daughter's hand. "I'm just a text away."

NINE

Nikki started the engine and typed in the address Hernandez had sent her, trying to figure out why it sounded so familiar. Summit Avenue was St. Paul's incredible historic street. Several of the city's historical figures had lived on the street or in the neighborhood, including the writer F. Scott Fitzgerald, who wrote one of his novels in the brownstone row house that was now known as the F. Scott Fitzgerald House. The brownstones had been built by a renowned architect in the late nineteenth century, and, if Nikki remembered correctly, there were eight brownstone row houses altogether.

Curious, she zoomed in on the directions pulled up on her satnav and switched to street view. "Holy crap."

Hernandez's friends didn't just live in one of the brownstones. They lived in the same one that Fitzgerald had lived in when he wrote *This Side of Paradise*.

"Mom, you would be so excited right now if you were still here," Nikki said to herself as she exited Rory's driveway. When she'd been forced to read *The Great Gatsby* in high school, Nikki couldn't see what everyone raved about, including her mother. Before her death, Nikki's maternal grandmother used to tell stories about Fitzgerald and his wife, Zelda, that she'd heard from Nikki's great aunt, who'd allegedly run in the same wealthy social circles as the couple before Fitzgerald's untimely death.

Nikki remembered her mom rolling her eyes whenever the stories came up. She'd never believed her aunt, and Nikki doubted the stories held water. Still, it had been a cool family story to tell at parties. She and her mother had loved the homes on Summit and made it a point to drive through the area every time they came to St. Paul.

Despite the severity of the situation, Nikki was kind of excited about finally going into one of the homes she and her mother had daydreamed of owning. When she finally turned onto Summit Avenue and saw the unique brownstones, Nikki felt the same familiar awe she'd had so many years ago.

Hernandez had told her to come to the door, so she parked behind his sedan in front of the house. Nikki took a moment to focus on her breathing and center herself in the moment. After Hernandez's call, she'd climbed out of bed and quickly got ready to leave, almost on autopilot. She didn't take the time to think about the significance of such an intense case. A child was missing, and that's all Nikki needed to know.

She'd expected to feel a little rusty after so much time off, but now that she was about to hit the ground running, the magnitude of the day had begun to settle on her shoulders.

Nikki had never doubted her skill as a profiler or FBI agent. But everything she'd gone through had changed her. Nikki was still learning to navigate those emotional changes, and she couldn't let them interfere with the investigation.

The front door opened, and Hernandez stepped out. Most days he wore a quick smile, but his grim expression made it clear just how important this case was to him.

Nikki quickly grabbed her bag and exited the jeep. She practically jogged to the front steps, barely noticing the colorful annuals planted along the sidewalk.

"Thanks for coming." He extended his hand. "I've got a bad feeling about this."

Hernandez might not be a profiler, but he was good at reading a situation. Most bureau chiefs, in Nikki's experience, had earned the position because they were good at managing controlled chaos. Few that she'd dealt with had much field experience, but Hernandez was different. He'd put himself through college by working as a security guard and bouncer. He'd started out with the St. Paul police and worked his way through the ranks to special teams. Hernandez had spent six years as a successful crisis/hostage negotiator before the FBI stole him from the St. Paul police more than a decade ago. Last Nikki heard, some St. Paul cops still held a grudge against Hernandez since he'd broken ranks and joined the FBI.

Their loss had been the FBI's gain. Nikki couldn't imagine having to deal with an inexperienced bureau chief in a situation like this.

"Bring me up to speed, if you don't mind."

Hernandez leaned against one of the impressive brown stone pillars. "Sonia Ashley is the one who called me. She's a writer, and she comes from a wealthy family; she was left with a considerate sum after they passed."

"Are we looking at a kidnapping for ransom?" One of the first things Nikki had noticed when she arrived in the area was the lack of canvassing officers. A missing child was an all-hands-on-deck situation. "Is that why there's no one out knocking on doors?"

Hernandez shook his head. "Sonia called me personally. They want to keep the press out of this. I've got two plain-clothed police officers searching the immediate area, but since the victim didn't come home last night, I've focused the search around the area where she worked. Her car is missing and we're currently waiting for the security footage to be examined by our tech guys at the lab. No action on her phone or credit cards since yesterday afternoon."

Hernandez explained that he was coordinating with the St.

Paul police on the search, but that the FBI was running point. "Before you ask, no, the St. Paul PD aren't happy, mostly because I'm the one calling the shots. If they give you any trouble, kick them over to me."

"No argument on that." Jurisdiction between local police and the FBI could be a touchy subject, and she didn't need to deal with the politics. "But we need the press. They can be crucial in cases like these. What do we know so far?"

"Joyce Ross disappeared after leaving work early this morning," Hernandez said. She works second shift at a twenty-four-hour emergency vet clinic. Joyce is the surrogate for Sonia Ashley's baby, and she's due in less than ten days. She's also dealing with gestational diabetes, and she and the baby need to be monitored."

"That complicates things." Nikki knew there wasn't much regulation with surrogacy. Depending on how the surrogate was found, the agreement was usually facilitated by both parties and their attorneys. "Is there a chance Joyce left on her own, intending to ransom the baby?"

"I doubt it," Hernandez said. "They're paying all the medical bills; she's staying with them during the pregnancy and they agreed to a lump sum for Joyce—eighty thousand dollars. She's only been paid half of it."

Nikki could see why Hernandez didn't think Joyce would try to manipulate the situation, but she was the logical starting point given the surrogacy situation. What if she had bonded with the unborn child? Taken half the money and run?

"What do the biological parents actually know about Joyce? How did they find her?"

Hernandez sighed. "Let me introduce you to Sonia and Tony. They can explain the situation better than I can."

As soon as Nikki and Hernandez stepped into the house, a small woman with silky, straight black hair and amber-colored skin practically pounced on Hernandez. "Please tell me you have some news."

"Agent Hunt is here." Hernandez pulled away enough for Nikki to see Sonia's face. She was a beautiful woman, roughly Nikki's age, but she had a petiteness to her that made her seem fragile.

"Thank you for coming." Sonia latched on to Nikki's outstretched hand. "You have to find them." Her soft voice cracked.

"I promise to do everything I can," Nikki said softly. "Are you able to answer some questions for me?"

Sonia nodded wordlessly and led them down the hall to the impressive kitchen, where a slim man with bed hair sat at the table, staring into space. The massive Great Dane lying at his feet perked up and hurried over to Sonia.

"Wow, he's the size of a small pony." Nikki tried to sound relaxed. She wasn't a fan of strange, big dogs, but she'd always heard Great Danes were gentle.

"His name is Fitz." Sonia patted the dog's dark fur. "Tony's the Fitzgerald fan."

The man at the table finally moved. He looked over at them with tired, bloodshot eyes. "Is this her?"

Hernandez introduced Nikki, and she, Hernandez and Sonia took the other seats around the table while Fitz the Dane took his spot on the floor, near the head of the table. He was so tall he didn't need to sit on a chair to be part of the conversation. Lacey would have been so excited right now.

Anxiety rushed over Nikki. She knew Lacey was in good hands and that Rory wouldn't hesitate to ask his parents for help with her, but this was only the second day Nikki had worked since Tyler, and she worried the day would eventually take its toll on Lacey.

"Joyce has been having Braxton Hicks for the last week, and the gestational diabetes increases her risk for early labor," Sonia said worriedly. "If he's born early, he might need medical attention."

Tony reached over and squeezed her shoulder. "Honey, if this is a kidnapping for ransom, they won't hurt him." He looked up at Nikki. "Plus, there are safe havens. Churches, fire stations, hospitals. Newborns dropped safely with no repercussions."

"That's only if the mother or someone with her permission leaves the baby, and Minnesota's safe haven laws have designated places with medical treatment at safe havens," Nikki said, closely watching Tony's reaction. Parents were always among the first suspects in the disappearance of a child, and Nikki didn't plan on treating this case any differently.

He hung his head, still holding Sonia's shoulder. "They could still leave him somewhere safe."

"Absolutely," Hernandez said. "We're currently contacting all the hospitals to see if Joyce was admitted, and they will all be on the lookout for Joyce or a baby brought in as abandoned."

"What about churches and fire stations?" Sonia asked through teary eyes. "I thought they were safe too."

"The police will check with those places," Nikki said. "But I'm sure if he's left like that, they will immediately report it."

"What if he's not?" Sonia's voice trembled. "I don't know what I'll do if we lose him."

"Sonia, don't get ahead of yourself," Hernandez said gently. "Joyce may not go into labor. Her due date isn't for ten days."

"Has she given birth before?" Nikki asked.

Both parents shook their heads.

"That's good," she told them. "I'm sure you know that most first pregnancies go past their due date, and women with gestational diabetes go full term all of the time." Nikki knew the odds were against Joyce, but it was pointless to tell Sonia that right now. She shifted the subject back to what they knew. "Agent Hernandez mentioned Joyce worked at the emergency vet clinic."

Sonia nodded. "The Animal Emergency Center of St. Paul. It's in the West Seventh neighborhood."

"I can remember when that neighborhood was blue collar,"

Hernandez said. "Hard-working people who liked to party a bit too much on the weekends. Now it's the cool place to be, at least in parts."

"Did she enjoy working at the clinic?"

"She loved it." Sonia dabbed her eyes with the tissue. "She's been working the front desk the past couple of weeks. This is supposed to be her last shift until after Patrick is born." Her lips trembled. "We named him after my paternal grandfather."

"It's a very good name for a little boy," Nikki said. "Agent Hernandez told me Joyce worked rotating shifts and that she was currently on a late shift. She's rarely home before midnight on those shifts."

"Sometimes it's closer to two a.m.," Tony said. "She was always so quiet we rarely heard her come home. That's why we didn't realize it until Sonia noticed that Joyce's car wasn't parked on the street this morning."

Nikki knew Hernandez had already issued a BOLO on the blue Kia Soul. "And that was around five thirty this morning?"

Sonia nodded, petting the dog's head. "I woke up out of a sound sleep, and I just had the feeling something was terribly wrong. I went to the bathroom and looked out the window. Her car wasn't there. We called her cell phone first and it went straight to voicemail. Then we called work and found out she'd left around midnight. Her car wasn't in the lot, and they checked their security videos. She left in her car, alone." Sonia's hand tightened on the dog's broad head. "I just can't believe this is happening."

Hernandez patted Sonia's hand. "We'll find her."

Nikki kept her gaze on Tony, trying to figure out if he was under the influence of something or in shock. He didn't seem inclined to offer much comfort to his wife, nor did he appear to care that Hernandez's hand still rested on Sonia's.

"Tony, what do you think?" she asked quietly, her gaze sliding to Hernandez and Sonia's hands. He quickly pulled away and crossed his arms over his chest.

Tony jerked at the mention of his name. "I feel the same way as Sonia. It's like we're trapped in a nightmare."

Nikki knew there were centers specializing in surrogacy, but she had a feeling Sonia hadn't gone through those channels. "Did you meet Joyce at the veterinarian's office?"

"Fitz likes to counter surf and garbage dive," Tony said, nodding. "He helped himself to a bone-in ribeye and had an obstruction."

"We almost lost him," Sonia said. "They did emergency surgery, and it took hours. Joyce came out a couple of times with updates. I was a wreck and blabbed on about Fitz being our baby because we couldn't have any. Another lady whose dog was also in surgery asked about surrogacy, and the three of us started talking about it. I didn't know much about Minnesota laws, but the lady in the waiting room had a friend who'd been a surrogate. By the time the surgery was over and we knew Fitz was out of the woods, I'd convinced Tony to look into the surrogacy."

"Did you approach Joyce, then?" Nikki was pretty certain she already knew the answer, but she wanted to clarify exactly how the agreement was made.

"No," Sonia said. "When I came in to bring Fitzy home, she asked if we'd looked into it further. We were still on the fence. Joyce asked if we could meet for coffee later that day because she'd done some research and wanted to show it to me."

"Joyce offered to be the surrogate," Tony cut in sharply, seemingly annoyed with his wife's play-by-play. "She had managed to put herself through school to be a veterinary tech, but she really wants to be a veterinarian. But she didn't want to be in debt for the rest of her life, so she'd been trying to save money."

"She saw her chance to pay for school," Sonia said. "It was a win-win situation for everyone."

"Did she name the price?" Hernandez asked.

Sonia shook her head. "She showed us the research she'd done, and we did plenty on our own. The average cost is eighty thousand plus medical expenses. We were more than generous in our offer."

"They do have a legal agreement," Hernandez said, looking at Nikki. "Joyce's background check came back clean, and every person Sonia and Tony spoke with had nothing but good things to say."

"That's why we offered for her to stay here," Tony said. "She was living out of a tiny apartment in a sketchy area. Living with us was healthier for both her and the baby, plus we could keep an eye on her."

"And she never gave you any cause to worry?" Nikki asked.

"No," Sonia said. "She even agreed to be on our phone plan so that we knew where she was at all times."

But GPS only works when the phone's turned on, Nikki thought, eyeing Tony. He'd gone from almost frozen in shock to fidgety, his slipper tapping against the tile floor. "Tony, what aren't you telling us?"

He stiffened and then slowly turned his head to stare at her. His face looked calm, but he couldn't hide the fear in his eyes. "Uh... nothing."

"Tony," Nikki said, her patience gone. "Your baby is missing, which means any expectation of privacy has to be set aside. Whatever you're hiding, we need to know, no matter how small it might seem to you."

Sonia looked between them, her dark eyebrows knitting together. "Agent Hunt, I know you're very good at your job, but Tony wouldn't hide anything."

"Agent, I'm sure that Tony would have told us anything else," Hernandez said firmly.

Nikki ignored him, keeping her gaze pinned on Tony. He stared back defiantly for exactly five seconds, and then his shoulders sagged. "Her background check did come back clean. But..." he said, glancing at his wife, "there were only two years on it. She had no history prior to that. I was going to ask her about it, but by then Sonia was so excited, and things were being put into motion. So, I brought up the idea about her living with us and the phone tracker stuff. When she agreed without any issue, I assumed she was on the up and up. She never once acted like a person with something to hide."

Sonia stared at him, tears forming in her eyes. "Why didn't you tell me this when we realized she was gone?"

"Because I don't think Joyce has anything to do with this," Tony said emphatically. "She's a victim. She wouldn't do anything to put Patrick in harm's way. I'm sure there's a reasonable explanation for the history being missing."

Sonia shook her head and pushed away from the table, tears streaming down her face. "Excuse me."

Hernandez shifted in his chair as though he might run after her, but Tony was already on his feet.

"We'll need a copy of that background check," Nikki said quietly.

Tony nodded and hurried after his wife, Fitz following obediently behind.

Hernandez sighed and rubbed his temples. "Damn, Tony. This changes things."

"It does, but Joyce could still be a victim," Nikki said. "We need to know who this woman really is asap. That's the only way we're going to have a fighting chance at finding them." Nikki couldn't hide her anger. "Who gets a report back like this and doesn't realize something is wrong?"

"I don't know, but if I didn't know better, I'd think she was in WITSEC. It would explain why her record is blank."

"Why?" Nikki asked.

"Experience," Hernandez said. "I put two gang members in witness protection while I was a cop. And contrary to television dramas, very few witnesses are killed if they follow the rules. I'll call the US Marshals and the Attorney General. If she's in WITSEC, they'll know."

Nikki ticked off the things she knew Hernandez had already coordinated with local police. "We've got the BOLO out. Checkpoints have been set up on the routes she would take to leave the vet's office. What about security videos?"

"Our audio-visual guys are in the process of getting a big dump of closed camera footage from the Department of Transportation, and we have boots on the ground everywhere."

"I know the family doesn't want the publicity, but we need to get her picture on the news. We don't even have to tie it to them right now, just Joyce and the baby."

Hernandez perked up a bit. "That's true. What do you think about Joyce being behind this? Maybe angling for more money?"

"It sounds like the family's been generous, but we have to consider that possibility, especially if we want to have any shot at finding her and the baby before it's too late."

Hernandez's eyes snapped to hers. "You don't sound very hopeful."

"Hope isn't my job," Nikki said flatly. "Finding people is my job. Experience tells me that if Joyce is involved, we are fighting a mountain instead of a molehill."

"Right. I want to see that background check. We'll run Joyce through every single database we have and see if we can get a hit."

"Tell them we can't hold off on the media anymore," Nikki said. "They're one of our best resources. Like I said, there's just no privacy at this point. Every decision made has to be about Joyce and their baby, period."

"I'll tell them, and I'll get the information to the media." Hernandez stood and started toward the direction the two had gone in but then stopped and looked at Nikki. "I know you're trying to prove this doesn't affect you, but please don't go so far that you lose your ability to empathize, even if you have to fake it for someone who doesn't deserve it."

"Understood," she answered, trying to listen to Sonia and Tony's muted voices in the adjacent room. "I'd like to see Joyce's bedroom before we head to her work."

"It's on the second floor, the room with the pink rug," Hernandez said. "I'm going to talk to Sonia and Tony again."

She felt her phone vibrate.

Mommy? U ok?

Nikki smiled at her daughter's shorthand. Rory was probably helping her because he often texted like that just because he knew it annoyed Nikki. "I promised Lacey she could text me once an hour so she knew I was okay. Let me just text her back."

I'm fine. Love you.

Nikki nodded to Hernandez and cut through the large butler's pantry toward the front of the house. She climbed the impressive staircase slowly, taking in the Victorian-era red and gold wallpaper. She wasn't a historical expert, but Nikki could tell the wallpaper was a fairly recent addition, most likely a replica of early nineteenth-century wallpaper patterns.

Nikki stopped on the second-floor landing and got her bearings. She could tell one room had been converted to an office, but the other two doors were closed. She knocked gently on the closed door across from the office and then peeked inside. She saw more sleek, gleaming floors, but no pink rug.

Joyce's room was at the end of the hall, and Nikki guessed that Joyce didn't have much say in the decor. The antique, four-poster bed and matching dressing bureau were exquisite, and the pink theme continued into the adjacent bathroom, which could be accessed from both the bedroom and the hallway.

The room appeared to be as Joyce had left it, with a hastily made bed and a dog-eared romance novel sitting on the nightstand. The drawer was filled with the usual bedside staples: Chapstick, lotion, earplugs, a couple of very personal items, and a few other odds and ends.

She didn't find anything unusual in the dresser. Joyce's clothes were all neatly folded, and the small closet was equally as organized. Two pairs of shoes sat on the floor: a pair of flats and heeled boots for fall. Nikki had been in enough old houses—including the one she'd grown up in—to know there were all sorts of nooks and crannies to hide things in. Nikki had kept private things under a loose floorboard, but she wasn't sure Joyce would have done anything to damage any of the original fixtures of the historic house, so she would have to be careful checking for loose floorboards. The closet shelf held only winter clothes and old books, none of which provided any clue into Joyce's mindset or previous life.

"What are you doing?"

Nikki jumped, nearly whacking her head on the low-hanging closet bar. Tony stood in the doorway, holding a leash.

"Just trying to get a feel for Joyce as a person. Are you taking Fitz for a walk?"

"A friend's picking him up," Tony said. "He doesn't like all the people coming in and out of the house." He eyed her. "Joyce was taken by someone from work. What does her bedroom matter? You should be out looking for her."

Something about his tone set Nikki on edge. Joyce was carrying this man's child, and his defensiveness didn't sit well. "Everyone has secrets." Nikki closed the closet door, her gaze on Tony. He stood in the middle of the small room, arms crossed over his chest. Nikki took a couple of steps closer to him. "Everyone." She emphasized the word. "And those secrets are usually tied into the bad things that happen. If there's something you know that can help us, but you don't want your wife to find out—"

"Did you find anything in here?" Tony asked, looking at the floor.

"Not so far," she answered. "You're certain that you and Joyce never had a single conversation about the years missing from her background check? Did you do any additional investigation into her background?"

Tony's mouth twitched. "I didn't see the point. I thought I'd taken all precautions. Why haven't we got a ransom call by now?"

"I don't know. It looks like a ransom situation, especially since it appears that all of her personal items are still here." Nikki slipped past him and walked to the other side of the room, opening the door that led to the bathroom. It was clean and tidy, but Joyce's toothbrush and other toiletries were sitting on the shelf above the toilet. Nikki opened the medicine cabinet, noticing over-the-counter allergy medicine and prenatal vitamins. It didn't look like she had gone willingly.

She turned her attention back to Tony, who'd followed her to the bathroom. "Hernandez said not many people knew about the pregnancy, but people at work must have realized she was pregnant. Did Joyce tell people at work she was a surrogate?"

"I assume so," he said. "It just seems like you should be out looking for her instead of doing this."

"I could say the same about you," Nikki said. "You sure there isn't anything you've left out? This is your child she's carrying. Any detail might help, even if it seems small."

"I've told you everything," he said firmly. "I'm going to check on Sonia. I'd appreciate it if you stopped wasting time and found my son."

Tony thumped down the stairs, leaving Nikki wondering why he hadn't mentioned Joyce's name. Did he expect them to find only the baby?

Her phone dinged with a text from Liam saying that he was downstairs, and Nikki sighed with relief. Hernandez was a good agent, but he wasn't a profiler. Liam also didn't have any personal ties to the case like their boss.

Nikki texted that she'd be down in a minute and for him to catch up on things with Hernandez. Then she opened a browser on her phone and typed in the house's address, hoping to find some sort of floor plan. She was certain that she remembered reading about the house going on the market a few years ago. The previous owners had lived in the house for decades and had learned several interesting tidbits about Fitzgerald, including a story about the third floor...

"Bingo," she whispered. The previous owners had mentioned the third-floor bedroom had been Fitzgerald's, and he'd written much of *This Side of Paradise* in that room. He'd also had to sneak out on the balcony to smoke.

Nikki could hear Tony downstairs, so she tiptoed upstairs. The bedroom took up most of the third floor, but it had been outfitted as an office. The old roll-top desk was locked, but the room was clearly being used. Several books on writing were scattered on the desk and in the reading nook beneath the window, as well as worn-out copies of Fitzgerald's works. A picture of the writer and his wife hung over the desk, along with a few others of Fitzgerald throughout the years.

One of the stairs squeaked, and Nikki turned around, prepared to go another round with Tony. She sighed with relief as Liam's tall, lanky frame appeared.

He scanned the room with raised eyebrows. "Wow."

"Right?" Nikki moved to the bookcase that lined the wall. She skimmed the titles, noting the various classics along with more modern works from all genres. "I wish we could pick the lock on that desk."

"Hernandez wants to talk to you again before we go to the vet's office," Liam said. "He's going to stay here and coordinate the search with the local police."

Nikki took one last look around the room, feeling like she was missing something. "Hopefully he can get away from Tony long enough to sneak up here. I assume he brought you up to speed?"

Liam checked his notes. "A twenty-eight-year old black female who happens to be the surrogate for Sonia Ashley and her husband. She's due in ten days, but she's got gestational diabetes. Her last numbers look good, but early labor—especially stress-related—is still a real possibility. Hernandez says they don't have a landline, so there's no real need to set up a trace."

Even the FBI couldn't track an incoming call without help from the network operator, and that would take a court order. "If a ransom call comes in, we'll get a warrant," Nikki said. "Our AV guys are already going through the security footage from the last twenty-four hours."

They walked quietly down the stairs. "What's your impression of these people?" Liam asked.

"We aren't getting the whole story for sure," she answered quietly. "Unfortunately, we need more information to force the truth out of them, and Joyce and the baby may not have much time left."

TEN

Hernandez had set up in Sonia's office on the second floor, across from the master bedroom. Unlike the rest of the home, Sonia's office was decidedly modern, with sleek lines and cream-colored walls. Instead of immaculate and uncomfortable antique furniture, Sonia's modern executive desk sat adjacent to the arched windows, allowing natural light to filter into the room without shining directly onto the desk. Vibrant plants had been placed throughout the room, including a massive fern that seemed too wide to get through the narrow doorway.

"This is exclusively Sonia's home office," Hernandez said. "It's the only place in the house that's truly hers. Tony's determined that every other room reflects the history of the Fitzgerald era." He rolled his eyes.

"What do you know about him and Sonia?" Liam asked. "Agent Hunt said she contacted you personally this morning instead of the police."

"I know it sounds weird," Hernandez said. "But Sonia's a very private person. Her father was the CEO of a local Fortune 500 company for nearly fifty years. Before she passed a few years ago, Sonia's mother was one of the best-known cardiologists in the country. As an only child of traditional Irish American and Indian parents, she was expected to follow in their footsteps. But she never wanted to do anything but write."

Nikki had skimmed Sonia's website before leaving Rory's this morning. Sonia had started out as a freelance writer, doing small articles on local businesses. She'd worked her way up the chain, eventually traveling all over the country doing investigative journalism. In the past few years, she'd had two nonfiction books on the bestseller lists, both dealing with various women's issues. She'd worked hard to become a respected writer, establishing a career separate from her family.

Nikki asked the question that had been bothering her all morning. "Why didn't she call the police immediately? Why take the extra step of calling you?"

"Sonia grew up wealthy and sheltered. When things went badly, her parents always knew someone who came into their lives and fixed it without making a huge fuss, no matter how serious the problem was. She still operates on that level."

Where did Hernandez come into all of this? She still wasn't certain that it mattered, but Nikki had also solved cases based on small details and bizarre connections. "Sir, we all know how urgent this situation is, so I'm going to be blunt. Why did she call you specifically? Is there anything we need to know that might affect the case?"

Hernandez snickered. "Always be blunt, Agent. Sonia and I met several years ago when she was a freelance reporter for the paper and I was still a street cop. Before you ask, yes, we did date for a while, but found we were better as friends. I'm one of the few people who actually knew about the surrogate, so she called me first."

"That was my next question," Liam asked. "What about Sonia's and Tony's friends? Is there something—or someone—in either's background that might have put Joyce and the baby in danger?"

"They're wealthy," Hernandez said simply. "Sonia is, anyway. As for Tony, he's the wild card."

"You don't like him." Nikki had to wonder if the dislike was based on more than just his impressions of Tony. If Hernandez still had a thing for Sonia, his opinion was likely to be skewed.

"Not particularly, but I did run a background check on him before they got married. It came back clean."

Nikki could feel Liam's eyes on her and knew he was thinking the same thing: why run a background check unless he had a vested interest in Sonia not marrying the guy? Whatever had gone on—or was going on—between Sonia and Hernandez likely didn't have anything to do with the kidnapping, but still, she couldn't treat him any differently than she would anyone else who might have knowledge of a case. "Do you still have that background check on Tony?"

"I've emailed it to you."

"You think he's after her money?"

"It's not that," Hernandez said. "I mean, he teaches elementary school art, so she's definitely the breadwinner. But as far as I know, he works hard and doesn't rely on her for money." He gestured at the room. "It was Sonia's idea to buy the house, supposedly. She let Tony decorate because he's good at it and enjoys it. I've never seen or heard anything that makes me think ill of him or that she was unhappy."

"And yet you still have a bad feeling about him?" Liam asked.

Hernandez held up a half-empty sheet of paper. "I'd gotten over it, until now. Look at this joke of a background report." He passed the paper over to Nikki.

Joyce's social security number was listed, but the work and residential history were less than two years old.

Liam had been reading over her shoulder. "WITSEC, then?"

"That's what I thought, but I just talked to the Attorney General's office in D.C. They are the ones who keep those records, and there's no one who matches her name or physical description."

"She could have changed her own identity," Liam said. "It's not that hard if you know what you're doing, and there's plenty of websites with information on how to disappear."

Hernandez nodded. "I added her personal information and photo to all of our databases, listing her as a missing person with a possible alias. We've got tech using facial recognition to expedite the process, but it's taking time Joyce and the baby don't have."

"What about the security footage from the vet's?" Liam asked. "I know there's a BOLO out for her vehicle but if they have a good angle of the parking lot, we might know which direction she went."

"I spoke to them earlier," Hernandez said. "She left the building at two seventeen a.m. Her car was parked directly under a security light. At one point, she stopped and listened as though she heard something, but then kept walking and got into the car. They reviewed the footage to see if she was followed out of the parking lot. She wasn't, but seconds after she left, a black sedan that had been parked across the street pulled away and went in the same direction. Unfortunately, the camera was too far away to get a clean look at the license plate, but we're hoping to figure out at least a couple of numbers. All the footage has been emailed to our people. Maybe we'll get lucky and they'll find something."

"What did the traffic cameras pick up?" The vet's location on West Seventh Street meant there should be plenty of CCTV from the numerous traffic cameras.

"I emailed you the few security videos we have," Hernandez said. "Joyce turned left out of the parking lot, and she should have taken the next exit to get on the interstate. You two head over to the vet's and see what you find out from the employees. I'll stay here and continue to coordinate with local law enforcement."

Hernandez stood and motioned for them to follow him downstairs. They could hear the murmuring of voices in the kitchen. "They have a cleaning lady who comes once a week. Fortunately, she's due to come today, so I'll talk to her."

"We have to check out everyone Joyce worked with too," Nikki said. "Some of them must have known she was a surrogate for a wealthy family, and if that vehicle followed her, her kidnapper knew she was at work."

"I had the vet on call send me all the employee information,"

Hernandez said. "We're checking them all out as we speak. So far, nada."

Heavy feet thumped toward them, and then Fritz the Dane rounded the corner.

"Is that a pony?" Liam whispered, inching toward the front door. Tail wagging, Fritz sniffed Liam's shoes and then stood up, paws on his chest, to sniff his face.

"Fritz, off." A red-faced Tony had followed Fritz. "We need to talk before you leave."

"Has something happened?" Nikki asked. "Did you get a ransom—"

"No," Tony snapped. "I want to make sure that you understood that I completely disagree with getting the press involved. We don't need that sort of madness."

Before she answered, Nikki introduced Liam. "We can keep the press away from the house," she said. "Unfortunately, they're a necessary evil in cases like these."

Tony narrowed his eyes. "With all due respect, I'm not as confident in your ability as my wife. I've followed your career over the past year, and you've gone through hell. This is your first case after your husband's murder and your daughter's kidnapping, right? It was all over the papers."

Nikki felt like she'd been sucker-punched, but she managed to keep her calm. "I appreciate your concern, and I assure you that you don't have to worry. We work as a team, and Hernandez is running this investigation, not me." She crossed her arms over her chest, her shirt already damp from the heat. "I did want to ask you a few questions, though, so I'm glad you caught us."

A bead of sweat ran down his sharp nose. "What is it?"

"Obviously we know Sonia's family wealth could very likely be a target. Is there anyone you can think of, maybe someone you've lost touch with, or who is upset with you? Someone who might use Patrick for revenge?"

"I assume you're asking this question of both Sonia and I," he said.

"I'm asking you, right now," Nikki said, without breaking eye contact.

Tony put his hands on his hips and shook his head. "The answer is no. I'll leave you alone so you can do your job and find my son."

Hernandez gave Nikki a knowing look. "No stone unturned. I have complete faith in your judgment." He followed Tony back into the brownstone.

Nikki dug her keys out of her back pocket and tossed them to Liam. "You drive my jeep. I want to look at Hernandez's emails."

Nikki opened her email and looked at the security videos first. The parking lot was well lit, and she could see Joyce's dark blue Kia parked underneath the light. Joyce walked outside, wearing maroon scrubs, her belly straining against the material. She shuffled more than walked, her bag hanging off her arm as though it was almost too heavy to carry. Joyce was clearly exhausted after a long shift, but she didn't seem wary of anything in the lot until she was just a few feet away. Joyce's head turned sharply to the left, and she listened for a moment before going on to her car. Despite the severity of looking for a missing child, Nikki was still grateful to have something other than her own life and Rory's dead ex-girlfriend to focus on for a while.

"The black sedan pulls away from the curve after Joyce leaves the parking lot," Nikki said. "Looks like there are some big shrubs at the corner of the driveway. If the sedan was actually following her, my bet is that he scouted the area, knew where to park and when she would leave."

"She works second shift, but if the place is always open, she's probably working past her shift sometimes," Liam said. "Places like that are always busy."

"Hard to be confident in someone's routine unless you have inside information," Nikki said, thinking of Tony. "Have you spoken to Miller this morning?"

"Why?" he asked.

"Because he needs to know you have a case and probably won't be able to assist him with Becky's case until we find Joyce and the baby."

"Oh, right," Liam said. "I'll let him know this morning. How's Rory doing?"

"He's very stressed about getting back to work," Nikki said, trying not to wonder what Liam thought of Rory. "I know that sounds terrible, but this is a huge job."

"Did you know the family who owned the farm before? Back when you were in high school, I mean?" Liam's tone was casual, but she could see his hands tightening on the steering wheel.

"Not personally, but we went there a lot when I was kid. They had a pumpkin patch. I think the house sat empty for a few years after the last McFarland died. Why?"

"Just curious since you grew up in Stillwater. Rory worked there, didn't he?"

"So did half the town," she said flatly, using Reynolds's line.

ELEVEN

Liam parked the jeep at the end of the vet's small parking lot, in the shade of a big maple tree. "Doesn't look like it backs up to anything useful to hide in," he said. "No woods or anything."

"I looked on Google Maps on the drive over," Nikki said. "They have a decent sized backyard for the animals, with a privacy fence. I expect they have plenty of security cameras too."

"All vet clinics smell the same," Liam said quietly as they walked inside. "Not bad, but chemical. Like some kind of special cleaning stuff."

"It probably is." Nikki held up her badge to the tired-looking woman behind the curved counter. "Agents Nikki Hunt and Liam Wilson with the FBI."

"Have you found Joyce?" the woman asked hopefully. "We're all just devastated to have heard that she's gone missing."

"Not yet." Nikki was disappointed to hear that the entire staff had already been told about Joyce. She liked to deliver the news to potential witnesses and suspects because those initial reactions were a key part of figuring out whether to believe someone's story. "We'd like to speak to as many of the staff as possible."

"I'm the office manager, Linda," the woman said. "Both of our vets are in surgery, but Doctor Meier should be done shortly."

"I see you're busy," Liam said. "Agent Hunt and I will split up to talk with the employees so we can let you get back to work. Do you have a couple of extra exam rooms available?"

"For the moment," Linda said. "We might have to play musical rooms, but we'll figure it out."

With Linda's help, they managed to speak to all fifteen employees on site in less than two hours, but the process was still tedious because the staff had to deal with the morning rush of sick and injured animals. Nikki heard essentially the same thing from each person she interviewed: Joyce was outgoing and friendly with everyone. She was proud of being a surrogate and seemed to enjoy living with the parents.

Liam came into the exam room that Nikki had been set up in with a scowl on his face. "Everyone likes her, she never caused issues. She was excited about being a surrogate."

"That's pretty much what I heard as well," Nikki said. "It doesn't sound like she shared a lot about her private life other than the obvious. She never really talked about where she worked prior to this."

"Sorry to keep you waiting." A tall, thin woman dressed in jeans and a scrub top appeared in the doorway. She sat down at the cluttered desk, smoothing the stray hairs that had escaped her long ponytail. "I'm Doctor Meier. Do you know any more about what happened to Joyce?"

"Unfortunately, not much," Liam said.

Nikki checked her notes. "Your office manager said that Joyce has worked here for two years?"

"That's right," Dr. Meier said. "She's one of my best employees. Joyce was so warm and caring, people gravitated to her. And she had a way of making people feel comfortable. She's always the one to sit with the clients who have made the choice to euthanize."

"She was good at reading people," Liam said. "Of knowing what they needed to hear?"

"You could say that, yes."

"Did she mention where she grew up? What she did before she worked here?" Nikki asked.

"She said she was born and raised in the Twin Cities."

"Did she ever mention living anywhere else?" Liam asked. "We'll need her former employers and her references too."

"We don't have that," Dr. Meier said. "Joyce admitted that she didn't have a lot of work experience during the interview process, but she was anxious to prove herself. We were short-staffed, so I started her on a trial basis. She picked up things very quickly. I think I'd hired her permanently by the end of the first week."

A petite woman in powder blue scrubs knocked on the front door. "Doctor Meier, is now a good time?"

"It's the perfect time," the vet said. "Cat, this is Agent Hunt and her partner, Agent Wilson. Cat worked last night, and she's really the only person who knows much about Joyce outside of work." Dr. Meier stood and motioned for Cat to take her seat. "I'm double-booked," she said apologetically. "If you need anything more from me, send Cat to look for me when you're done talking to her." The doctor hurried out of the room, and Cat took her place, looking worriedly at Nikki and Liam.

"I can't believe anyone would want to hurt her. It has to be about the baby, right?"

"We don't know yet," Nikki said. "Did you and Joyce spend a lot of time together outside of work?"

"Some," Cat said. "Before she decided to be a surrogate, I'd get her to go out and have some fun every once in a while."

"She didn't like going out?" Liam asked, scratching something in his little notebook. "She ever tell you why?"

"Not really. She just always said she wasn't into the party scene or whatever. But she didn't even like going out for a couple of drinks or coffee. She always said they were a waste of money and she had to save every dime, which I totally get." Cat sniffled and retrieved a tissue from her pocket. "I'm so worried about her I can't concentrate for very long."

"I understand," Nikki said gently. "Can you think of anyone

she might have mentioned, somebody perhaps bothering her or maybe following her around?"

"Not that I can think of," Cat said. "Wait, that's not true. Right around the time she and the parents found out the baby was a boy, Joyce told me she was certain that she'd seen the same guy loitering around near the house at odd times."

"Such as?" Nikki prompted.

Cat's cheeks turned pink. "I don't want to gossip. It was a theory of hers."

"There's no such thing as gossip in this kind of case," Liam said. "Everything is vital."

"It's just that the Ashley-Halls are good people and—"

"I'm sorry, Ashley-Halls? As in, both have the hyphenated last name?" Nikki asked. "I didn't realize that."

Cat nodded. "Tony's idea, I think. Anyway, Joyce liked them both. She never had any bad stuff to say but she thought Tony might be seeing someone behind Sonia's back. She always saw the guy around when Sonia wasn't home and one night, Joyce was absolutely certain she saw him walking in the back garden, near Tony's little greenhouse. She told Tony about it, and he said that he checked the security cameras and didn't see anything. He said she must have been dreaming, but Joyce told me he was flustered when she approached him. And she was positive the guy would have been caught on one of the back security cameras."

"Why did she assume an affair?" Nikki asked.

"Tony's openly bisexual." Cat shrugged. "Sonia knows, of course, but Joyce was positive he was sneaking this dude in, and the only thing that made sense was cheating."

Nikki thanked Cat and the others for their time and handed out business cards. "My colleague or I will likely be back to talk to the later shift, but please let them know to call asap if they have any information."

Nikki shaded her eyes as the late morning sun attempted to burn a hole in her retinas as she and Liam walked to the jeep. "I knew Tony was hiding something. It might not have anything to do with the kidnapping, but it doesn't speak well to his character that he didn't mention it to Hernandez even though his surrogate and baby are now missing."

Liam looked down at his scribbled notes. "Cat said that Joyce saw the guy she assumed Tony was sneaking around with around the time they found out it was a boy. How far along are you when you find out the sex?"

"Around twenty weeks, depending on the baby's position. But they have 4D ultrasound now, and sometimes people can find out earlier."

"So like four or five months pregnant," Liam said, doing the math in his head. "She saw this mystery man with Tony around February, then?"

"Around there," Nikki said, checking the notes she'd taken earlier. "Tony and Sonia told Hernandez that the security cameras only store so much, and they only keep a couple of weeks' worth of footage at a time. They have one mounted on the porch and back door, facing the backyard. And then a third in the far corner of the yard that focuses on the house. And Joyce was right. Those cameras would have picked up someone in the backyard. Tony lied to her, and we need to find out why."

Nikki pulled up a satellite image of the house on Google and showed it to Liam. "There's a small walkway from the back door that opens up into their closed-in yard, which isn't that big. If I remember correctly, that privacy wall is six feet. Easily scaled by the right person."

Nikki checked in with Hernandez to see if they had any updates on Joyce and fill him in on what they found out at the vet's, which hadn't amounted to much of anything. "You're on speakerphone, sir."

"We might have something. Our tech team identified the black car as a BMW, and they managed to figure out the last two digits of the license plate. It matches a 2019 M6 Gran Coupé that was reported as stolen by a Mae Kendrick a week ago. I'll text you her address. Get over there and see what you think. Is she a suspect or do we need to find the person who stole her car?"

"What do we know about the Kendricks?" Liam asked. "Why does that name sound familiar?"

"Because he's the guy Nash and I talked to yesterday," Nikki said. "It could be a really weird coincidence, unless Joyce's disappearance has something to do with the traffickers Nash is investigating. Did you have any luck with missing persons?"

"Checked our state and the national database," Hernandez answered. "No matches. The state police are searching for Joyce's car. We've checked all medical facilities in a fifty-mile radius, but no Joyce and no baby left in accordance with safe haven law."

Nikki promised to keep Hernandez updated and ended the call. Swearing, she cut into the passing lane to avoid a woman in a minivan talking on her phone and swerving.

"The car was stolen from Kendrick's driveway at three a.m. And they had proof. A security video on their property caught a man dressed in black sneaking onto the property. Ski mask, average height and weight. The door to the car was unlocked."

"Who leaves a car unlocked at night these days, especially a luxury car?" Nikki wondered. "That BMW has to retail at six figures."

"According to this, Mae thought she'd locked it. She hadn't been feeling well and went to the twenty-four-hour pharmacy." Liam balanced his tablet on his lap. "I'm going through the bureau's file on the tax fraud case, but there isn't a lot of information."

"I know." Nikki had learned over the years that those guys didn't trust anyone or any systems. "What you're seeing is basically a summary. Tax crimes and financial investigations are usually kept as confidential as possible, and the investigating agent doesn't log a bunch of information into the database until after the case is closed and the person sentenced. Fortunately, Tyler was working his case. Kendrick claimed he saw his wife go to a hotel and come back out with two teenagers, but that security tape was conve-

niently lost. Don't bother contacting his boss. I have copies of all
his notes and files in storage."

He looked up from his laptop. "Where are we, anyway?"

"Southern Washington County," Nikki said. "Super rich, big
homes, very exclusive golf course. Kendrick's place is just around
the corner."

She maneuvered the sharp curve, and Liam let out a low
whistle as the house came into view. "This isn't a house. It's a mini-
castle."

Nikki murmured her agreement and pulled into the bricked,
circular drive. She parked behind the red Range Rover sitting in
front of the house.

"At least she still has the SUV," Liam said dryly.

"Look at the bricks in the driveway," Nikki said. "The stone
matches the bricks on the house."

Nikki checked her phone for Lacey's text and quickly replied.
"I'll take my jeep over that any day." Nikki couldn't be certain the
cases were linked, but she had to figure out if she trusted Mae's
account of the stolen car. Had she really been robbed? Or was she
as sketchy as her husband?

Two massive planters of red geraniums sat on either side of the
front door. Nikki knocked on the heavy glass and waited. Seconds
later, a tall woman in her thirties with shoulder-length, shiny
blonde hair answered the door. "Can I help you?"

"Are you Mae Kendrick?" Nikki and Liam both showed their
badges, and Nikki made the introductions. "We're following up on
the report about your stolen BMW."

"The FBI?" Mae asked in surprise. "I know my husband's
being investigated for tax evasion, but we haven't been given any
notice about seizing our property."

"Actually, we're investigating a possible kidnapping," Nikki
said.

"A kidnapping?" Mae looked between them. "That pregnant
woman on the news?"

Liam nodded. "We have reason to believe your stolen vehicle might have been following her. May we come in?"

"Yes, of course," Mae said. "Although I should warn you, my daughter and I are going through old clothes and the house is a mess."

"No judgment." Nikki and Liam followed Mae into the tiled entryway. Nikki saw movement out of the corner of her eye. She glanced into the large family room where various clothes and other items littered the furniture. Mae was dressed casually in cut-off jean shorts and a Twins tank top, but Nikki also noticed several designer bags. "You're selling designer handbags?"

"Downsizing," Mae said cheerfully. "I just have too many useless things, and I'm starting to realize it's just sinful."

She was also part of a tax investigation and could lose everything, Nikki thought. Mae was likely selling things in hopes of hiding cash from the IRS. Tyler had run into similar situations several times, and Nikki was always amazed at how petty the Feds were about assets. He'd seized cash more than once. It all seemed like overkill to Nikki, but Tyler was a by-the-books guy.

"Sylvia," Mae called. "We have guests."

A brown-haired girl who appeared to be around twelve came into the room, looking at the floor. "Do you want me to get them something to drink?"

"No, thank you," Nikki said. "We won't take up much of your time, Mrs. Kendrick."

"Please, call me Mae." She looked over at her daughter. "Honey, why don't you go upstairs and start on the guest room closet?"

Sylvia looked like she couldn't leave the room fast enough. "She's very shy," Mae said. "And she's not happy about getting rid of things."

Nikki smiled. "My daughter is almost six and has the same problem with toys."

"I remember those days," Mae said. "Time goes so fast, but I don't miss having a little one. Girls are much more fun when they get older."

Nikki remembered her mother saying the opposite, but every kid was different. "We just have a couple of questions and then you can get back to sorting. We want to know a little more about the missing car you reported. My colleague mentioned it's been involved in a kidnapping. You told the police you forgot to lock it? Do you have an anti-theft system?"

Mae rolled her eyes. "Before my soon to be ex-husband ran off, he disabled it. Honestly, I assumed he snuck onto the property and took it out of spite."

"The two of you are separating, then?" Liam jotted something down in his small notebook.

"He's a crook, and I'm not going down with him," Mae said simply. "I never had anything to do with the business, anyway."

"That's not what your husband said," Nikki replied. "He told us that you took care of the books."

Mae scowled. "Lying sack of you-know-what. That's not true, and I can prove it. He's a manipulative bastard who will do whatever he has to in order to stay out of prison."

"You turned over the security video of the car being stolen," Liam said. "Did you recognize the man in the recording? Is it possible it was your husband?"

Mae snorted. "He would never have the balls to do it himself. Excuse my language. I'm sure it was one of his lackeys. Or at least I was sure. So you think my car was used in this kidnapping?"

"We don't know for sure," Nikki said. "All we know is that it was involved in some way. Your husband mentioned he'd moved into a penthouse."

"We separated weeks ago," she said. "He hasn't called to talk to his daughter since he left. Not that he was ever much of a father. He's probably off gambling in Atlantic City. That's why he got into tax trouble in the first place. He loses money as fast as he makes it."

"Can you give us his new address and phone number?"

Mae nodded. Nikki could have asked Nash, but he had already

messed her around several times. She'd have to update Nash on the couple's possible involvement in her case, but she didn't need to rely on his information.

"Mrs. Kendrick, we have to ask where you were last night," Nikki said, bracing for outrage.

"Right here," Mae said. "With Sylvia. We watched that movie with the actor who plays Captain America. It's a murder mystery. James Bond is in it too."

"*Knives Out*?" Liam asked. Nikki was glad he understood the references. She wasn't exactly up to date on pop culture unless it involved something a five-year-old was interested in.

Mae snapped her fingers. "That's it. Good movie."

"Would you mind if I speak with Sylvia?" Nikki asked.

"Of course not." Mae walked over to the bottom of the stairs and called her daughter's name. Seconds later, the girl jogged down the stairs, her arms weighed down with clothes.

"There's a lot of stuff in that closet," Sylvia said. "I'm still working on it."

"Agent Hunt wanted to speak with you," Mae said.

Sylvia chewed on her lower lip. "Okay."

"Mrs. Kendrick, could I look at your garage while Agent Hunt's talking with your daughter?"

Sylvia looked frightened at the possibility of being left alone with a stranger. She stared at her mother, waiting for the answer.

"Are you allowed to speak with her without me present?" Mae asked.

"With your permission, yes," Nikki said.

Mae fluffed her daughter's shiny, dark hair. "Are you okay with that?" she asked her daughter and Sylvia nodded.

"The garage is off the kitchen," Mae addressed Liam. "I'll show you."

Nikki waited until Liam's tall frame had disappeared into the kitchen. "My name's Nikki."

"I know who you are. You were on TV."

Nikki smiled and sat down on the couch, motioning for Sylvia to sit next to her. "It must be hard with your parents splitting up."

"He's not my father," Sylvia said quickly.

"I'm sorry, I didn't realize," Nikki said. "Do you get along with your stepdad?"

She shrugged. "He was nice when he was home. He traveled a lot."

"I guess his moving out isn't as much of an adjustment as it could be then," Nikki said.

"Not really." Sylvia sat on the end of the couch, her hands between her knees. She looked at Nikki with dark, serious eyes. "Is that all you wanted to know?"

"Actually, I wondered what you and your mom did last night."

Sylvia's eyes lit up and she confirmed Mae's story. Since the girl had been upstairs when they'd spoken to her mother, Nikki was confident Sylvia was telling the truth.

When she returned with Liam from the garage, Mae gave them Kendrick's address and cell phone number and promised to let them know if he called.

"What do you think?" Nikki asked Liam as they headed back to the jeep.

"No sign of anyone trying to break into the garage," Liam said. "I'd like to know where Kendrick was last night. Did Sylvia back up what her mom said?"

Nikki nodded. She had been thinking about Kendrick's claim that he saw his wife picking up teenaged girls from a motel. At the time, she hadn't made much of his accusations, but Joyce's disappearance shed new light on it. "I want full background checks on both Kendricks. I don't believe Mae was driving that car, but there's something suspicious about both of them."

"You going to call Nash first or Kendrick?" Liam asked.

Nikki made a face. "I should give Nash a heads-up, but I don't feel like I owe him anything."

"Really bugs me that the anti-theft was disabled and the car was left unlocked," Liam said.

"Me too," Nikki said. "But the Kendricks are splitting up, and he's being investigated for tax fraud. She assumes he had it stolen. We don't know if the car was involved in Joyce's disappearance, but we need to confirm Kendrick's alibi for last night. His new address is in the Downtown East area of Minneapolis. Call the MNPD and see if he's home."

"He won't be," Liam said. "I overheard Nash tell the sheriff that Kendrick had left the meeting and headed for the airport on a business trip to New York."

Stuck behind a slow-moving car, Nikki ground her teeth. Nash couldn't have known Kendrick was a suspect in the kidnapping, but most agents wouldn't let a person being investigated for tax fraud leave the state. "I've got Kendrick's number. Hopefully he takes my call." Nikki merged onto the freeway. "Let's head back to the Ashley-Halls' to touch base with Hernandez."

Nikki chewed the inside of her cheek, trying to figure out how to broach the awkward subject hanging between them. "Have you talked to Miller today?"

Liam sighed, never taking his eyes off the road. "Please don't put me in this position, boss. I've already told Miller that I've got to help you with Hernandez's case, but you know I can't share any of the information I do know about Becky's case."

All Nikki really wanted to know was if they had other suspects yet. She wanted to convince him into telling her with every bone in her body, but she knew she couldn't. It wasn't fair to Liam or to Becky and her baby. She couldn't compromise their case before it got started. "Miller thinks he's got a good chance at catching her killer, doesn't he?"

"I don't know, honestly. But you know him better than I do. You trust him, don't you?"

"Of course," Nikki said, a headache starting in her temples. "We'll go back to the house and figure out our next move. Let's hope Hernandez has good news about Joyce."

TWELVE

Summit Avenue was much busier when they returned, as rush hour traffic clogged the streets. A news van had taken up residence in front of the historical row of brownstones, and Nikki spotted it with surprise.

"So much for just using Joyce's name. Who in the hell gave away her address?"

Liam grinned. "Well, you know how cunning investigative reporters can be."

Nikki rolled her eyes. "Just because your girlfriend stops at nothing to get the story doesn't mean every reporter does. My bet is one of the local beat cops tipped off the media."

She turned left and drove down the alley behind Summit Avenue.

"Is that Hernandez's?" Liam asked. "Looks like our department-issued vehicles."

"He's driving his personal car," Nikki said. "It's probably additional agents he's brought in to assist with the search." Nikki eyed the street ahead, expecting to see reporters from the news van come charging around the corner. She didn't want to deal with the media. Hernandez would handle the current case, but once a reporter saw Nikki's face, she knew they'd get excited and never leave them alone. "Can you do something for me?"

Liam grinned. "You want me to sacrifice myself to the reporters out there."

"And then let me in the back." She pointed down the street. "There's a gate."

"Give me five minutes." Liam exited the jeep and walked briskly around the corner, and Nikki sighed with relief. She grabbed her things, locked the vehicle and then headed toward the back gate.

Number 599 was in the middle of the row of brownstones, with some having open yards and others fenced. This was the only rowhouse with a retaining wall of sorts instead of a fence. Nikki found the black metal gate and settled in to wait for Liam.

A few passersby look at her strangely, and Nikki realized she didn't exactly look trustworthy hanging around the back gate, and she definitely didn't look like an agent. She'd thrown on her running shoes, jeans and a gray T-shirt this morning, brushed her teeth and roughly combed her hair. It was up in a bun right now, but Nikki still felt like she was starting to melt.

She checked the time and then heard the back door of the house open and close. She looked up with a grin, expecting to see Liam.

Instead, Justin Nash strode toward her, carrying a set of keys. "Fancy meeting you here." He unlocked the gate with one of the keys and held it open for Nikki. "I heard Kendrick's car might have been involved in this kidnapping."

Nikki had been planning on calling Nash when she got back to the Ashley-Halls'.

But something had been niggling at her the entire drive back from the Kendrick home. Joyce's odd connection to Kendrick and her blank past didn't sit well with Nikki. Someone only had a clean slate like that if they were in WITSEC, and the only reason she wouldn't be able to find that out would be if Joyce was involved in a current, high-profile case. If WITSEC had moved her, Hernandez would have been informed by now. Nash definitely wasn't working with WITSEC, so why was he here now?

Nikki's stomach dropped. Was Joyce Nash's informant? The woman who had informed the police that a major trafficking operation was running out of the Twin Cities?

It would be just like Nash to dole out information in breadcrumbs. He'd always liked having the spotlight all to himself, and so far Nikki hadn't seen any evidence that he'd changed much. She shaded her eyes and glared up at Nash. The time for diplomacy had passed. "Why are you here?" She didn't give him the chance to respond. "Is Joyce your informant? WITSEC and the Attorney General's Office have never heard of her, and yet here you are, nosing around my missing person case."

Nikki was glad to see the bags beneath Nash's eyes. He motioned for her to follow him, but Nikki refused to move until he answered her question. "She is, isn't she? Why in the hell isn't she in the system?"

"Just come inside the house," Nash pleaded. "I'll explain it to all of you at the same time."

Nikki resisted the urge to shoulder check him as she stalked toward the back door. If Kendrick turned out to be responsible for Joyce's kidnapping, then Nash was to blame. If anything happened to Joyce or the baby, Nikki would find a way to hold him responsible. If she was his informant, he had a duty of care.

They joined Liam and Hernandez in the kitchen. Nikki glanced around. "Where are Sonia and Tony?"

"Resting upstairs," Hernandez said, his eyes on Nash. "Your friend said he had information about this case. I can't wait to hear it."

Liam caught Nikki's eye. "She is the informant, isn't she?"

Nikki dropped her bag onto an empty chair. "Yep. And he let Kendrick get on a plane."

"Excuse me?" Hernandez folded his arms across his broad chest. "You let a kidnapping suspect leave the area?"

"I didn't know anything about the kidnapping until this morning. How could I have known he was a suspect?" Nash demanded.

"Just start from the beginning," Nikki snapped. "We don't have time for any more runaround."

Nash loosened his tie and opened the top button of his blue dress shirt. The cocky swagger from yesterday had completely dissipated. "A few years ago, I was working in the bureau office in North Dakota."

Nash looked at her, clearly waiting for her to question why he was working in one of the states that agents jokingly referred to as punishment assignments. Those states didn't have much crime, which meant boredom. She didn't have time to wonder what Nash had done, however.

"I went through their open files to see if there was anything I could help with, and I came across Joyce Ross's statement," he continued. "When she was fifteen, she came into the North Dakota branch claiming a white man had abducted her when she was five years old and kept her captive in the Twin Cities until she escaped."

"For how long?" Nikki demanded.

"Ten years." Nash shook his head in disgust. "Back then, the old guard didn't believe anyone who looked untrustworthy, especially in piddly Bismarck. The file says that Joyce appeared to be under the influence, so she was told to come back when she was sober, and they'd talk to her then."

"But she didn't, because she knew it would be a waste of time," Liam guessed. "Did you try to find her?"

"After I read the notes, yes. Joyce said the man who took her gave her a new name and made her sleep in his bed. He molested her for years until she got old enough not to interest him anymore. Joyce told the North Dakota police that she'd been the only kid for a few years and endured her kidnapper's advances. Then new girls started showing up. Joyce was told to stay away from them."

"How old were these new girls?" Liam asked.

"At the time, around twelve or thirteen. As Joyce got older, she was transitioned into a caretaker role. By the time she was four-teen, she'd seen dozens of kids come through the house. None of them stayed more than a few nights, but she heard them at times, crying for help and begging for someone to 'stop.'"

"What did Joyce call her kidnapper?" Liam asked. "Did he convince her that he was her only family?"

Nash nodded. "He told her no one ever looked for her and that they were meant to be together. I first reached out to her months ago, and she refused to talk to me at first. No one had believed her the first time, and she was starting the surrogacy process."

Nash looked down. "I was shocked by how well she was doing and her strength, but I think she was relieved someone was finally taking her account seriously."

"I can't blame her," Nikki said. "Especially after she was basically told to take a hike all those years ago. Is Joyce her real name?"

Nash shook his head. "He gave her that name and told her to stop thinking about her life before him. She was so young when he took her..."

"Did she remember what he looked like?" Nikki asked. "How did she escape?"

"They moved a lot the first few years," Nash said. "Eventually they moved into a house with a big backyard and a privacy fence. She didn't even know the town she lived in, and if she did get to leave the house, he made her lie down in the backseat and cover up with a blanket until they'd driven far enough away from the house," Nash said. "She escaped when he blew a tire on a rural road and had to get out and change it. Joyce hit him with the tire iron and ran like hell."

"Does she remember where that happened?"

"She ran into the woods and hid until morning," Nash said. "Joyce had been planning her escape for a while, so she'd saved what little cash she had for a bus ticket. She cleaned up in a park bathroom and then went to the nearest bus stop."

"Which park?" Nikki asked.

"She was so stressed about getting out of town that she didn't pay a lot of attention, but she remembered a steep ravine. She got on the bus in Cottage Grove."

"That's Washington County," Nikki said. "Did she have any idea how close they were to the place he kept her when she escaped?" She briefly thought of Becky and her baby buried in the field. She'd disappeared just a few years earlier than Nash's first known trafficking victims, and the Washington County connection couldn't be ignored.

"Fairly close," Nash said. "That's part of the reason I wanted to talk with the sheriff about the women found last year. Kendrick lives in Washington County, doesn't he?" His skin had an ashy sheen.

"Yes," Nikki said. "But his house isn't anywhere near the area you're talking about." Neither was the McFarland farm where Becky had been found, but she had no idea where Rory's ex-girlfriend had lived growing up. She made a mental note to pass the information on to Miller. "Why wasn't Joyce in WITSEC?"

"I tried to get her into WITSEC," Nash said, his voice cracking in frustration, "but since the North Dakota guys never verified her story, and I initially couldn't track her down, that was impossible. And when I did finally find her, she'd already started the surrogacy process."

"So, she got a new identity on her own," Liam stated. Nikki knew it probably wasn't that hard for her to do given she'd never had an original identity. "What about her real family? Is there a missing persons report?" Liam asked.

"It's hard to find when he tricked her to forget what her real name is or even where she disappeared from," Nash said testily. "He told her he took her from Wisconsin, but none of that matched with what she remembers. Same with Minnesota."

Liam shoved himself off the wall and closed the distance between him and Nash. "Hard, but not impossible. Didn't anyone ever teach you that the tedious details are usually the ones that can break a case wide open?"

Nash clearly found Liam's comments patronizing; she could see his blood boiling.

"Drop the attitude, Justin," Nikki said. "You're already on thin ice. The only reason I haven't called your superior is because we have to focus on finding Joyce and the baby."

"I just want to find Joyce," Nash said.

Now that Nash had finally come clean, Nikki could already begin working on a profile for one possible suspect: the man who kidnapped her as a child. His relationship with Joyce would be complex. It would be about control. Since he didn't kill her as a child, he was unlikely to kill her now, but she was pregnant this time, and all her medical needs made the situation more complicated. Even if Nikki didn't think the man was intending to murder her, they needed to find her soon. The longer he had to cover his tracks and find a new hiding place, the less likely they were to ever see her again.

"What about Kendrick?" Liam asked.

"He flew to New York," Nash said, and Liam and Nikki both swiveled to look at him angrily. "He even gave me the name of his hotel. I've got two agents on the ground looking for him right now. He won't be getting on any international flights."

"What else did Joyce tell you about her kidnapper?" Nikki asked.

"He had an inner circle, people he was trafficking these girls for. Some of them preferred teenagers, some younger. She remembered a couple of them living in the house when she was young, but they really talked to her. They weren't allowed to talk to her."

"Did she attend school?" Liam said.

"She was never allowed to go out of the house except for the backyard, which had a big privacy fence."

"She didn't remember the names of any of the others he brought into the house?" Nikki asked. "Or any of the men she might have met or heard in the house? She doesn't remember anything about where she was taken from?"

Nash sighed and stuck his hands in his pockets. "Fleeting bits of memory that she isn't even sure are real. Like I said, the kidnapper spent years saying her family abandoned her and he found her, alone."

Joyce had been so young and traumatized it was a miracle she remembered anything from her childhood before she'd been taken. "Have you gone through missing persons databases to try to identify her?" Nash nodded. "Let's do that again," she told Liam. "Did she remember anything specific about the last place he kept her before she escaped?"

"She said it was an old farmhouse with creaky steps," Nash said. "Two stories, light brown, fenced-in yard, privacy fence. That's it. She was rarely allowed outside, and never by herself."

That described dozens of houses in the area. "What about the other girls who came through the house over the years?"

"A blur of faces. That's about it." Nash looked dejected. "She didn't recognize the two Washington County victims when I showed her photos of them, but they would have been taken and killed when Joyce was young. She and I went through the missing persons database a dozen times and never found anyone else she recognized."

He paused. "I don't know if the parents filed a missing persons report. I've searched the databases but haven't found one that matched Joyce's memories."

"Did you talk to any of the cops who worked the initial case?" Liam asked.

"One's dead," Nash said flatly. "His partner retired to Florida and says he doesn't remember anything. I'm pretty sure he's got some early-onset Alzheimer's."

"Have you ever worked a missing kid case?" Nikki asked.

"Why does that matter?" Nash demanded, hands on his hips.

"Because I don't think you would be so quick to dismiss the effort put in by original investigators if you had. I know there are still major problems with law enforcement that need fixing, but missing children cases take everything out of an investigator, especially if the kid isn't found. Assumptions like yours don't help anyone, especially Joyce."

"Email me a copy of her initial missing persons report," Liam said to Nash. "I'll have our people go through the database again, starting with the surrounding areas. They might find something you and Joyce missed."

"Minnesota and Wisconsin. It's twenty minutes to the state line, and people go back and forth all the time," Nikki reminded him. She'd been watching Nash closely the last half hour, and something about his story bugged her. "I'm going to check in and let Miller know we have yet another connection to Washington County. Hopefully, he can spare someone to keep an eye on the Kendrick place too. They're both pointing fingers at each other, so as far as I'm concerned, they're both suspects right now."

"On it." Liam had already fired up his laptop.

Nash dug a pack of cigarettes out of his back pocket. "I need to get some air."

Hernandez scowled, watching Nash leave. "Just so we're all on the same page, Nash claims Joyce was kidnapped when she was five, by a man running a large trafficking ring. She escaped, which means she might be able to help locate her kidnapper." He looked at Nikki. "Nash said WITSEC didn't get involved because they couldn't verify her story and Joyce had already started surrogacy. If the DOJ was involved, I have a hard time believing they would be so accommodating to a star witness." Hernandez cursed. "I've got some contacts out there. I'll call and see what I can find out."

"Call New York and ask them to find Kendrick," Liam said. "I don't trust Nash to talk to the right people at this point."

"Neither do I, but I'll make sure that actually happens," Hernandez said indignantly. "We're stretched thin with every available body searching for Joyce." He looked at Nikki. "Call Sheriff Miller and let him know what Nash said about Joyce. See if he can put some deputies on the Kendrick place."

Nikki paced the kitchen, her cadence nearly in time with

Liam's typing. She forced herself to stop and take a breath. "Are you going back to the St. Paul police station?" Given his history with the SPPD, working so closely with former colleagues had to drain Hernandez's energy.

"Unfortunately," Hernandez said. "I could cut the tension there with a knife, but they're doing everything they can to help find Joyce and the baby. They're establishing search grids in both St. Paul and Minneapolis. Parks, lakes, empty fields. Any place a body or a baby could have been left." He leaned against the counter. "What's your impression of Nash now?"

"I don't know," Nikki said. "The Justin Nash I knew was spoiled and flew on his parents' coattails. He said he was in the North Dakota field office when he discovered Joyce's file, and I highly doubt Nash was working in North Dakota on his own volition. Is there any way you could talk to someone in the field office out there too?"

"Tomorrow," Hernandez said. "It's almost six p.m. No one's going to answer."

No wonder Nikki's stomach was growling. "I hate feeling this helpless. We're looking under every rock for her, and she's just vanished. I feel like—" She managed to stop herself from admitting to him that she felt almost as stressed and powerless as she had when Lacey was taken. "Liam, try to find Joyce's missing persons report, and search for any reports in Minnesota and Wisconsin with similar disappearances." Nikki explained her strategy of finding other victims with living family members who knew additional details that might help them find Joyce's kidnapper. "I think at least one of us should stay here tonight in case something happens."

"Sonia already suggested that," Hernandez said. "I've got to get to SPPD. Hunt, can you talk to both of them again now that we have new information? See if they knew any of it and didn't tell us."

Nikki nodded, glancing at Liam's computer, expecting to see

the missing persons database. Instead, he appeared to be studying an aerial photo of a familiar-looking farm.

"What do you want to do about Nash?" Hernandez asked. "D.C.'s an hour ahead of us, so I doubt I'll be able to talk to anyone at the DOJ until tomorrow."

"Hopefully I can convince him to stay here too. That way we can keep an eye on him." Nikki's gut told her Nash still hadn't shared all his information. She peered over Liam's shoulder. "Is that the McFarland place? I thought you were looking at missing persons."

Liam looked like she'd caught him sneaking money out of her bag. "Yes. It's an old image Miller sent me, before a lot of the surrounding development."

Nikki could see the area Miller had marked in red, and she knew it was the area where Becky had been buried. "Wow, there's the old house before it was torn down. I'd forgotten how much open land there was back then."

"Yeah." An awkward silence hung between them. Nikki sighed, knowing she had no right to pressure him to share information. "Since you're helping Miller, why don't you let him know what Nash just told us and ask if he can spare deputies. I'm sure I don't have to mention that there were only a couple of years between Becky and the victims found last year. Doesn't mean there's a real connection, but he'll want to know about it. It's probably best it comes from you."

Liam scowled. "I still don't think we're getting the whole story from Nash."

"Neither do I," Nikki said. "I'm going to talk to Sonia and Tony again, see if I can get them to eat and relax enough to talk more. I just don't think we're getting the whole story from them either. Since she requested it, let's set up here for the night."

Liam nodded, then looked down at his phone. "Uh, you might want to check your phone. Hernandez just texted us."

"He can't even be out of the driveway yet," Nikki said. She

yanked her phone out of her back pocket, her heart dropping as she read the text.

> Joyce's car found. Not good. Don't say anything yet. Meet me at address.

THIRTEEN

Liam drove while Nikki talked to Lacey on the phone. Hernandez had given them an address in the West Seventh neighborhood, less than half a mile from Joyce's work. "I'm so sorry, bug. I really want to come home, but a lady and her baby are still missing."

"It's okay, I guess." Lacey's little voice shook. "Granny said I should have a slumber party with her tonight, anyway."

Relief washed over Nikki. "That sounds like a great idea. Has Rory stopped by yet? Did he tell you he would come back today?"

"He was pretty stressed when he brought me over. It was okay until he got a phone call. I helped him clean his leg, and there really are eighteen stitches, Mom. It's so gross."

Nikki laughed. "You don't have to look, silly." She said her goodbyes to Lacey and texted Rory to call her when he could, trying to ignore the constant nagging guilt she felt. But this was her job, and she still had to provide for Lacey. Nikki just wasn't the sitting around at home type, especially when someone was missing.

She checked her text messages for the umpteenth time, hoping to see something from Rory. She didn't mind him bringing Lacey to Ruth, but the phone call her daughter had mentioned worried her. Had Miller found something new? She doubted Courtney had established paternity yet. She pushed the thought to the back of her mind. It had probably been a work-related call. Rory spent half his days putting out fires, and she had a pregnant woman to find.

Hernandez's text hadn't given any details other than the scene wasn't good. Nikki's heart ached for Joyce and Patrick, praying they hadn't run out of time.

Nikki's stomach was in knots when they pulled into the empty parking lot where Joyce's car had been abandoned. Hernandez stood on the perimeter as Dr. Blanchard attended to the back seat of the car. The trunk was open, and Nikki sighed with relief when she saw that it was empty.

"Was she in the car?" Nikki asked bluntly.

"No, but there's a lot of blood," Dr Blanchard replied. "I think it's afterbirth. There are definitely remnants of placenta. We'll have it tested." Dr. Blanchard leaned against the hood of the car, looking more emotional than Nikki had ever seen her. "It's dried, but given this baking heat, it could only be a few hours old. Either way, I think that baby has been born."

"Get this on the news," Nikki said. "Let the media know we found the car and believe Joyce may have delivered the baby. They both may need medical attention. It changes the figures we need the public to be looking out for."

Nikki approached the car, trying not to gag from the smell of baked blood. She said a silent prayer for Joyce and little Patrick. "Oh God," Nikki said when she saw the backseat. "That's a lot of blood. Do you think she bled out?"

"No, but she was in bad shape when she left the car at the very least. It looks like there was some sort of hemorrhaging, but that's impossible to tell without seeing the victim."

Nikki was thinking about what Nash had told them. If his information checked out, the baby would only be a nuisance to the kidnappers. "If the same guy who abducted her as a kid is responsible, he doesn't want her to die. He wants her to live so he can make her life miserable," she said, walking back over to Hernandez.

"Word's out to all the hospitals in the state and Wisconsin," Hernandez said, looking worried. "If she or the baby shows up, we'll be notified."

The front seat of the car looked pretty clean, and Nikki couldn't see any real signs of a struggle. Blanchard had moved aside to bag some of the biological evidence she'd taken, so Nikki edged up to the driver's side backseat. Most of the blood seemed to be centered in that area, with some running down the side of the car. Nikki shined her flashlight on the fresh blacktop, searching for any sign of a bloody shoe print. If Joyce had bled in this car and walked off on her own volition, Nikki would expect to see a blood trail. "Doctor Blanchard, with all of this blood loss having the baby, is it possible Joyce left the vehicle and walked somewhere for help?"

"Highly unlikely," Blanchard said. "She was either cleaned off or carried. She would have left some kind of blood trail."

Sweat trickled down Nikki's spine, and the setting sun seemed to shine right into her eyes. She slipped on latex gloves and opened the glove compartment. She found Joyce's registration and the car's manual and little else. Nikki tried the center console next. Its design was similar to the jeep, with a shallow compartment that lifted to reveal a deeper one. Hoping to find Joyce's cell phone, Nikki lifted the inner piece. "Damn." She stood up and wiped the sweat off her face. "I assume the keys were left in the car. It doesn't look like you pried the trunk open."

"They were," Blanchard said. "I bagged them for evidence. Might be able to get prints."

"We called Courtney on the way over. She's swamped, but she sent a couple of her guys over to get the car. She wants it all to go to the lab," Liam said.

Nikki walked over to Blanchard's already bagged evidence. Gum, breath mints, pepper spray. "Where did you find the pepper spray?"

"Center console," Blanchard said.

If Joyce had been forced to pull into the parking lot and carjacked, she likely had time to at least try to grab the pepper spray, but Nikki could tell that it hadn't been used. "She didn't use the spray. It's never been opened."

"Maybe she couldn't get to it. Or she was already in labor and couldn't think straight."

"That's entirely possible," Nikki said. "She could have gone into labor and pulled over, thinking she'd call for help. Joyce doesn't know she's being followed, and she's blindsided, with no time to go for the pepper spray."

"Doctor Blanchard, could you tell if her water broke while she was driving?" Liam asked.

The medical examiner shook her head. "It would have dried faster than the blood. But your lab should be able to test for it."

Nikki now knew for certain that Joyce hadn't run away; she'd been taken. And Nikki or the agents on Hernandez's team had been with Tony and Sonia since they'd reported her as missing. They were definitely looking for someone else. Maybe even a man who had been looking for Joyce for a long time.

On the drive back to the Ashley-Halls', Nikki and Liam strategized. They had to push them harder than they had earlier.

"We need more people on the streets," Liam said. "We don't know if Joyce was allowed to care for the baby, or if he has just been left somewhere. Joyce lost a lot of blood, and who knows if the baby was healthy?"

"Agreed, especially as both mother and baby are extremely vulnerable until they can be given proper medical attention," Nikki replied, unable to voice what they were both thinking: if the baby had even been allowed to live. As far as she could tell, little Patrick might simply be collateral damage—unless it turned out the biological parents were involved. "I think Sonia will be cooperative. Tony's the one I'm concerned about. I've been kicking myself for not asking about the man Joyce saw earlier, but this might work out better." Nikki intended to put him on the spot in front of

Sonia. Between herself, Liam and Hernandez, she hoped they could get the answers they needed.

"I know the boss doesn't want to hear this," Liam said, "but something's hinky with this whole thing. It doesn't add up to me."

"What do you mean?" Nikki asked. "If her kidnapper found out where she was, he's probably been planning this for a while."

"But how did he find that out in the first place?" Liam asked. "It's thirteen years later, Joyce is going by a new name. After all this time, why come after her now?"

"Pride," Nikki said. "You know these guys think of these girls as possessions. But you do have a point. Let's forget about Kendrick's and Nash's stories and look at things from a different angle."

"Sonia and Tony," Liam said. "They're the most logical, and because Hernandez essentially vouched for them, we've focused on other things."

Nikki knew their boss wouldn't have let any personal connection cloud his judgment, but she and Liam had to look at every option. "You're thinking Sonia and Tony have Joyce taken and plan to be reunited with the baby at some point, while Joyce is disposed of?" She just didn't see the reasoning when the Ashley-Halls had already spent so much money on her. "They knew Joyce had gestational diabetes and that Patrick needed to be born in a hospital. Why take such a risk so close to her due date? Plus, they paid her half of the eighty thousand dollars and took care of her living expenses for months. Maybe they're trying to get out of paying Joyce the rest of the money, but that seems like a stretch."

"I know, and the whole thing puts the baby at risk, and Sonia doesn't seem like she'd take that risk." Liam flipped through his notes. "I just feel like we're missing something."

"See if Tony or Sonia has a life insurance policy on Joyce or the baby," Nikki suggested. "It would make sense given she's the surrogate, but I'd like to know whether or not they'd be honest about it." Nikki hadn't pegged Sonia or Tony as involved, but people continued to surprise her, and they still needed to ask Tony about the mystery man.

Nikki parked behind Hernandez's car, and she and Liam walked to the brownstone together. "Sir, since you're a friend of the family, maybe you should be the one to give them the news," Nikki said as they caught up with him outside the house.

Hernandez nodded wordlessly as he trudged up the stone steps. He probably was the best person to deliver the news, but that wasn't the reason Nikki had suggested it. She wanted to be able to observe both Sonia and Tony receiving it.

Nikki was disappointed to see Nash sitting with the couple, a half-full bottle of vodka and two shot glasses sitting on the glass table. "Anything new?" Tony asked.

Hernandez nodded and slowly pulled out the chair next to Sonia. "I don't want you to panic, but we found Joyce's car abandoned. There was lot of blood, and biological material, including the placenta."

Sonia covered her mouth and howled. Tony dropped his shot glass, and it shattered onto the floor.

"Listen to me," Hernandez said. "This doesn't mean Patrick is dead, or Joyce for that matter. All the hospitals are on high alert. We've got as many people as possible searching for them. It's not time to give up hope."

Nash stared at Hernandez for a minute, as though he were unable to comprehend what he was hearing.

Tony wrapped his arms around Sonia and held her close, tears streaming down both their faces. Tony brushed his wife's dark hair off her face and kissed her forehead. "He'll be okay. Joyce too. They'll find them."

His voice cracked, bringing fresh sobs from Sonia. Her keening howl made Nikki's throat ache. She knew the pain intimately, knew how it embedded into your stomach and ate away at the soul. Time had stopped when Frost took Lacey, and Nikki had spent every agonizing minute trying to figure out what to do next. The helpless feeling still kept her awake some nights. What if she hadn't found Lacey?

"Nicole?" Hernandez's voice brought Nikki back to the present.

Nikki shoved the memories down and tried to focus. "I know it's a really difficult time, but I have a few more questions for you."

Sonia and Tony still clung to each other, but she wiped her face with her shirt and nodded.

"Did Joyce ever mention anyone named Kendrick?"

They both shook their heads. Liam fiddled with his phone for a few seconds and then extended it to the couple. "This is the same BMW model seen behind Joyce last night. Does it look familiar at all? Maybe one of Joyce's friends has one?"

"I don't think so," Sonia said. "She never had friends over to the house, but I don't think anyone she knew drove a new model BMW."

"Why?" Liam asked.

"Joyce always seemed kind of awed by anything extravagant," Sonia said. "She rarely talked about friends, and when she did, we both got the impression they weren't financially well off."

"I assume you spoke with Joyce about what happens after the baby is born," Liam said. "How long did you intend to let her stay with you?"

"We told her she was welcome to stay for the first three months," Tony said. "She hadn't decided yet."

"Why do you think that is?" Nikki asked. "Where else would she have to go?"

"What does that matter?" Nash asked. "How are her plans for the future going to help us find her?"

Nikki ignored him and tried to think of the right way to word her questions. Her gut said the Ashley-Halls weren't involved, but she had to push them to make sure. "When is Joyce due the remainder of her surrogacy fee again?"

"After he's born," Sonia said. "We have it set up to deposit on his due date."

"Did Joyce ever ask for more money?" Liam asked. "Try to change the terms of your contract?"

Tony and Sonia looked at each other, confused. "Just the opposite," he said. "She tried to pay for rent and groceries all the time, and we told her to save the money."

"Very altruistic," Liam said.

Nikki knew he was deliberately trying to goad them into slipping up if they were involved, but she could tell that Nash wasn't picking up on the tactic.

"I don't like where you're taking this." Sweat beaded across Nash's forehead. "Why would Joyce ask for more money?"

"It was just a question," Liam said, looking at the couple. "If she had, would it have been an issue?"

"Of course not," Tony said, his cheeks pink. "Obviously Sonia's the one with the money, but she would have given Joyce anything she asked for."

Nikki could tell that Nash was going to interrupt again, so she decided to be blunt. "Your financials will confirm there are no issues with paying Joyce the remainder of her fee, I assume?"

"Of course," Sonia said. "Why wouldn't they?"

"She's trying to ask you if the two of you are involved," Nash snapped. "Even though all evidence points to the contrary."

Nikki wanted to throttle him, but she kept her attention on Sonia and Tony. "I wouldn't put it that way, but if there is anything else we need to know, now is the time to tell us."

"If we knew anything more, we would tell you." Tony threw his hands up in desperation.

Nikki seized her opportunity. "Who was the man Joyce saw on the security cameras a few months ago? Around the time you found out the baby's sex?"

Tony stared at her, pink starting to bloom in his cheeks. "What?"

"Her friend at work said Joyce saw a man in the backyard one night, sneaking around. You told her the security cameras were clean, but she knew what she saw."

"That was February," Nash said.

Hernandez's gaze slid over to Nash, his eyes narrowing. "Did Joyce tell you this?"

"Yes," Nash said. "She wasn't worried."

Sonia was staring at Tony. "I already knew about him. I have access to the security cameras too." She turned her body away from her husband. "That person was a friend of Tony's."

"You have a lot of guy friends come visit late at night?" Liam asked.

Tony stood. "I don't have to listen to any of this. Sonia and I have been completely forthright. You are wasting time while Patrick is out there."

"This is routine procedure," Hernandez said. "We have to eliminate you as suspects."

"Consider us eliminated," Tony snapped. "The friend Joyce saw that night is out of the country right now, anyway. And when do you think we had time to follow Joyce when we've been here, watched by your agents, this whole time?"

"Why didn't you tell her who it was?" Nikki asked.

"It's a private matter between the two of us." Sonia's voice was hard. She picked up her phone and swiped to unlock it. "You don't need a warrant to run our financials. I'll show you everything right now."

"There's no need for that," Hernandez said. "And legally, we need a warrant."

"We also need the name of this male friend so we can confirm he's out of the country," Liam said, addressing Tony.

"But I want us off the suspect list so you can find them," Sonia said. "This is doing nothing but wasting precious time. That man's name is Logan Dunn."

Nikki could tell by the sickly look on his face that Tony hadn't realized his wife knew about Logan's visit.

"I promise we are looking at every angle," Hernandez said. "We have cops all over the area out on the streets, and we'll have fresh eyes out this evening after shift change."

"Good," Nash said. "Because treating these poor people like suspects is a waste. The same person who took Joyce as a kid has her now. Get back to the facts."

Hernandez stood up, his solid bulk far more intimidating than Nash's wild eyes. "I'm calling the DOJ and the North Dakota office first thing in the morning. I suggest you sit down with Agent Hunt before I see you again."

Nash grabbed his cigarettes and lighter off the table. "Yes, sir." He stalked out of the room, presumably going to smoke.

"I don't understand what's going on," Sonia said. "Is he lying?"

"About Joyce's past?" Nikki shook her head. "I don't think so. But we don't have the whole story yet."

"Get it before he leaves today," Hernandez said flatly. "We don't have time for his games."

FOURTEEN

Nash appeared shortly after Hernandez left, stone-faced. He spent the next hour helping Liam and Nikki go through everything Nash and Joyce had tried in order to find her kidnapper. Joyce had done such a good job of blocking out his face she couldn't remember enough details for a good composite sketch. Nash explained that he and Joyce had spent countless hours going through missing persons files, trying to find any of the girls she remembered being in the house. Nash had hoped that finding one or two of the other victims would back up Joyce's story, and he would be able to open a formal investigation. But nothing had worked, and Joyce had been ready to give up, but Nash had convinced her that Nikki's skill as an investigator and knowledge of the area could help them find her captor.

"I assume last night wasn't the first night she was supposed to stay with you when you came to town," Liam had asked. "Why didn't she tell these people she wouldn't be home?"

"She told me she'd call when she got off work because they'd be sleeping, and she wouldn't have to listen to Sonia worry about her being out at night."

"Was there tension between them, then?"

"Nothing serious," Nash had said. "Joyce never had a bad word to say about either of them. She had her opinions on Tony, but it wasn't anything nefarious, including about Tony's buddy. She saw the guy twice, the second time leaving the house. Right out the front door."

"What about Sonia?" Liam asked. "It's pretty clear that Tony wasn't aware she knew about Logan."

"Joyce just said that she was positive that Tony was hanging out with this guy, and she had no clue if Sonia knew. She figured it was none of her business, anyway."

Nikki worked through the timeline in her head. "Sonia said she'd woken up at five thirty a.m. out of a deep sleep and knew something was wrong."

She glanced into the living room. After Hernandez left, Tony gave them Logan's contact information and then disappeared upstairs. Sonia remained on the couch in the parlor, staring into space. "You guys keep going through stuff. I'm going to talk to Sonia again."

Sonia didn't seem to realize Nikki was in the room until she spoke. "How are you holding up?" She sat down next to her on the couch.

Sonia's light brown skin appeared sallow, dark circles beneath her eyes. "I think I'm really just numb right now."

"I understand," Nikki said. "Waiting for news is the most hopeless feeling in the world."

Her dark eyes focused on Nikki. "But you found your little girl."

"We will find your son and Joyce too."

Sonia reached for another tissue. "I wanted to be there when he was born. That sounds so selfish but it's true."

"It's not selfish at all," Nikki said. "You're his mother."

"I can't believe Tony didn't tell me about the background check," Sonia said. "I know he meant well and thought he had the bases covered but..." She choked back a sob. "I guess not."

Nikki seized the opportunity to push her on the couple's relationship. "Did you know about Logan Dunn before Joyce saw him on the security cameras?"

Sonia nodded. "Tony and I have an arrangement. I just didn't know he was sneaking his friends over here." She looked down at her hands, twisting the diamonds on her left ringer finger. "I was too caught up in the pregnancy to deal with it. Sometimes it's better just to let things get swept under the rug."

"How did you and Tony meet?" Nikki asked.

"I know you're thinking we make an odd couple," she said, brushing a tear off her cheek. "A half-Indian woman from a wealthy family and a freelance writer who should be teaching." She shook her head. "He's an art teacher, but I convinced him to take a year off and write his novel. I'm sure you've figured out he's sort of obsessed with Fitzgerald."

"A little bit." Nikki smiled encouragingly. "Have you known him for a long time?"

"I met him about four years ago," she said. "It was a blind date set up by a mutual friend. I can't say that we clicked right away, but Tony grew on me. He's very smart and sensitive. He'll make a great father."

"Is he as excited about having a baby as you?"

Sonia stiffened. "What do you mean?"

"I'm not suggesting he's unhappy," Nikki clarified. "But sometimes one spouse really wants a child and the other might be on the fence. That doesn't mean he won't love Patrick."

"He's more scared than me," she said. "I know how to take care of a baby, but Tony's never been around young children. I think he just needs time to get used to Patrick once he's back home. If he comes home."

"Are you and Joyce close?" Nikki deliberately used present tense.

"I don't know if I would say close," Sonia said. "I always felt like she held a lot back with me, but she was so accommodating with everything we asked her to do during the pregnancy, including dosing down on her medications."

"Medications?" Nikki asked. "I didn't see any in her medicine cabinet."

"She finished them before the procedure," Sonia said. "All with the doctor's guidance. She's had some spells, but we're using a holistic approach right now to treat her depression and anxiety."

"Did she ever talk in detail about her issues?" Nikki asked. "Like what caused them?"

Sonia shook her head. "She just said it ran in her family, but she'd been wanting to get off the meds anyway. Everything was monitored by the doctor. She never told me about her childhood."

Nikki wanted to tell Sonia about Joyce's past, but she didn't want to reveal anything that might impede her investigation. She couldn't be certain that Sonia wasn't a suspect yet.

Nikki tried to keep her talking. "Joyce liked to read, didn't she? I saw a romance novel in her room."

Sonia smiled faintly. "She said they were her escape, but she read everything. Even sad things like real stories from women who've survived abuse or other terrible things. I never understood how she could stand to read them."

"How's Tony doing?"

"He's holed up in his office. I should check on him." Sonia sighed and started to stand, but Nikki stopped her.

"Let me check on him," she said. "Why don't you go grab something from the kitchen? I know nothing sounds good right now, but you need to eat something."

Nikki trudged up the stairs, wondering how many damn steps were in the house. She had her answer thirty-eight steps later. Huffing, she went to the third-floor office door, but Tony had locked it. She banged on it. "Tony, open the door, please. Sonia's worried about you."

He still didn't answer, but Nikki was determined to talk to him tonight. "I can also pick a lock in under a minute."

"I'm fine," he finally answered. "I just need to be alone."

"We won't stop looking until we find them, I promise." Nikki was growing impatient with Tony. He was hiding something, and Joyce and Patrick were paying the price.

Screw it.

Nikki banged on the door again. "Liam confirmed your friend was out of the country." She pitched her voice low, hoping her words didn't carry all the way downstairs to Sonia. She heard his feet stomping across the wood flooring and then the rattling of the old lock. Nikki took two steps back, uncertain. She didn't trust him.

The door finally opened, but instead of going on the offensive, Tony appeared completely defeated. "Sonia and I have an agreement. I wasn't supposed to bring anyone home, but I did it anyway. Joyce never approached me. She wasn't trying to blackmail me. Joyce wasn't like that."

Nikki suddenly felt sympathy for Tony. Perhaps she was reading his impatience wrong; maybe he was scared. "She could still be alive," Nikki said. "Your son too."

Dark circles ringed his bloodshot eyes, and the smell of marijuana clung to him. "I don't have much faith in that, no offense."

Behind him, the room's large window was partially open, a warm breeze blowing inside. Nikki could just barely make out the small enclave in the house's sloped roof. "Fitzgerald snuck out there to smoke cigarettes, right?"

"Yeah," Tony said. "He wrote *This Side of Paradise* in this room, mostly because he wanted to make enough money to marry Zelda."

Nikki hoped her miniscule knowledge of the writer and his mentally ill wife would be enough to gain Tony's trust. "My mom loved Fitzgerald. Romanticized the hell out of the time period."

"Me too," Tony said. "Life was simpler back then. People didn't worry about their children playing outside, creeps didn't prowl the street ruining people's lives."

Nikki leaned against the doorjamb, curious about Tony's choice of words. "Did you see someone around, Tony? I believe you about Joyce respecting your secret and not using it to her advantage," she lied. She hadn't ruled that out yet but telling Tony wouldn't help gain his trust.

His gaze snapped to hers. "I already told you that I didn't. Why do you keep asking the same questions?"

"Because it's my job." Nikki kept her tone neutral. "You'd be surprised how many people withhold details because they're embarrassing and they don't think the information would help, but they're often wrong. The littlest details are the ones that matter most."

"Agent Hernandez looked at our security footage already. It didn't pick up anything unusual."

"Except for Logan—"

"Weeks ago," he interrupted her.

"Did he know about the surrogacy?"

Tony shook his head. "We didn't exactly discuss personal stuff. It was a few times, blowing off steam." He sighed and walked over to the roll-top desk, finally allowing Nikki to see the entire room. She inched closer, trying to see what he'd kept locked in the roll top.

"That is one hell of a pipe collection," she said, disappointed. Tony might be trying to write his novel up here, but the only secrets he was keeping in the damn desk were weed-related.

"Thanks," he said, writing something down on a sticky note. He thrust the note toward her. "These are the only two men I've entertained in the past six months. Do what you have to."

"I'll be discreet."

"It doesn't matter now," he said softly. "Sonia's never going to forgive me."

"If you're talking about the cheating—"

"I'm not." Tension layered his voice.

"Then what are you talking about?" Nikki pressed.

He looked past her, a vacant look in his eyes. "The background check. She's so upset about it."

Nikki had been thinking about everything Nash had told her in the last couple of hours. How had Joyce's kidnapper even found out she'd returned to the area, much less actually found her? He likely had resources and allies who were just as invested as him in making sure Joyce stayed silent. If he were smart, he'd taken Joyce and run, severing all ties with anyone who could testify against him. And if he'd really stayed under the radar for more than a decade, he was smart.

But in her experience, ego often trumped intelligence. He'd want to punish her, and unless he'd run with her right after she gave birth, it would have been next to impossible for him to get through airport security or the checkpoints in and out of the metro area. He was likely lying low, biding his time. Hiding.

Nikki had just noticed the dark smudges on Tony's hands. "Charcoal?" she guessed. "You're an art teacher, right?"

"I was. I love teaching it, but my skills as an artist are pretty pathetic. I used to tell Joyce that she had a real gift and should do something with it."

"What sort of gift?" Nikki asked. "Painting, drawing?"

"Drawing," he said. "She had an incredible memory. The three of us would take Fitz for walks around the neighborhood, and she'd come back and draw the people we interacted with in amazing detail."

"Really?" Nikki asked.

"Sonia used to tease her about having a photographic memory," Tony said. "But Joyce insisted that wasn't it. She said..." He stared at his hands for a few seconds. "She said she just liked to draw faces." He grew quiet, staring into space. "Of people that she didn't want to forget."

Tony reached for a pre-rolled joint and then glanced at Nikki. "I'm going to light this. Arrest me if you want."

"I'll keep my options open." Nikki's heart raced, fresh adrenaline working its way through her. It was a long shot, but if Joyce had drawn any of the other girls she'd seen trafficked, then they could release those to the media. Finding out the circumstances of the other kidnappings might help them find Joyce. Some traffickers also let people go after they'd been used up and gotten older. It never ceased to amaze Nikki at how many victims said they were just dropped off in another state and left. They were so mentally broken, and many had become forcibly addicted to drugs. Very few turned their captors in at that point.

"Do you know where Joyce kept her drawings? The ones she'd make after taking walks?"

"In her room, I guess. You looked in there, right?"

Nikki nodded. "I searched the closet for compartments and tested the floorboards to see if she'd hidden something below them." She'd checked under the mattress and bed, searched all of Joyce's drawers and storage boxes.

"Old houses." Tony balanced the joint on his lips. "Always some place to hide things. Fitzgerald didn't live here during prohibition, but he'd hide bottles in here, so the story goes."

"I'm going to search Joyce's room again," Nikki said.

"Knock yourself out." He lit the joint and slowly inhaled.

Nikki backed up towards the door, not wanting to smell like a walking joint. "Sonia is getting something to eat. You should try to eat something as well."

He held up the joint and exhaled a plume of smoke. "This is all I need."

Nikki left him to it and went in search of Liam. He hadn't moved from his spot in the kitchen. "Where's Nash?"

"He said he was going to grab some sleep." He looked at his phone. "Damn. We have at least a hundred people out looking for this woman and the baby. Why haven't we found them?"

"Think about it," Nikki said. "Traffickers run extremely tight operations; they know how to hide. They're not your average criminal—they're organizations." Nikki had to remind herself that Liam hadn't worked on a case like this before—they hunted serial killers, individuals, but this was the first time they were dealing with someone who might have connections to a criminal organization.

"She betrayed him," Liam said. "What better punishment than to bring her back to where he kept her as a kid so she can see he's still doing what he wants."

"My thoughts exactly," Nikki replied.

FIFTEEN

Nikki and Liam found Nash with his eyes closed on the couch. Nikki didn't trust the man, but it was clear he hadn't slept since Joyce had gone missing. He opened his eyes as Liam went to search Joyce's room—Nikki had already looked herself, but perhaps he'd find other hiding places—and she quietly explained Joyce's drawings to Nash.

"Joycie never mentioned any drawings to me," he mumbled, digging a pack of cigarettes out of his pocket. "I'll be back."

Nikki felt her stomach flip.

Joycie?

She hadn't heard anyone else call Joyce by that nickname. Exactly how close had Nash been to Joyce? She followed him into the small back garden. "So when did you start smoking?"

Nash shrugged. "I only smoke when I'm stressed." He didn't look at her, but she could tell by the rigid state of his shoulders that he was more than a little upset. He kicked a loose piece of rock across the patio and swore.

"How long have you and Joyce been seeing one another?"

Nash didn't answer immediately, and Nikki wondered if he'd seen her question coming. She stepped in front of him and grabbed his cigarette, stomping it out on the ground. "I know that your parents are high up on the food chain, but frankly, so am I. And if you don't tell me everything you know right now, I will make sure you're back in North Dakota within twenty-four hours."

"I have told you everything you need to know, *Special Agent Hunt*." He started to pull another cigarette out of the pack, but Nikki smacked it out of his hand.

"A helpless baby is out there." She raised her voice loud enough for the neighbors to hear. "You're withholding information that could help us save him. I could charge you with accessory."

His nostrils flared. "Unbelievable."

"Yes, you are."

"I'm talking about you," he sneered. "You're such a superstar you got your daughter kidnapped and your husband killed."

Nikki swung out of blind rage. Her fist connected with Nash's jaw, and pain shot through her hand. He'd always known how to cut a person down, but this was plain cruel. During their academy days, Nash's cushioned, sheltered upbringing had allowed him to think he could say and do whatever he wanted. He'd clearly never fully grown out of that mindset.

He clutched his jaw, wide-eyed. His right arm tensed instinctively, and Nikki put her hands up, ready to block the blow. Nash stilled. "Oh Christ, I'm sorry. That was cruel as hell."

She pressed her aching hand to her chest. "Yeah, it was. But I shouldn't have hit you."

"It's okay. I deserved it."

"I know you did. I meant my hand." She tried to grin at him, but the joke fell flat.

"Five years old," Nash said. "Joycie was five years old when that piece of trash destroyed her life. She doesn't even remember her early life because he put her through so much trauma." He yanked out a fresh cigarette with unsteady hands. "Most of her memories before ten are spotty. As she got a little older, he left her alone more and more. Until he started loaning her out. That's how he found out how much money he could make." All the fight seemed to have drained out of him. "Nik, I swear the information I left out won't help you find her."

Still rubbing her hand, Nikki decided to try another tactic. If Nash and Joyce had been involved, then he was likely making decisions based on his emotions.

"Justin, I'm not judging you for being involved with her. But trust me when I say it's extremely difficult to make clear decisions when you're so close to a case. That's part of the reason Tyler is dead." Her voice shook. "I have to live with that every day, and I wouldn't wish that feeling on my worst enemy."

"I'm sorry I said that about him," Nash said. "It was totally out of line."

"That doesn't mean it's not partially true," Nikki said. "If I'd removed myself from the case, then Tyler might still be alive. My daughter wouldn't be traumatized. My point is, it's not too late for you to come clean about everything. If you're worried about losing your job, I can put in a good word for you. So can Hernandez."

"Everything I said was true," Nash said. "I just left out the part about the two of us." He rested his forehead in his hand. "When I finally tracked her down, she was only a couple of months into her surrogacy, and she refused to talk to me at first. But I was persistent."

"She was your ticket out of North Dakota, and you thought her information would land you on the task force," Nikki guessed. "Did it?"

Nash shook his head. "I admit that was my intention in the beginning, but things changed." A flush had started to creep up on Nash's neck.

Nikki was getting impatient, but she knew Nash needed to be handled with kid gloves. "When did she finally start talking to you?"

"After I got the tip from Tyler about Kendrick, I decided to talk to her again. That's when she told me the rest—and I haven't left anything out. Everything between us happened after that." Nash exhaled a cloud of smoke. "I tried for weeks to get someone to take

Joyce's story seriously. But time had passed and, well, my reputation didn't help. I've made a lot of dumb mistakes."

Nikki asked the question that had been bugging her. "If there is no DOJ task force, then why would Tyler send you the tip? Did he know you were in the North Dakota office?"

Nash nodded. "We reconnected at a conference in New York a few years ago. You guys were in the middle of your divorce, and I took him out to have some fun. We stayed in touch after that."

Nikki knew she shouldn't feel betrayed. Tyler hadn't done anything wrong by not telling her about Nash. But she thought he'd told her everything, even during the divorce. They'd had a mediator, and the entire process had gone more smoothly than a lot of their marriage. They were better people and parents divorced. Tyler had remained Nikki's main confidante, but it was unfair of her to assume that he felt the same way about her.

"He said you didn't know we got to be friends," Nash said. "He didn't think you'd care, but he knew how you felt about me, so—"

"I never had a problem with you," Nikki said. "You were kind of a womanizer, but I knew that."

Nash's lips twitched. "We were really good together. I wish I had a better answer, but we didn't talk about you much."

"It's fine," Nikki said briskly, willing her self-pity away. "Did you and Tyler talk about the case at all?"

"He called me the day after he sent it," Nash said. "He felt guilty about not telling you instead, especially since I was in North Dakota. But everything was going on with Frost, and he decided to wait. I told him I'd check it out..." Nash's voice caught. "I should have come to the funeral. But I..." He paused. "I'm a coward."

"Don't worry about it," Nikki said, warming to Nash for the first time that week. Tyler's funeral had been beautiful, but Nikki didn't want to think about it. She had to stay focused on Joyce and the baby. "Tyler never gave you any other information about Kendrick?"

Nash shook his head emphatically. "I'd tell you that. Yesterday I wasn't sure about Kendrick's involvement, but after seeing that damn car following her, I feel like an idiot for letting him get on a plane."

"Technically, you didn't have the means to stop him. He hasn't been formally charged. When was the last time you spoke to Joyce?" Nikki fanned her shirt. The humidity had yet to break, and she felt grimy from sweating.

"Yesterday afternoon," he said. "After our meeting with Kendrick.

She was supposed to meet me at my hotel last night when she got off work. I wasn't too worried initially since she worked at the emergency vet. It's not exactly regular hours. But then she didn't answer her phone. The hours went by, and I got madder and madder."

"She knew you and I were speaking to Kendrick? Did she recognize the name? I assume you showed her his photo."

"She knew, and no, she didn't recognize him. She saw you on the news after you caught Frost, and I told her we went to the academy together. I knew if Joyce came with me, and you heard her story, you'd want to help. I convinced her to sit down with you today." Moisture built in his eyes. "I thought she'd changed her mind and just wasn't taking my call. And now she and that baby might be dead."

As much as she wanted to blame him, Nikki couldn't put that on someone. It was a terrible feeling. "None of this is your fault. I wish you would have told us the whole story earlier, but I'm not sure it would have made much of a difference. I'm going to fill Liam in. You might want to come in and let him know you're really on our side too."

SIXTEEN

Liam had listened to Nash's information in silence. She knew he'd been steaming for the past hour, and Nikki had been impressed with how neutral he'd been toward Nash considering everything.

"If you had told us this earlier..." Liam began.

"I don't think he held us up," Nikki said. "If anything, he could have sounded the alarm about her not showing up at his hotel, but his reasoning made sense. I probably would have thought the same thing. You too."

"Why all the bluster and subterfuge?" Liam directed his question at Nash. "How are we supposed to believe you now?"

Nikki had left out the part about Nash's friendship with Tyler. It wasn't relevant, and she couldn't focus with his name being tossed around all the time. "He's got no reason to make this up. He and Tyler were friends," she added softly. "I didn't know. Justin was afraid to tell me."

Liam chewed the inside of his cheek, his eyes on Nash. "You should have told her. She can handle it, and we might feel like we could actually trust you."

"I just want to find Joyce and the baby," Nash said. "Call my boss in North Dakota after this, have me suspended. I don't care. Joyce and Patrick are all that matter to me."

Liam still didn't look completely convinced, but she knew he would go with her judgment, at least for now.

Nikki knew what Liam was thinking. "I still need to go through all of Tyler's paper files on Kendrick. They're in storage and doing so will take time." She watched Nash for his reaction, but he was quiet, appearing to be lost in his thoughts.

"Where's the storage at?" Liam asked. "We might be able to get someone over there."

"Stillwater," Nikki said. "It's the same unit my aunt had. There's stuff in there that belonged to her and my parents. Tyler's things are all packed in boxes that probably aren't marked accurately."

"What about Rory?" Liam asked. "Couldn't he go over and look? It's a long shot, obviously, but it just seems like we should see the file he had on Kendrick."

It wasn't a bad idea, and Nikki needed to check in with Rory anyway. "Check in with Courtney and see if she's getting anywhere on the car. And tell her I'll call her in the morning."

Liam grunted and reached for his phone. "Pizza should be here in a few minutes."

"Save a couple of pieces for me. And breadsticks." Liam could eat all day and still be hungry. Nikki had seen him plow through a takeout order without even thinking about whether he had the right food. "I'm going to check in with Rory and Lacey."

Nikki expected to see text messages from Rory, but she only saw Lacey's asking if Nikki was okay. Instead of replying, Nikki called her cell phone.

"Mommy, I was afraid you weren't going to call me tonight."

"I was afraid you'd be asleep," Nikki said. "What did you do today?"

That was enough for Lacey. She told Nikki all about planting and helping Granny Ruth. "Rory never came over," Lacey said. "Is he okay?"

Nikki was beginning to wonder that herself. "He's working long hours, honey. That's all."

Lacey was silent for a few seconds. "I miss Daddy most at night."

Nikki's throat burned from fighting back tears. "I know, bug. I miss him too. But he's still here in spirit, watching over us." She rolled her eyes at the cliché. It had never made her feel any better.

She and Lacey talked for a few more minutes, and Nikki promised to text her in the morning. She decided to see if Rory would answer the phone. She clicked video chat, wanting to see his face.

"What?" he answered groggily, glaring at the phone with one eye open.

"I didn't expect to wake you up," she said.

"You didn't." Rory took a drink of beer, and she realized he was sitting in bed, drinking. He was drunk.

"Everything okay?"

"What do you think? I spent two hours in the sheriff's office being interrogated about Becky again." His glazed eyes burned with anger.

"Interrogated?" Nikki asked nervously. "You already gave your statement."

"Yeah, but Miller had more questions because he talked to her lying friends. So he started digging in like he thought I had something to hide."

"Do you?" Nikki couldn't keep the question from slipping out of her mouth. "I don't think you had anything to do with Becky's murder, of course," she clarified. "You just seem very antagonistic."

Rory drained his beer. "Yeah, well, being a murder suspect will do that to a person."

"You're not a murder suspect." Nikki was getting irritated. "Miller is doing his job."

"Keep telling yourself that," he grumped. "You talk to Lacey tonight?"

"Yes," Nikki said. "This case isn't going well at all. It looks like the surrogate went into early labor and had the baby. We still have no idea where they are."

Rory cracked another beer and stared at the open can. "I keep thinking about how I'd feel if my son was missing. God, poor Becky."

"Hey, Nik." Nash walked up behind Nikki, his face in the camera frame. "I'm going to crash for a while... oh, sorry. Didn't know you were on the phone." He sniffed the air. "Did someone order pizza?"

"It's in the kitchen." Nikki was still stuck on Rory's last words. Had he really said 'son'? Hernandez had released Joyce's name to the media, but decided to hold back on the sex until they had reason to believe the baby had been born. Right now, all the focus needed to be on Joyce.

"Who was that?" Rory asked.

"Agent Nash." She was still processing what Rory said. "He's helping with the case."

"The dude from yesterday?"

Nikki nodded, her stomach turning at the question she was about to ask. "How'd you find out that the baby Becky was carrying was a boy?"

Rory didn't answer right away, but he visibly flinched. "Miller, I guess." He took another swig of beer without looking at the camera. "I'm about to fall back asleep."

"Right," Nikki said. "I should try to sleep for a little bit myself. I'll talk to Miller tomorrow."

"Don't bother," Rory said. "You need to focus on your case. But I'm not going back down to the station again. He wants to talk to me, he can arrest me."

Nikki didn't know what to say, and Rory's belligerent tone was getting to her. "I'll talk to you tomorrow. Stop drinking and go to sleep."

"How long will the paternity test take?" he asked quickly.

"As far as I know, Courtney's rushing it," Nikki said. "But the lab is always swamped, and I can't give you an ETA."

"Sounds about right," he said. "Talk to you tomorrow."

He ended the call before she could say goodbye. A heavy pall settled over Nikki. She'd tried to tell herself that Rory would get better once they knew if he was the baby's father, but she didn't know what to think, especially since he seemed to know the baby's sex. Miller must have told him, Nikki reassured herself, even though she knew that was the sort of information Miller would never reveal to a suspect. It was just the alcohol talking. He wasn't used to so much of it. Rory usually had a beer or two after work, but he rarely got drunk, and when he did, the night usually ended with incredibly satisfying sex.

She had to cut him a break, at least for tonight. She'd ask him about the storage unit tomorrow when he was clear-headed.

A woman screamed, her voice carrying down the stairs. Jolted awake, Nikki peeled her eyes open, trying to find her bearings. She'd been going through her notes on the couch, looking for anything they might have missed. She didn't expect a ransom call at this point, but she'd decided to accept Sonia's invitation to stay at the house in order to keep an eye on both parents. When had she fallen asleep? The scream came again, and Nikki jumped to her feet as Nash and Liam stumbled out of the kitchen, bleary-eyed. Upstairs, Sonia and Tony's footsteps pounded on the wooden floors.

Nikki raced up the steep stairs, Liam on her heels. "Sonia, what's going on?" she shouted.

Sonia burst out of the master bedroom, tears flowing, still in the clothes she'd been wearing earlier. "The hospital just called. Patrick is okay."

"What about Joyce?" Nash asked.

"I don't know." Sonia ran back into the bedroom, where Tony was stumbling around, trying to put his tennis shoes on. "Patrick is being taken to the hospital, and Tony and I have to get to him."

Nikki's cell started ringing, followed by Liam's and Nash's.

"Agent Hunt," she said crisply.

"Joyce walked into some dive up north and handed Patrick

over to the owner, and then she left." Hernandez sounded exhausted.

"Alone?" Nikki asked.

"Sounds like it. I'm meeting Sonia and Tony at the hospital. I'll text you the location. I've got people searching the area for any sign of Joyce, but you and Liam get out there and talk to the woman."

"On our way, boss." Nikki ended the call. "Sonia, do you and Tony need a ride to the hospital, or are you safe to drive?"

"We're fine." Tony finished lacing up the shoes. He grabbed Sonia's shaking hand. "Please let us know if you hear anything about Joyce. This isn't over until she's home safe too."

SEVENTEEN

Nikki called Rory on the way to the location to ask him if he could look through Tyler's storage boxes, but his phone went to voicemail. She knew Lacey was with Ruth, but it wasn't like Rory not to answer. She left him a message, asking him to check the storage and call back if he could.

"He's probably still asleep," Nikki said after she ended the call. Rory's slurred words from last night played on repeat in her head.

My son.

Nikki was certain Miller wouldn't have told Rory the baby's sex. Had he just made a lucky guess? Or did he know more than he'd admitted? She wasn't worried about his guilt, but withholding information wouldn't exactly make him appear innocent to Miller or Liam.

"I thought this was supposed to be the populated part of Minnesota," Nash said from the back seat. "Aren't the boonies farther north?"

Nikki snorted. "Not quite. It's even more sparsely populated, but there are plenty of rural lakes and resorts in the area. I looked at the reports earlier—the trafficked victims found in Washington County last year were buried less than three miles from the place

Joyce left the baby. And Joyce was five when she was taken and fifteen when she escaped in 2007, right?"

"Yes, I think so," Nash said. "Why?"

"It's the timing," Nikki said. "The victims you identified last year were taken before Joyce escaped. She might have seen their faces, assuming your trafficking theory is right." Nikki glanced at Nash. "You said that Hardin was a pain in the ass when you talked to him last year. How exactly?"

"I wanted to look for more bodies," Nash said. "He told me ground-penetrating radar didn't find any other bodies, and they had a K9 out, too, supposedly. Problem was he did all this when I wasn't around, and I wasn't sure I could believe him."

Nikki had worked with Hardin when she first returned to Stillwater—their personal history dated back to her parents' murders. He'd been a decent cop, but he'd made plenty of mistakes. He'd run the sheriff's office like a mini dictatorship, so she wasn't surprised Hardin hadn't allowed Nash to dig for more victims.

"Thankfully, Hardin's out of the picture, and Sheriff Miller is easy to work with. I texted him before we left and asked him to meet us here." Nikki turned onto the narrow road that wound around the lake. Sun glinted off the water, and she could just make out a boat in the distance. The road curved sharply, and the marina appeared, along with the bar and grill/bait and tackle store. She parked next to Miller's cruiser. "Looks like he's already inside."

"Boon's Bar and Bait." Liam pointed to the sign. "This place is bizarre."

Nikki snickered. "Clearly you aren't familiar with the north woods. This is typical."

Nash caught her eye from the rearview mirror. "This is an FBI case. Why is a county sheriff here?"

"Because I asked him," Nikki answered.

Nash started to open his door, but Nikki hit the child locks. "Wait just a second."

"For what?" Nash demanded. "Joyce was in that place less

than an hour ago. She could still be close, and you're fine with some county sheriff who isn't even involved in Joyce's case—"

"Sheriff Miller knows Washington County better than anyone else," Nikki said firmly, glaring into the rearview mirror. "He's an avid outdoorsman, and he's already sent deputies out to help search for Joyce at our request."

"He's a county sheriff." Nash looked at her in disbelief. "He's out of his element."

"This is also his jurisdiction," Liam said, the muscle in his jaw twitching.

"I've worked with Sheriff Miller on three high-profile cases," Nikki said. "He's more than capable, and I want you to understand that. There isn't going to be any jurisdictional bullshit. This is about finding Joyce alive. Understood?"

"That's all I care about," Nash snapped.

Nikki shut off the engine. "Then let's go."

Boon's Bar and Bait looked exactly like Nikki had expected: small and run down but somehow still clean and cozy. The interior smelled like a river, likely from the barrels of live minnows that were lined up against the back wall.

Miller was standing at the wooden bar talking with a white-haired woman. "Agents, this is Sharlene Denton," Miller said. "She owns the bar and bait shop."

The short woman slid off the tall bar stool. "Nicole Walsh, as I live and breathe. I never thought I'd see you in here."

Nikki stopped in her tracks. The only people who ever called her by her maiden name were the ones she'd known in another life, before her parents had been killed. "I'm sorry, do I know you?"

"You wouldn't remember me," Sharlene said. "But your dad loved to fish up here, and he'd bring you with him every once in a while. You were just a tiny sprout, not even five. But you sure could catch fish. Your dad spent the whole time baiting the hook and taking off the fish."

Nikki smiled. "I still don't like doing those things."

"Well, I suppose you want to know what happened," Sharlene

said. "I never saw anything like it in my life, and if I hadn't seen it with my own eyes, I probably wouldn't have believed it. The bar opens for lunch, but the bait shop opens at ten. Used to be nine, but I'm old and like to sleep in. Anyway, I was outside, fiddling with an old boat motor I'm trying to sell." Sharlene pushed her coarse hair off her face. "I got that feeling you get when someone's watching you. Trying to sneak up on you. It's survival instinct, you know?"

Nash had been hanging back, pacing. He crossed his hands over his chest and sighed loudly. "Can you get to the point? We're here about the woman."

"Excuse him," Nikki said, gritting her teeth. "He's not used to being out in the field."

Sharlene waved him off. "He don't bother me. I deal with yuppies every day. As I was saying, I got that feeling, so I turned around. Had my wrench in my hand, and I was ready to knock someone's fool head off. But it weren't no creep. It was this poor black lady, looking like she was damn near too weak to walk and holding a pile of sheets. At least that's what I thought it was. I begged her to come in and rest, let me call for some help, but that poor thing was scared to death. Kept looking over her shoulder, but I didn't see anyone. That's when she handed me the pile, and I see a brand-new baby inside. Poor thing needing cleaning up." Sharlene shook her head. "He is so small. But he was squirming and whining, seemed alert. She followed me inside and sat down while I went into the office and called for help. When I came back, she'd left the baby on the bar and disappeared."

"How long did you take to call for help?" Nash asked.

Sharlene shrugged. "Long enough, I guess." She broke eye contact, pink forming on her cheeks. "When I have to go, I have to go, or I'll have a mess."

Nikki wanted to kick Nash for embarrassing the poor woman. She rubbed her shoulder. "It's okay. Did she say anything at all?"

"Not a word," Sharlene said. "At first, I thought she might have been on something, but when I got a good look at her, I knew it was worse than that. That girl's broken. But she did feed that baby, cause I'm pretty sure he had dried milk on him, and she left a little bottle of what the paramedics said was breast milk."

"Is Patrick going to be all right?" Nikki asked Miller.

"Paramedics said he was in good condition, but he'd probably stay in the hospital for a couple of nights." Miller pointed to the ceiling, where a single camera had been mounted. "Doesn't work."

"I been meaning to replace it," Sharlene said. "Money's tight, you know."

"We understand," Miller said, looking at Nikki. "We've searched everything in a three-mile radius, which is all rural. No sign of Joyce or anyone, for that matter."

"You won't find her," Nikki said. "He chose this area because it's probably far away from where he's keeping her."

"You all need anything more from me right now?" Sharlene asked. "Customers will be coming in soon."

"I think we're good for now," Miller said. "But if you think of anything else, call immediately."

"Are there any traffic cameras around here?" Liam asked.

"Too rural," Miller said. "County says they wouldn't make enough money to warrant having them out in the rural areas."

Little Patrick was safe, but Joyce had vanished into thin air, again. Frustrated, Nikki leaned against the bar, looking blindly at the names and dates that had been carved into the bar over the years. For a moment, she hoped her father's name would be gouged into the wood, but it wasn't.

"I know your people are stretched thin." Miller was talking to Liam. "I've got volunteers searching all over the county, but it's really starting to feel like a needle in a haystack."

"Nikki." Nash's sharp voice cut into her thoughts. "What now? You're the damned expert."

She grabbed a half-mangled paper clip off the counter and imagined stabbing him in the eye. "Where are the sheets that Patrick came in with?"

"Bagged as evidence," Miller said.

Nikki explained the timeline that Joyce had laid out for Nash. "Becky disappeared in 1997. The two Washington County victims who were found last year disappeared within two years of her. I know you can't talk about the specifics of Becky's case, but has anything come up that might tie to this one?"

Miller chewed the inside of his cheek, clearly debating what he could share. "I've talked to Becky's dad and brother, along with her friends. She had her issues, but she came from a supportive home. Her friends all liked the family. I haven't heard anything that made me think Becky might have been trafficked, no. I did notice there was an uptick in missing teens in the early 2000s. Most of them were girls, and several had run away and were found. But there are a few unaccounted for. Have you ruled out the parents, then?"

"I don't think they're involved. I just don't get that impression from either of them, and we haven't uncovered any solid evidence against them. Both seem to care deeply about Joyce. And she told the biological father that as a kid, she drew pictures of people she didn't want to forget. If we can find any of those drawings, assuming they even still exist—"

"You can use them to compare against other missing persons," Miller finished. "That's like finding a needle in a haystack, though."

"I know," Nikki said. "But if we can track even one of them down, we might be able to figure out where Joyce was kept the first time. I think it was somewhere in Washington County, and I think the person who took her is toying with us."

Miller's dark eyebrows knitted together. "I don't follow."

"He buried at least two bodies near here—girls Joyce likely would have been aware of if he'd taken them while she was still under his control. He's gotten away with so many things, including kidnapping this girl twice. He feels nearly invincible, so he has her leave the baby here as a message."

"What sort of message?" Nash demanded.

Nikki struggled to put the ideas floating around in her head into the right words. "That he can do whatever he wants because he's so many steps ahead of us. That's why finding living victims is crucial. There are just too many things we don't know."

"You're thinking some of these victims might have been let go or got away and could provide information about who took Joyce?" Miller asked.

"Possibly." Nikki explained how Joyce eventually escaped. "They'd been living in a house with a large back yard and privacy fence. She said it was an old farmhouse on a rural road. The tire blew on the road, and he'd already made her lie back down, so I think they were close to the house. She hid in the woods and then got on a bus in Cottage Grove. That's part of the reason I asked you to meet us here. You know the area better than anyone on my team."

Miller nodded. "Any idea how long she had to walk from her hiding spot to the bus station?"

"Twenty minutes," Nash answered. "She thought it was around a mile."

"That means the house she was held in was probably in Washington County, right?" Nikki asked, thinking about the McFarland house's location. In the nineties, there had been a few farms in that area, and she wasn't sure if any houses remained, but Miller could easily find out.

"I'd have to see everything marked on a map," Miller said. "But it's definitely possible. I'll start looking at property records and see if I can come up with someplace. Let's just hope the house is still there. A lot of that area has been built up."

"I know," Nikki said. "But if we figure out which house, we should be able to tell who lived in it during that time period. We need to dig deeper into Joyce's life somehow."

"There isn't any deeper to dig," Nash said angrily. "Joyce didn't trust anyone enough to really let them in. And she always felt like an outsider, because absolutely no one in her life could fathom what she'd gone through. Even the girl from work, and her life was bad too."

"Who?" Liam asked. "Cat? That's the only person at work

Joyce spent much time with, and that was before she became the surrogate."

"Maybe," Nash said. "She only mentioned her a couple of times when we first met. I think Joyce said that someone in her family abused her. Her friend from work, I mean. She said they kind of bonded over it. But she hasn't talked about her in months."

"I'll call the vet's and see if Cat's working today," Nikki said, pulling her phone out of her pocket. Out of the corner of her eye, she saw Miller motion to Liam, who nodded and followed him outside.

Unease flickered through Nikki. Were they discussing Rory? She hadn't had a chance to talk to him yet today. She barely noticed when the call was answered.

"Hello?" A female voice came through the speaker.

"This is Agent Hunt with the FBI. I spoke to several employees yesterday about Joyce."

"Did you find her?"

"Not yet, I'm afraid. Is Cat working today, by chance?"

"She's off today, but I can give you her cell."

"Does she live near the vet's office?" Nikki asked.

"I'm not sure, but she's probably not home. She usually spends her day off at the women and girls' shelter on Grand Avenue. Family Alliance, I think it's called."

Grand Avenue was in the heart of St. Paul, adjacent to Summit Avenue. Depending on the location of the shelter, the Ashley-Halls were likely within walking distance of the shelter. She ended the call and grabbed Nash's elbow. "Let's go." Outside, she blinked against the bright sun and then saw Miller and Liam leaning against Miller's cruiser, talking.

"Liam," Nikki called. "Cat volunteers at Family Alliance on Grand. Let's go."

He and Miller walked over to the jeep; Liam's head was down, his hands stuffed into his pockets.

"What is it?" Nikki asked. "You're about to tell me something I won't like, right?"

"I wondered if Liam could ride with me for a couple of hours," Miller said. "I'm going back to the station to regroup with the volunteers, and I was hoping Liam would help me coordinate some things. We can work on figuring out where the house might be too."

"That's fine," Nash piped in. "Come on, Nikki."

She nodded, trying to act like she wasn't fully aware that Miller wanted Liam's help with Becky Anderson's murder. "I'll call you after I talk to Cat."

"Meet at the hospital in a couple of hours?" Liam asked. "Give or take? I want to check on Patrick and talk to the parents again."

Nikki's gaze lingered on Miller's grave expression. What weren't they telling her? What had Rory gotten himself into?

EIGHTEEN

An awkward silence hung between Nikki and Nash during the drive back to the metro area. Nikki was used to volleying ideas back and forth with Liam, but she didn't have the same relationship with Nash. Her mind raced between imagining an exhausted, traumatized Joyce bringing the baby to safety and thinking about the strange looks on Liam and Miller's faces. She tried to tell herself that it was just her imagination, but she felt the same sinking feeling she'd had the day they found the remains.

Her phone rang through the Bluetooth system, and she glanced at the touch screen, hoping to see Rory's name. "It's coming from the hospital," she said, trying to hide her disappointment as she answered. "Agent Hunt."

"It's Tony. The baby's okay. Did you find Joyce?"

"No, not yet. We're following a lead right now."

"Agent Hernandez told Sonia the case isn't over until Joyce is found. So you're staying on to find her, right?"

"Absolutely," Nikki said.

"Good." Tony cleared his throat. "The nurse said Patrick had been well cared for. I don't know how Joyce convinced her kidnapper to let the baby go, but she put herself before him. You have to find her."

"We're doing everything we can," Nikki said. "I'll see you at the hospital." She ended the call, her gaze on the road but her mind going in a dozen directions. Tony and Sonia could be playing things up right now, but she believed their concern for Joyce was sincere. If they'd been approached by the kidnapper and blackmailed, involving the FBI didn't make sense. Taking Joyce while she was pregnant put a spotlight on her disappearance, and they were both smart enough to know the FBI would immediately consider them primary suspects. Sonia had already told them that she'd set up the transaction for the remainder of Joyce's surrogacy fee to be paid on Patrick's due date. Given her wealth, it was hard to imagine Sonia had put her baby in danger to get out of paying the rest of the fee.

"Becky Anderson was found on your boyfriend's construction site, right?" Nash had been so quiet that his voice startled Nikki out of her thoughts.

"Yes, why?"

"Miller didn't seem to think that her murder was related to Joyce's case."

"It's probably a long shot, and Miller made a good case for her not being trafficked," Nikki said. "But it's a possibility we shouldn't rule out."

"Is your boyfriend a suspect?"

Nikki glanced over at him. "Did I tell you Rory and I were seeing each other?"

Nash shrugged. "I think I read about it when his brother was freed." His tone was light, but she could see him fidgeting out of the corner of her eye.

"Why would you ask if he was a suspect?" Nikki tried to keep her tone as neutral as possible.

"Because Miller asked for Liam's help instead of yours, and it was pretty obvious they didn't want to share information with you," Nash said.

"It's not about whether or not they want to," Nikki said. "It's following protocol. Technically, Rory is a suspect because Becky was his ex-girlfriend. But it's just a technicality. And I have to stay out of it." She wished Rory would make it easier and stop being so surly about the investigation.

"You aren't worried about him being arrested?" Nash asked in surprise.

"He's innocent," Nikki said. "I have full confidence in Miller. You should too."

Nash didn't say anything, and Nikki racked her brain, trying to think if the news articles had mentioned her relationship with Rory. "Did Tyler tell you about Rory?" she blurted.

Nash reddened. "I didn't want to bring his name up."

"It's fine." Nikki's hands tightened on the steering wheel. If Tyler had told him about her dating someone, then he'd probably talked about how he felt too. Nash would probably tell her if she asked him, and she desperately wanted to, but she also knew that hearing about Tyler's disappointment in her dating would only add salt to the wound that had only begun to scab over.

"You want me to see if I can find anything out about Miller's investigation?" Nash said. "He might be more inclined to share information that he wouldn't with you."

Nikki wished that were true, but Miller wouldn't fall for it, especially after Liam had finished telling him how much of a pain in the ass Nash had been. "Thanks, but I'm not worried. If the connection's there, Miller will find it."

Family Alliance was housed in a beautiful old house overlooking Grand Avenue. Set back off the road, the home had a beautiful front yard with colorful flowerbeds. Nikki squeezed into a spot close to the house, and she and Nash headed up the sidewalk towards it. The young woman tending to a flowerbed stopped weeding and watched their approach. Family Alliance was a haven for domestic abuse victims and at-risk teenagers, and Nikki could tell by the girl's wariness that she didn't trust strangers.

Nikki held up her badge. "Hi. I'm Agent Hunt; this is Agent Nash. We're looking for Cat. Is she volunteering today?"

"I haven't seen her," the woman answered. "If you go in the front door, there's a little office to the left. Cindy should be in there. She'll know."

Nikki thanked the girl for her help. Nash followed her up the uneven concrete steps and into the house. The front room was empty, but Nikki could hear women chatting down the hall, talking about what to serve for lunch. Little ones piped in, asking for grilled cheese.

Nash looked decidedly uncomfortable. He'd grown up sheltered, with access to virtually anything he wanted. He'd probably never been inside a place like this.

"Why are there so many moms with kids here?" he whispered to Nikki.

"Because they need help, and shelters like this are their only option." The office looked like it had probably been some kind of storage area or closet. She showed her badge to the woman working the front desk and introduced herself and Nash. "Hi. Cindy, right? We're here to talk to Cat. Is she volunteering today?"

Cindy looked over her reading glasses, unfazed by the appearance of law enforcement. "She was supposed to, but we haven't heard from her today. What's this about?"

"A missing person case," Nikki said. "How often is Cat around?"

"She used to come twice a week, but her attendance recently has been spotty."

"Did you ask her why?" Nash asked.

She gave him a tight smile. "We don't badger our volunteers."

Nikki spoke before Nash could say anything. "What can you tell us about Cat?"

The woman leaned back in her chair thoughtfully. "She's great with teenaged girls," Cindy said. "She never told us a lot about herself, but I've heard her telling some of the older girls that she was bounced around from man to man for a long time when she was their age. I assume she's had some difficult relationships and experienced some trauma."

"Are any of those girls available now?"

Cindy narrowed her eyes. "Yes, but they aren't going to talk to you. It's like pulling teeth to earn a tiny bit of their trust."

"That's okay," Nikki said. "I'd still like to give it a shot."

Cindy nodded. "Wait here."

"What's your plan?" Nash asked when she'd left. "I doubt they're going to trust us enough to tell us anything."

"Listen," she said, glancing up at Nash, "no offense meant, but I'd like to do the talking here. They're more likely to feel comfortable with a female agent."

He held up his hands. "Go for it. I don't want to say something wrong that sets them on edge or something."

Nikki was pleasantly surprised. If Nash could ever fully let go of his ego, he could be a good investigator. He'd likely moved up so quickly through the ranks on his parents' names that he'd missed out on the chance to just observe and learn.

Cindy returned with two girls. "This is Agent Hunt and Nash with the FBI."

Both girls appeared to be around fifteen, and both looked at Nikki with dark, distrustful eyes. "Cat's awesome," the taller girl said defensively. "We aren't going to help get her in trouble."

Nikki smiled at both of them encouragingly. "She's not in trouble, I promise. A friend of hers is missing. We met Cat yesterday at the vet's office, and she told us what she could about her friend. I just have a couple of follow-up questions."

The tall girl shrugged. Her friend edged back, her eyes on Nash. "If you have questions for Cat, what do you want with us?"

"How about this?" Nash said. "I'll wait outside for Agent Hunt. Would you guys feel more comfortable if I wasn't here?"

"Yes," Cindy answered for them.

Nash nodded. "I'll be on the porch."

Nikki nodded in surprise. Once Nash had gone, she tried another tactic. It was risky, but she needed to earn these girls' trust in a short amount of time.

"You look familiar," the shorter girl said. "Have you been to my house before?"

"No," Nikki said, smiling. "I have had some high-profile cases lately. Maybe you've seen me on the news."

"That doesn't mean we are going to say anything about Cat," the first girl said defiantly.

"What are your names again?" Nikki asked.

"I'm Callie," the tall girl said. "She's Anita."

"Okay, Callie and Anita." Nikki sat down on the only extra chair in the room, letting the teenagers stand taller than her and showing them they were in control. "I'm going to break some rules because I really need you to trust me. Have you heard about the missing pregnant woman on the news?"

Both girls shrugged.

"Well, Cat is a friend of this woman, and we think Cat might have information that could help us find her. I'm not asking you to betray her confidence, but I need you to think really hard. Did she ever say anything about Joyce or how she might have known her prior to the vet's?"

"No." Callie looked at Cindy. "Can we go?"

"You're free to do whatever you want," Cindy said.

"Nice meeting you, Agent. Let's go, Anita." She grabbed her friend's arm, but the other girl didn't budge.

"Are you talking about the black lady in the scrubs?" she asked.

"Probably," Nikki said. "Joyce and Cat worked at the same vet's. Did Cat talk about their past at all?"

Anita chewed her bottom lip. Callie pulled on her arm. "Come on. We don't owe these people nothing."

"I know, but Cat's been different lately," Anita said. "This is the second time she didn't show up when she was supposed to, and that's not like her."

"Big deal," Callie said. "People are a constant disappointment."

"You're right," Nikki said. "Some people are, and it sucks. It sucks that you girls are here, and I can't imagine what you've experienced. I know that's why Cat's important to you, but I promise she's not in any trouble. Cat might be in danger."

Callie was unfazed, but Nikki could tell that she was getting to Anita. "Joyce came to see Cat one day, a week or so ago."

"Anita—"

"Shut up, Callie. This is the right thing to do," Anita snapped. "They got into an argument on the porch. Joyce was really angry at Cat for something—saying something about a farm, a terrible place where they met. With some man. I didn't hear much of what they said, but when Cat came back inside, she was wrecked. Like, freaked-out PTSD wrecked. She cried in the bathroom, and I knocked on the door, asking if she was okay." Anita's mouth trembled, but she didn't cry. "Cat said she was and to give her a minute, but when she came out, she was different. And she's been different ever since."

"Thank you very much for trusting me," Nikki said. It sounded like Cat had been kidnapped too—had she been another of the girls held by the man who took Joyce? Nikki hoped Callie wasn't going to be too hard on Anita.

"It's cool," Anita said. "Just make sure Cat's okay."

"I will." Nikki left her card with Cindy and asked her to call if they heard from Cat. She knew the shelter wouldn't have Cat's address on file, and the vet's office probably wouldn't give it to her thanks to privacy laws.

Nash looked like melted chocolate by the time Nikki came outside. The humidity seemed to have increased in the short time she'd been inside. "Thanks for doing that," she told Nash. "It made all the difference."

She explained what Anita had told her. "I'm confident there's a lot more to their relationship than just working at the vet's office. Did Joyce say anything about Cat upsetting her?"

"No." Nash shook his head. "Where does Cat live?"

"I'm not sure, but the St. Paul police will be able to find out.

We'll have them do a welfare check while we get to the hospital and talk to Sonia and Tony. If she's home, they can let her know we need to talk to her." Nikki wished that she could shed the feeling that Cat wouldn't be home, but her gut told her that Cat was also in trouble.

NINETEEN

Nikki arrived at the hospital before Liam and Miller. She tried not to let it bother her—they were likely still trying to locate the house Joyce had been held in as a child. Still, she couldn't shake the feeling that something was terribly wrong. "Why don't you go in and find their room," she told Nash. "I need to make a call."

Rory didn't answer. She thought about texting him, but if he really was busy, then she didn't want to be a nag. With Patrick found, Nikki would be able to go back to Stillwater tonight. She'd look through the storage unit herself.

She heard the beep to leave a message and spoke without thinking. "Listen, I shouldn't do this, but if Miller didn't tell you the baby was a boy, don't tell him that you know. It won't help things." Nikki ended the call, already feeling guilty. She had no business advising Rory, but he was innocent. Still, Hernandez would have her ass if he found out.

"I won't say anything else," she said to herself as she entered the hospital. She didn't see Nash anywhere, but she knew they would be in the maternity ward.

"Nikki." Nash popped out of an open doorway, looking relieved to see her. "In here." She could tell by his expression that something was going on. "They want me to get them out of the hospital," Nash said in a low voice. "I don't know what to tell them."

Nikki managed to stop herself from criticizing Nash and entered the maternity suite where Joyce should have given birth. Tony and Sonia sat on the couch, cradling the baby.

"Ah, swaddling," Nikki said with a smile. "My daughter never took to it. She was constantly moving."

Sonia looked up at her, beaming. "He seems to like it."

"How is he?" Nikki asked.

"The doctor said he's great," Sonia said. "So far there are no signs of complications, but we have to keep an eye out for it. Would you like to hold him?"

Nikki firmly believed that holding a baby had some sort of magical therapeutic property. "I would love to, but given everything he's endured, I don't want to expose him to more germs. And he's looking awfully content."

"Have you gotten any word about Joyce?" Tony asked.

Nikki shook her head. "I'm just thankful she convinced her kidnappers to let her leave the baby with someone."

Fresh tears built in Sonia's eyes. "I know. If you find her—when you find her—I'm going to make sure she has everything she needs to recover from this. Tell her she can stay with us as long as she needs. She doesn't need to worry about money or medical bills, either."

Tony nodded in agreement, although he had yet to take his eyes off the baby. He reminded her of the way Tyler had been with Lacey. He never let her out of his sight. She shoved the thought out of her mind. "What's this about going home?"

"They won't let us leave until the DNA tests come back." Tony finally looked up at her. "Even though Joyce is the one who brought him to that place, we still have to wait."

"The hospital's going to protect itself," Nikki said. "I promise there's no exception on this one. It's law. Plus, it might be good for you all to stay here, together, the first night. Regardless of how he got here, this is your first night caring for an infant. The nurses deal with new parents all the time, and they can really help the first couple of nights, especially if he is having trouble sleeping."

"We won't let him out of our sight," Tony said. "I'm sure all of the staff are fine, but we just can't do it."

"I understand," Nikki said. "Before we leave, I wanted to ask you if Joyce talked much about her friend Cat. She's not working today, and she isn't at the shelter she volunteers at, and Nash is certain that if Joyce confided in anyone, it would have been Cat."

"She told me that she and Cat had more stuff in common than other people," Sonia said. "Cat's one of her oldest friends."

"How old?" Nikki and Nash asked at the same time.

"Since they were kids. I think Joyce said they met in middle school."

Nikki's phone vibrated and she anxiously pulled it out of her bag, hoping to see Rory's number. Instead, the St. Paul Police Department's generic number flashed on her screen. "This is Agent Hunt."

"Yeah, this is Officer Thompson with SPPD. We went to the address you requested and knocked, but no one answered. Landlord happened to be around, and he let us in. Apartment's empty, no sign of duress."

"Thanks for the fast response," Nikki said. "Any chance the building has security footage that we can look at so we can establish the last time she was home?"

"Unfortunately not," Officer Thompson said. "She lives in subsidized housing."

Nikki thanked the officer again. "Agent Nash and I need to go," she said, looking at Tony. "But I will let you know the minute I hear anything about Joyce."

She shut the door and walked briskly down the hall, her mind moving on to the next thing. "Cat's not home, no sign of foul play. No security cameras," she told Nash.

"Now what? You said he would want to control Joyce, that this was about her and not the baby. She's still alive, right?" Panic laced Nash's voice.

"I hope so," Nikki said gently. "From a psychological point of view, I think there's a strong chance she's alive, but that's just my opinion. You have to prepare for the worst."

They walked in silence to the jeep. Nikki cranked the air up and called Liam to update him on Cat and find out if they'd made any headway on figuring out where Joyce had been held as a child. After two rings, her call was sent to voicemail, something he rarely did.

"It's Nikki," she said after the beep. "Cat's MIA, but it sounds like she and Joyce might have known each other a lot longer. Call me asap."

Next to her, Nash leaned forward, resting his head on the dashboard. "Where do we go from here, Nicole? All we've got are a bunch of bits and pieces that don't help us at all."

"They do," she said. "We just aren't putting them together in the right order. I'll drop you off at your hotel and then go to my storage unit and see if there's anything in Tyler's notes about Kendrick that might help us. It's probably a waste of time, but if he'd been compiling a case against Kendrick, there might be information in the files we could use." She texted Rory that she would be at his parents' after she searched the storage unit. She knew they likely wouldn't find anything useful, but she couldn't just ignore the files if they might contain a sliver of information that could help them find Joyce.

"No way," Nash said emphatically. "I can't just sit around at the hotel and wait. Let me go with you. Please."

"Fine, but we'll pick up your car first. I don't think Rory would appreciate you sleeping on his couch."

Nash picked up his car and followed Nikki to the storage units in the old part of Stillwater. Since her aunt had purchased the unit decades ago, it was smaller, older and at the back of the lot. It didn't have a keyless entry like the new ones, and Nikki always struggled to get the lock to work. She managed to get it on the third try, without scraping her fingers like she usually did.

"Let me help." Nash grabbed the handle and started lifting the roll-up door until it jammed halfway.

"That's as far as it goes." Nikki ducked inside and immediately sneezed. The last time she'd been in the unit, Rory had to climb on the boxes to reach the string that turned the bulb on. He'd replaced the string and wrapped it in glow-in-the dark tape, and Nikki found it easily.

"Dang." Nash looked around in surprise, sweat beading on his upper lip. "You need a bigger unit."

"Lacey and I weren't ready to go through Tyler's things, so I put all of it in here." One day, Nikki thought, she'd look at everything with Lacey. She wanted her to feel connected to the other members of her family, but right now she was too young. Only just now starting to really accept that Tyler was gone. Nikki's throat constricted. She didn't want to cry in front of Nash, so she shimmied between her parents' old dresser and a stack of plastic crates full of God only knew what. Most of Tyler's personal things had been jammed into the back left corner, including the six cardboard boxes of paperwork.

Sweat stinging her eyes, she made her way to the boxes. Tyler had been neat almost to the point of being obsessive, so she knew that he would have everything in alphabetical order. Sure enough, Kendrick's paltry file was exactly where she expected it to be. Nikki pulled the file and started bobbing and weaving through stuff. Even with the door partially open, the inside of the unit felt like a sauna, and Nikki was already feeling the effects of the heat and humidity. She stumbled, knocking her hip on the corner of her grandfather's old and heavy wooden desk. She bounced off and hit the plastic bins. The Little League trophy that had been sitting on top of the bins clattered to the floor, the impact separating the bottom of the trophy from the base.

"Oh my God, no," Nikki muttered. She dropped to her knees

and grabbed the trophy. Part of the bat had broken, too, and the base had cracked in half. "This was Tyler's. His only one from Little League because he only played one year." Her voice rose, and her body suddenly felt like she'd been wrapped in bone-crushingly tight ropes. "I'm sorry, Tyler. I'm so sorry."

She felt the dam cracking and knew the grief wouldn't be ignored this time. Nikki gathered the pieces and clutched them to her chest, sobbing. She wished Nash wasn't around to see her so vulnerable, and she fought with her emotions to try to keep them in. She heard him shuffling around things.

"Nicole, it's okay." Nash knelt beside her, his hand patting her back awkwardly. "I mean, it's not okay. What happened to Tyler is terrible. I mean it's okay to cry. Letting it out has to be better than bottling it up every time."

"It's my fault." Nikki rocked back and forth on her knees. "I wouldn't stop looking for Frost, even when Lacey was threatened. Even when I knew there was some kind of personal connection between us, I refused to step aside. My ego..." She swallowed hard, her throat on fire. "My ego got Tyler killed."

"No, it didn't," Nash said. "No one thinks that."

Still clinging to the trophy parts and the Kendrick file, Nikki struggled to get to her feet. "I need air." She appreciated Nash's kindness, but the storage unit was stifling, and the humidity made her feel like she'd been smothered. "I need to get out of here. It's so hot."

Nash offered his hand, and Nikki swallowed her pride. File in hand, she let him guide her through the crowded unit, out into the still-hot but fresh air. Nikki handed Nash the file, but she hung on to the broken trophy as though it were her only connection to Tyler.

Nash again patted her on the back. "What do you need?"

"I'm okay." Nikki's breathing had started to return to normal. She wiped her face with her shirt. "It's just a cheap trophy." She tried to sound lighthearted despite feeling utterly shredded.

"You okay to drive?" Nash asked out of concern.

"Fine. Is there anything in the file? It's pretty thin."

"He'd only been assigned to it for a few days." Nash opened the file. "It looks like a condensed version of Kendrick's tax returns for the last five years—the summary sheets, I guess. Bunch of hand-written notes, looks like his impressions of Kendrick."

Nikki gestured for him to hand over the file. "I'll go through it. Tyler had his own shorthand." Her stomach growled. "Did we eat today?"

"I don't remember," Nash said, sounding as tired as she felt.

Nikki hit the remote start on the jeep. They were only ten minutes from the Todds', and she could see Lacey while they grabbed something to eat. Before she could make the suggestion, Liam called.

"Hey, what's up?" Nikki asked, cradling the phone against her shoulder.

"Sorry we didn't get to the hospital," Liam said. "But we have good news. We've pinpointed the area where Joyce likely escaped from."

"You're kidding," Nikki said. "How?"

"We had to go back to the old maps," Miller said on speaker-phone. "Before that area was more developed. Going by what Joyce said—how long it took her to get to the bus station from her hiding place, and how close she believed they were to the house—we narrowed it down to three houses. One's been owned by the same family for eighteen years, and they're a popular, well-known family in the area because they live in one of the older, original homes."

"So probably not that one."

"Second house that was there when Joyce escaped was torn down last year. The third is condemned, has been empty for more than a decade. It's owned by a dummy corporation that's defunct. Neighbors—all houses built in the last ten years—want the place torn down, but there's been a hold-up for years thanks to zoning issues. Apparently, there may be historical relevance to the house, and the county wants to be sure before any development takes place. It's abandoned, definitely not a safe place for a hideout."

"But a good one to dump a body," Liam said.

Nikki glanced at Nash, sweating in the heat. "Text me the address. We'll meet you there."

TWENTY

Nikki glanced in her rearview mirror. Nash drove too close to her bumper, his fists clenched on the wheel. She almost wished that she hadn't told him where they were going yet, but she understood his actions, and she knew that he was praying Joyce might somehow be in the house—that he would get the opportunity to rescue her.

The house was in even worse shape than Nikki imagined. The lot size looked larger than the newer homes nearby, but the house was in disrepair. Part of the roof had started to collapse, and a corner of the porch sagged dangerously to the ground. Weather had stripped the wood siding down to the grains. The front door and windows were all securely boarded up.

She parked behind Miller's cruiser and joined the two of them in front of the house. "I can't imagine it's safe to go upstairs." Seconds later, Nash's car door slammed behind her.

"Oh, it isn't," Miller said. "We found a loose board on one of the windows. You can see the stairwell is coming down."

Liam drained a bottle of water. "I crawled through the window and checked out downstairs as best I could. No sign of inhabitants. And upstairs is likely where she was kept, assuming we have the right house."

"Why?" Nash demanded.

"It's a lot harder for a child to escape," Liam said.

Nash glared at the eyesore, his shirt still damp with sweat from the storage unit, his chest rising and falling with deep, shaky breaths. "Joyce might be in there."

He stepped forward, but Liam blocked his path. "Like I said, the bottom floor is clear. The stairwell's basically gone. No one is upstairs. The only way this place is useful is if we can confirm Joyce *was* kept here, and that's a tall order—literally. Chief, you think the fire department would come out and let us use their ladders?"

Miller snorted. "Their budget's been slashed more than ours. They don't have the extra manpower or equipment."

Liam gave Miller a pointed look that sent shivers down Nikki's spine. "We need a long construction ladder." He looked at Nikki. "Would you happen to know if Rory's around?"

Nikki knew what he was doing; Liam made no attempt to hide it, likely because he knew it was pointless. He and Miller wanted to talk to Rory again. Had he been ignoring their calls too?

Liam's eyes locked with hers, a mutual understanding passing between them. Rory wasn't going to be very friendly, but Nikki was determined to stay out of that investigation and focus on Joyce. "What do you think we're going to find up there?" she asked. "Getting a ladder and trying to walk around isn't worth it. If we can't get up there, then Joyce can't be there."

"I checked with the county, and the structural integrity of the second floor is believed to be about seventy-five percent," Miller said. "I think it's safe for one person to crawl through the window—"

"I'll do it," Nash said. "Joyce is my responsibility."

Miller shook his head. "Let me finish. It might be safe to crawl through a window to a single room but going near the hallway is a big risk. I'm not letting anyone take it."

"We can still get up on a ladder and look. Tell me you won't kick yourself for not looking when you leave here," Liam said to Nikki, "and I'll shut up."

"When did they decide the integrity was at seventy-five percent? Recently? Or will it have reduced further since then?" Nikki asked.

Miller checked his notes. "As luck would have it, couple of months ago. Neighbors heard a big crash early one morning. County came out and saw the stairwell had collapsed, so they checked the integrity of the second floor. If you stay away from the stairs, you should be safe."

Nash had grown impatient and started walking around the perimeter of the house. "Nicole," he called over to her. "Drive the jeep over here. If I can stand on top of it, I might be able to pull myself up."

"How?" Nikki waded through the tall weeds to where Nash was standing.

"The exterior is brick," Nash said. "I'm a rock climber. I think I can use those sheared-off ledges"—he pointed to the framing of one of the lower windows—"and the divots in the brick to get up and look into this window."

"What about the others?" Nikki asked. "You can't possibly find a place to climb up for every upstairs window."

Nash pointed to the second story window. "The plywood covering the window is rotting away. I can crawl up and get my footing on the casement, bust the plywood out and crawl in."

"No way," Miller said. "County said the stairs falling means the entire second floor could come down."

"I'm willing to risk it. I've got climbing shoes in the car. Always keep them around." He jogged back to his car.

"I don't know about this," Liam said. "A ladder is safer."

"But not faster," Nikki said. "And Rory isn't answering his phone. He's swamped today."

A beat of silence passed between them, and Nikki knew she'd been right: Liam and Miller had been trying to reach Rory too.

"Justin's an adult, and he cares about Joyce. You aren't going to stop him from going up there."

"You could," Liam said evenly.

Nikki shook her head. She walked around to the back of the falling-down house on the pretense of looking for an additional way inside, but inside she was steaming. Miller and Liam had surely known about the county's warning when they called and asked her to meet so they could investigate. Had they used this as an opportunity to try to get Rory to talk to them?

Nikki shoved the thought away. She needed some sleep. As much as she hated to admit it, ladders were a lot safer route than Nash's harebrained idea. She was so focused on the structure that she didn't see the twine until she tripped over it. Nikki fell forward and landed on her hands and knees.

She lifted the twine out of the tangled weeds. One end had likely been sheared off by the elements, but part of the rope was still embedded into the ground. Nikki stood and pulled the rope hard. Dirt sprayed everywhere, but she managed to yank it free from the ground. It was attached to the house somehow, but a mound of debris prevented her from seeing where the rope had been anchored. Nikki carefully removed the debris and rotting firewood until she could see where the rope was attached.

"Guys, come here," she called. "Justin, don't climb yet."

All three men jogged around the house to where she stood, still holding the frayed rope, surrounded by dried-up debris and firewood that fell apart when she picked it up. "There's a storm shelter, and it looks like someone put a lot of effort into hiding it." She held up the decaying rope. The other end had been wrapped around the handle, and the only way to get into the storm shelter was to slide the heavy cement slab off. "It looks like the door is made of heavy cement. They must have needed the rope to help open it."

"Which means it likely can't be opened from the inside," Miller said. "And it's not exactly easy to get to in a storm. My guess is that was by intention."

"Exactly," Nikki said. "I hope we can get it open ourselves. It might not budge."

The rope wasn't long enough for all four to hold on to, so Miller and Liam pulled on it while Nikki and Nash each took one side of the heavy slab. They inched the slab down, and Nikki shuddered at the spiders and other bugs fleeing for safety. She pressed her mouth and nose against her shoulder, waiting to smell the decay, but there was only the stench of old, damp earth.

They managed to get the slab down far enough to shine a flashlight into the cellar. It looked like her aunt's old, dank cellar, although it had about ten times as much debris as her aunt's place.

"Oh, Christ," Miller said.

Bones were scattered all over the cellar floor, and Nikki could see several holes where animals had been digging. She wiped the sweat off her brow. "Better call Blanchard. She'll probably send someone to process the scene and collect just like she did with Becky Anderson's remains." She shined her flashlight, looking for anything lying around that might help them identify the remains if they turned out to be human.

"If it's trafficked victims, we won't be able to identify them," Liam said, reading her mind. "Unless by some chance we have dental records or some personal item they still had on, like jewelry. And that's unlikely."

"They strip victims of anything that reminds them of their old life," Nikki said quietly. "Manipulation and trauma are extremely powerful weapons." She debated going into the cellar and doing her own digging, but she couldn't make reckless decisions like that anymore. Lacey only had one parent left.

Miller looked at Nikki. "You need to take a break. When was the last time you slept?"

"I honestly forget," she said. "I'll sleep some at Rory's tonight, I'm sure. You know I pretty much run on fumes all the time." She forced a grin. "Although I do need to spend time with my daughter tonight."

"Then why don't you catch up with Lacey, and I'll run point here? I can deal with the county people too."

Normally Nikki would balk, but she did need to see Lacey. This was the first time she'd been away from her daughter overnight since Tyler had been killed. Her stomach growled again, reminding her that she still hadn't eaten.

"He's right," Nash said. "I want to stay here and help however I can."

Nikki nodded. "Liam, walk with me to the jeep. I want to go over a couple of things."

Liam wiped the grime off his pants and followed her. Nikki's mind felt cloudy, and she struggled to figure out how exactly to ask her question without overstepping. Fortunately, Liam did it for her.

"Boss, Rory isn't taking Miller's calls."

"He isn't taking mine, either." She rounded on Liam. "I know what you were trying to do with the ladder."

He grinned. "I still think it was a good idea. But seriously, Rory isn't being very cooperative."

"I thought he already gave his statement and swabbed for paternity," Nikki said feebly.

"Miller has follow-up questions." Liam wasn't looking at her, and the vice around her lungs seemed to tighten.

"Liam, he's innocent."

He finally met her gaze. "Then he needs to connect with Miller again. Soon."

TWENTY-ONE

Nikki didn't go to the Todds'. Instead, she stopped at Rory's house, hoping to find him. She didn't see his work truck, but his motorcycle sat in its place in the garage. Maybe he really was busy, although he'd told her yesterday that his guys were sitting around, waiting to work.

She stripped off her clothes and took a quick shower. She hadn't thought to bring extra clothes yesterday, but thankfully she still had her emergency toiletry bag in the jeep, so she'd been able to brush her teeth and put on new deodorant at the Ashley-Halls'. Nikki could have stood beneath the hot water forever, but she didn't have that luxury. She dried off hastily and found a clean pair of cut-off shorts and a polo shirt from a forensics conference she attended a couple of years ago. Professional enough for the rest of the day, she thought. She had no idea what the next twelve hours would bring, so this time she packed a change of clothes.

Nikki made sure she had everything she needed and then headed outside. She stopped short when she saw the rusted pickup sitting in front of the old barn. It didn't belong to Rory, but she could see him in the passenger seat, talking animatedly. She tossed her things in the back of the jeep and walked over to the barn.

Rory jumped out of the truck, his face red. He looked shocked to see Nikki; what had preoccupied him so much that he didn't even notice her jeep? She raised her hand in greeting. "Hey. I've been trying to reach you."

"Sorry," Rory said. "I've been trying to clean out here, and an old buddy showed up. We went for a drive."

Nikki could tell by his breathing and the red dots on his cheeks that they hadn't just been driving around, chatting. Rory wasn't very good at hiding his anger.

"Introduce me, then," she said, walking past Rory. She stuck her head in the open passenger window. "Hi, I'm Nikki."

A heavily tattooed man around their age nodded at her, his worn-out hat pulled low, hiding most of his eyes. His Harley-Davidson shirt had holes in it, and what looked like fresh dirt caked his cuticles. "Jay. Rory and I went to high school together."

"Great," she said. "I went to Stillwater too, just a few years ahead of you guys."

"I know who you are." He was sizing her up, either trying to get a rise out of her or trying to piss Rory off even more.

"It was nice to meet you." Nikki faked a smile and then turned to Rory. "Can we talk in private?"

"He's just leaving." Rory's voice was hard. He glared past her into the truck. "Now."

Jay nodded again. He shifted to reverse and then hit the gas, spraying gravel as he turned and drove out. Rory seethed.

"What's going on between you two?" Nikki asked. "Why'd you ride off with him if you don't like him?"

"He wanted me to do something for him; I said no." Rory shrugged. "Not into his shady stuff."

"What sort of shady stuff?" Nikki asked.

He scraped the gravel with his steel-toed boot. "Misdemeanor stuff. He'd steal anything that wasn't tied down, underaged drinking and fighting. The kind of stupid crap you do when you're a teenager and hope you don't get caught."

"I did plenty of that." She grinned, hoping to set him at ease.

He was so keyed up she could see the tension in his muscles. "Is he the only reason you didn't answer?"

"What's that supposed to mean?" Irritation layered his voice. "Lacey's at Mom's, and I'm basically sitting around with my thumb up my ass until Miller releases the construction site. Figured I might as well clean this place out, and then he showed up. I didn't hear the phone."

"Okay." She twisted her still-damp, thick hair into a loose knot. "Are we going to talk about the elephant in the room?"

Rory smirked, reminding her of the lighthearted man she'd fallen in love with. He looked around. "Honey, we're outside."

"Cute." Nikki closed the distance between them, her heart racing as though they hadn't been a couple for months, and gingerly wrapped her arms around his waist. Rory hugged her back, resting his head on the top of hers. His body seemed to soften and mold to hers.

"The news said something about a baby being left somewhere," he said.

"Yes. One victim has been found. And he's healthy, thank God," Nikki said. "But we're still looking for Joyce. We've tied her to an abandoned house in the Cottage Grove area. It's condemned, so we can't search. Liam had the idea of calling you and asking to borrow your ladder so we could look in the upstairs windows."

Rory snickered, releasing her. "Not transparent at all."

"That's what I told him." She wished he would confide in her. "Did you get my message yesterday?"

Rory stuck his hands in his pockets and nodded.

"Are you going to tell me how you really knew she was having a boy?"

He looked at her with more emotion than she'd seen from him in days. "I swear I didn't hurt her. The baby isn't mine. Wasn't mine, I guess."

"Did you spend more time with her when she visited than you told Miller and Liam?"

Rory didn't answer. Nikki threw her hands in the air. "Oh my

God, what are you doing? Do you want Miller to suspect you? Because that's what your behavior is leading to."

"Of course I don't," he snapped. "But he can't help Becky now, and no one could help her then."

"Rory—"

"Nik, please, stay out of this," he implored. "I don't want this case messed up at trial."

She stared up at him. "You're worried about that? I've hardly been around."

"I know, and that's why I've tried to avoid you. It puts you in a crappy situation, and you don't need it," Rory said. "I can take care of myself."

Nikki wanted to tell him that he'd never gone up against competent law enforcement, that he didn't realize how Liam was once he sunk his teeth into something. "You need to cooperate."

"If they want to talk to me, they can do it through my lawyer."

"You hired a defense attorney? Why?"

"Because I'm tired of answering the same questions over and over," he answered. "I've told them what happened that night at least three times and signed the statement, but they keep hounding me. I'm not going to be the subject of some witch-hunt."

"This isn't a witch-hunt."

Rory turned toward the barn. "Nicole. I'm telling you to stay out of this. Becky's killer will be brought to justice."

Gooseflesh broke out over her arms. "You sound like a vigilante."

"Don't worry about me. Go find Joyce." He started walking and then stopped again, slowly turning around to look at her. "You and Lacey should stay at Mom and Dad's until this is over. For the integrity of the case. Lacey's all for it."

"You asked her if she wanted to stay at your mom's?" Nikki asked.

"Yes." Rory walked backwards into the barn, a fake smile plastered on his face. "Mom wants her there too."

"Great." Nikki didn't know what else to say. Given what his

brother had endured, she understood Rory's defensiveness, but he needed to listen to reason—for his own sake. What had happened to the calm, logical Rory she'd fallen in love with? "Why don't you call me when you want to tell me the truth." She turned and walked toward the jeep without looking back.

Ruth ran her hand through her tousled gray curls. Nikki hadn't been at the house for long, but it had taken seconds for the conversation to turn to Rory. She was concerned too.

"I'm just so worried about him. Some of his behavior reminds me of how he was back in those days, when he was dating her." She sat down at the kitchen table, and Nikki took the seat across from her, surprised. She didn't think Rory had a bad side. She knew that Rory had a tough time in high school despite being a standout athlete because of the stigma left from Mark's incarceration. It had been tough growing up as the little brother of the man who slaughtered two innocent people in their home. "He's just being irrational," Ruth said, a tremor in her voice. "He actually said this morning that he was worried the same thing that happened to Mark is going to happen to him. He was so angry with the questions Miller asked. But he doesn't have anything to worry about, right?"

"Of course not," Nikki said. "Miller is just following the evidence, and we both know it won't lead to Rory."

"He said that Becky was pregnant, and that it could be his." She reached for a napkin and dabbed her eyes. "If that turns out to be true, he'll even more of a wreck than he already is."

"Courtney's working on the paternity test," Nikki said. "Once she gets the sample from the fetal bones, the results should come quickly. Getting the sample is the hard part."

"I know you're busy with this case," she said. "But would you try to talk to him tonight and make him cooperate with Miller?"

Nikki nodded. Having already tried to reason with him, she wasn't sure what she could do, but she wanted to make Ruth feel better. "Of course I will. How well did you know Becky?" she asked, her interest piqued.

Ruth looked down and shook her head. "I wasn't very present during his high school years. Larry had his issues too. Rory had to learn to fend for himself about a lot of things... sometimes I think we failed him."

"You didn't fail him," Nikki said. "You did the best you could during a terrible time." Even though she and Ruth had bonded since Lacey's kidnapping, they hadn't had a serious conversation about Nikki's involvement in Mark's incarceration. She knew it was something they needed to do, but right now, she wasn't sure she had the energy.

"We didn't know Becky well," Ruth said. "I remember hearing him arguing with her on the phone at all hours of the night. I was relieved when she left town after graduation."

"You didn't like her?"

"It wasn't about liking her," Ruth said. "She had issues and so did Rory. They were just a bad influence on each other."

"Did you know her foster parents?"

"Sure," Ruth said. "She was the last one they fostered, I think. They wanted to retire and travel. Of course, she died, and he had an accident that put him in a wheelchair. Life is so cruel sometimes."

The back door opened, and Mark came in with Lacey on his shoulders and a sucker in her mouth. He was even worse about sweet stuff than Rory. He always had a stash of something, and he could never say no to Lacey, either. "She said she was starving."

Although she'd gotten used to seeing Mark every day, it still startled Nikki to see him with Lacey. She'd grown almost as attached to him as Rory, and Nikki suspected it was because Mark's stocky build and laid-back personality reminded her of Tyler. Her daughter also recognized a softie when she saw one, and Mark was so happy to have family in his life he rarely told Lacey no.

"I'm sure she did," Nikki said dryly. "And candy is so filling."

"Mommy, are we staying here like Rory said?" Lacey asked as Mark put her down.

Nikki flushed. "I'll talk to Ruth."

"Nonsense," Ruth said. "He already explained the situation. You know we've got the room in this place."

Lacey leaned against Nikki and pouted. Nikki wiped the sticky pink off her daughter's cheeks. "I have to leave again after we eat. We're still looking for the pregnant lady."

"You'll find her," Lacey said.

Nikki hugged her close. "Don't be upset if I don't come back tonight. We will probably work late."

"Promise you'll answer my text?" Lacey asked.

"Always."

"Okay." She whirled around to Mark. "Let's play monster hunter. I'll be the monster. You gotta find me."

She ran outside, the door banging shut behind her.

Mark downed the water he'd gotten out of the fridge. "I'm going to have to get in shape to keep up with her."

He lumbered after Lacey, and Ruth's eyes filled with tears. "Nicole, I know it's all been impossibly hard, and none of it was your fault. But we are so grateful to have you and Lacey in our lives. Mark is so happy with her around."

Nikki couldn't speak. She nodded and tried to stop the tears from forming in her eyes. "Let me help with dinner."

Nikki tried not to inhale her food, but she hadn't eaten anything all day. She tried to help Ruth with the dishes, but Lacey insisted that was 'her job.'

Nikki hugged her goodbye and gathered her things.

"Let me walk you to the jeep," Rory's dad said. He didn't speak a whole lot, but when he did, it was always worth listening.

He didn't say anything until they got to the jeep. Larry leaned against the vehicle, looking at the setting sun. "I think Rory's in real trouble."

"Why?" Nikki's legs felt weak.

"Because he's keeping secrets. I don't know what they are, but he ain't a good liar. I know he's not telling the cops everything, and I'm afraid he's going to do something stupid, like try to find out who killed that girl himself."

"Me too," she confessed.

"Becky was troubled," Larry said. "She had problems. Sometimes she'd be really outgoing, to the point she embarrassed Rory. Flirting with everyone and all of that. Next time he saw her, she might be totally different."

"Was she diagnosed with any sort of personality disorder?" Nikki asked.

"Not that I know of, but it wouldn't surprise me." Larry looked sheepish. "I'm not trained to spot things like you are, but that girl had issues with attention. She craved it, but then she'd hate it. Never seen anything like it."

"What about Rory?"

"He was enamored with her, I think. He and Jay—that's Becky's brother—used to run around doing stupid shit, like vandalizing windows and stealing smokes. Ruth liked to blame the family, but Rory didn't have it easy. He was acting out, I know."

"You did the best you could," Nikki said, thinking of the man she'd met earlier in Rory's driveway. Had Becky been as wild as her foster brother? "Rory's a good person. So is Mark."

"Oh, I know," Larry said. "But good people do stupid things that get them in trouble. Mark's a prime example."

Nikki remembered the hostility she had witnessed between Jay and Rory outside of Rory's house. "Is he still friends with her brother?"

"No, thankfully. He cut ties with him not long after he and Becky broke up for good. That's when Rory finally started getting his stuff together, he started working construction jobs, and then he built up his business." Larry coughed and looked at the ground. "Just promise me you won't let anything happen to him. With the system, I mean. He'd never hurt her, but whatever he got into with Jay, he's running from now."

"Do you think Jay would hurt his sister?" Nikki's mind was going in a dozen directions at once. Could Becky's death have been an accident, and her brother had convinced Rory to cover it up with him? She couldn't see the Rory she knew now doing that, but he had been eighteen, bitter and scared.

"I'd like to think he wouldn't," Larry said. "But I don't know the guy anymore. Never really did. He's just the opposite of Becky."

Nikki explained about the abandoned house and trying to figure out who owned it more than twenty years ago. She doubted Larry would have any information since he and Ruth had spent the last two decades focused on freeing Mark. "Can you think of who lived there around then?"

"Wish I could," Larry said. "But the place doesn't ring a bell."

Nikki promised to keep an eye out for Rory and thanked him for his time. She left the Todds' home feeling more unsettled than ever. She'd spent the last few hours trying to tell herself she'd over-reacted about Rory, but his father had just confirmed her fears.

TWENTY-TWO

Nikki stopped back at the abandoned house just before dark really set in. The medical examiner's office had cordoned off the property and set up Klieg lights so they could work in the dark and collect as much evidence as possible. They were certain now that the bones were human—the crime scene was connected to Joyce, but the bones created a connection to Becky.

Miller stood near the cellar opening, taking notes. Nikki showed her badge and ducked under the tape. "Déjà vu."

"There are at least three females buried here," Miller said. "Experts don't think any of them are older than fifteen or so. The bones have been dug up and scattered by animals, but the death investigator says the growth plates aren't fully fused."

"Pre-adolescent, then."

Miller nodded. "But old enough to get pregnant."

Nikki's stomach bottomed out. "You're certain?"

"Well, they'll have to run all the tests and match the fetuses to the mothers—if they even can. But they found two different sets of fetal bones."

"This is huge." Nikki's heartbeat accelerated, her chest tight with excitement. "You know Joyce told Nash that the traffickers killed any girl who got pregnant, and these bodies back that up.

They're also strong evidence that our cases are connected," Nikki said. "Depending on how good the evidence is, tests might find that all three were pregnant. Just not far along enough to find bones. Liam called Courtney, didn't he?"

Miller nodded. "She's in the middle of something and can't come out until tomorrow, so we decided to have these guys do their thing now. She'll come in the morning and work her magic. Most evidence is going to be under the dirt anyway. We didn't think dragging Courtney away from what she was doing would help find Joyce. I'm staying here until they're done, and then we'll have a deputy keep an eye on things until morning."

"Good call," Nikki said. "Where did Liam and Nash go?"

"Back to the city to shower and change. We told Nash to stay and get some rest, but I have a feeling he'll be back tonight."

"If he shows up, tell him to come to the station. I'm going to set up there and try to look at everything fresh. You'll have to share your files with me..."

"Will do," Miller said. "I don't suppose you talked to Rory?"

"I did."

"We really need to talk to him again, Nicole."

She shifted so she could look directly into his eyes and read his face as he spoke. "You don't really think he had anything to do with her murder? Especially now with so many similarities between Becky's case and Joyce's?"

"I think he knows something, and for whatever reason, doesn't want to come clean."

"He's afraid he'll get railroaded like his brother, I think. I told him you would never do that, but I know his being uncooperative doesn't make him look good."

"Thank you," Miller said sincerely. "I wish he'd believe you."

It was still muggy out, and bullfrogs in a nearby pond croaked their opinions. "Kent, how bad is it?"

Miller sighed. "Not great. We know he lied about that night. We have two different witnesses that tell the same story. Our cases may be connected, but I have no other persons of interest and neither do you. I don't think Rory hurt anyone, but he needs to tell us what he does know."

"I'll try to talk to him again," Nikki said. Maybe if Rory knew the cases were connected and his information could help find Joyce, he'd finally tell Miller everything.

"Tell him whatever it is, we can work with him on it. I'm not interested in old crimes. I don't care if he robbed a bank with her. I just need him to tell me the truth."

Nikki's phone rang loudly, startling them both. She'd forgotten she had turned it up in case Rory called. "This is Agent Hunt."

Nash's loud voice came over the line, talking too fast for Nikki to understand. "Slow down. What came for you?"

"A package from Joyce. It arrived sometime today. Postmarked the day before she disappeared."

Nikki hit the speaker button. "What did she send?"

"Her pictures," Nash choked. "They're old, but she was talented even as a kid. And there's a note."

"Read it."

Nash cleared his throat.

Dear Justin,

I hope that I see you before this arrives. I think he found me, and Cat may be in trouble, too. I want to come forward like we talked about, but I have to put Patrick first. I hope they leave me alone until he's born, but in case they don't, please keep these safe. They might be the only pictures of the girls that exist. He never knew that I drew them, because I always shredded each picture. But I drew each girl I saw over and over until I knew I wouldn't forget her face. I love you, and I'm sorry.

Joyce

"There's probably fifteen different pictures here, drawn from her memory," Nash said.

"Meet me at the Washington County Sheriff's," Nikki said.

"I'm already on my way," Nash replied. "What did they find in the cellar?"

"Female bones," Nikki said. "Two sets of fetal remains."

"That has to be the right place," Nash said.

"It doesn't tell us where he's keeping her," Nikki reminded him. "Let's pray that something she sent you will lead us to her."

Nikki reached the sheriff's station a few minutes before everyone else, so she signed in and went to the largest conference room. She'd tried Rory twice on the drive in, but he still hadn't answered. She left another message and then dug Tyler's file on Kendrick out of her bag. She'd skimmed it earlier and was confident it didn't have any address or numbers that might help them find Joyce, but she hadn't had a chance to look at his notes.

His oddball notetaking strategy had made sense once he explained it to her, but Nikki thought it was easier to write it out instead of trying to remember all the codes and abbreviations. She'd teased him relentlessly about his notes, and he always took it in his stride, like he did most things in life. Tyler had four large index cards on Kendrick, most related to their initial conversation. Nikki waded through the notes, studying every line to make sure she didn't miss anything. Kendrick hadn't told Tyler anything more than he'd told them at lunch the other day. The last index card had Tyler's impressions of Kendrick: boastful, big personality, finely tuned empathy.

"Finely tuned empathy." Nikki said the words out loud. Unlike a lot of white-collar crimes agents, Tyler took courses on profiling and psychology. He felt that working knowledge of human behavior was a vital asset to an agent in any department.

Tyler likely hadn't bought the story about Kendrick's wife. He only gave it one line on the index card, and it was clear he wanted both Kendricks investigated for tax fraud along with possible child trafficking.

Miller arrived with an excited Nash in tow. He'd showered and changed into jeans and a T-shirt, but he was as amped as Nikki had ever seen him. "I guess I shouldn't have touched anything but since she sent it to me for safekeeping, I'm not worried about messing up the bad guy's prints."

Nash started laying each picture out on the table. The edges of some were torn and wrinkled, but others were much newer. Nikki wondered how many times Joyce had drawn these girls' faces in order to commit them to memory.

"Recognize her?" Nash asked. "She's one of the ones I found here last year. Taken in '99."

"Do you recognize any others?" Nikki asked.

Nash shook his head. "No, but I'm hoping we can get them out to the media?"

"I don't know," Nikki said, studying the drawings. Most of the girls appeared to be females between twelve and sixteen.

Nash started to lay out another picture, but it was stuck to a second one. He carefully peeled them apart, his face going white. His fingers shook as he laid down a picture of two young black girls standing by a fallen log. Shock and fear lined their young faces.

"This must be when Joyce was taken," Nikki said softly. "It might be the only clear memory she has of the day."

Nash paced in front of the table. "Let's put this on the national news. I can contact the FBI's press liaison. She'll make it happen fast."

"Hold on," Nikki said. "These are good drawings, but that's all they are. I'm not sure it's a good use of time and resources."

Nash balked. "Then what should we do?"

"Missing persons," Nikki said. "Liam can upload these, and our system will let him compare the drawings to the ones we have. Especially this one." She tapped the picture of Joyce and probably her sister. "We haven't been able to locate her missing person's report, but the detail of this drawing might be enough for Liam to find it."

"That will take time," Nash argued.

"So will getting it out to the media, and I'm not sure that's the best strategy. This guy thinks he's still way ahead of us, and if we put these pictures out there, he's going to know we are getting close. That's not good for Joyce."

Nash rested his elbows on his knees, his hands on his head. "I let Kendrick get on a plane. He already had Joyce then, didn't he?"

"We don't know that. NYPD is still looking for him," Nikki said. "Kent, you have a unit on the Kendrick property, right?"

He nodded, skimming through the drawings. "I checked with them on the drive back. The wife left yesterday and came back with groceries. Other than that, there hasn't been a lot of activity."

"Sorry I'm late." Liam finally arrived. He'd showered and changed too. He stopped short, looking at the pictures spread over the table. He dropped his bag on the floor and peered at the same blonde girl Nikki had been studying. "That's Mae Kendrick."

Nikki smacked her hand against her forehead. "That's why she looked familiar."

"If this is Mae Kendrick, she's not just a victim anymore. She's an accomplice," Nikki said flatly. "We know this kidnapper makes his older victims into house mothers, and she's one of them. What if the two girls her husband saw her with were victims?" A sick feeling rolled through Nikki, and she went back to Tyler's file, praying she was wrong.

"These are summaries for the Kendricks' last several tax years," she said. "What's missing?" All three men looked over her shoulders.

"No dependents." Liam sounded as empty as Nikki suddenly felt. She sank into the chair. How could she have missed the signs? Sylvia had seemed so well adjusted, but Nikki knew what to look for, and she should have realized that the girl wasn't Mae's daughter.

"Catch me up," Nash said.

"Mae Kendrick's daughter was helping her downsize," Liam said bitterly. "Pretty girl, around twelve. But it would appear they don't have a daughter."

"How could I not see it?" Nikki asked. "I talked to her alone."

"You aren't superhuman," Miller said.

"I missed it too," Liam said. "You know as well as I do that a lot of these kids come from foster care or broken homes. They're vulnerable, and they know the only way to survive is to play along."

Nash rubbed his temples. "Joyce's kidnapper tried to convince her that he was her foster parent. He said he'd been sent to save her from her bad parents. That's the excuse he used every time he brought a new girl into the house. They were being fostered."

"Hold on," Liam said, flipping through the pictures. "Is it possible he actually used the foster system? Because if he did, then there should be records to trace."

"I don't think so," Nash said. "I've been going over that angle for weeks. No registered foster parent had nearly the amount of girls going through their house that Joyce remembered, which means at least some were likely kidnapped. I combed through all the records and complaints filed with DHS while Joyce would have been living with him and found nothing. Plus, if he had been a registered foster parent, doesn't that mean he's subject to random checks?"

"It does, but you have to understand the mental damage these girls experience," Nikki answered. "People who abuse and traffic kids like this are every bit as good at reading people as a profiler. They know what people are expecting to hear, and they have the confidence to back it up." She touched the pencil drawing with the two little girls. Their wide, frightened eyes haunted Nikki, but she was more interested in the older girl. "This is probably Joyce's sister. She saw the man who took her. Email our techs a copy of this drawing as well as the others and have them start combing through missing persons looking for a match."

Miller had been sitting silent, looking at his notes. He finally looked up at Nikki with tired eyes. "Becky Anderson was a foster kid for most of her life."

Nikki tried not to let her excitement show. "We already have four dead teenage girls who were pregnant at the time they were murdered, all found in the same county."

Nash was already halfway to the door. "I'm going to the Kendricks'."

"Hold it," Nikki said. "We can't just run over there. These people have been getting away with this for a long time. That house is surrounded by at least two acres, and there are security cameras all around. We only have one chance."

"And that has to be carefully planned," Liam said.

"Justin," Nikki said. "For Joyce's sake, listen to us, please."

Nash's shoulders dropped, and he stared at the ceiling. "Please hurry. I'll go get us coffee."

"Order it," Nikki said. "We need all hands on deck, and we do need to move quickly. Liam, see if you can get the SWAT team together. I'm not sure we'll need them, but I want them to be ready."

"On it," Liam said.

Twenty minutes later, with coffee in hand, Nikki stood in front of the smartboard, looking at the Kendricks' property. Aerial footage gave them a good idea of the terrain, but Google Earth had recent pictures of the house and surrounding areas. "When Liam and I were there the other day, she took him to the garage so I could talk to the girl. He noticed security cameras on the east side of the house, so we have to assume they're all around it."

She circled the property in the aerial footage. "Fortunately, there's no physical barrier around the property. And as luck would have it, the state owns the adjacent land, so we should have a solid route onto the property. I'll see what the SWAT leader thinks, but I say we go in with the assumption they will be alerted. We need the perimeter surrounded. Given the size of it, I think we need to utilize the SWAT team to hold the perimeter. We come in low, from the side, led by SWAT. One team goes to the back, the other in front—"

"We don't need SWAT." Liam stood in the doorway, pale and tired.

"Why not?" Nash demanded. "Did something happen? Is Joyce okay?"

Liam flinched. "I don't know, but the Kendrick place is on fire."

TWENTY-THREE

Nikki's hands hurt from her grip on the wheel. Liam had stayed at the sheriff's station, dealing with the NYPD and their search for Kendrick. Nash sat rigid beside her. She wanted to say something comforting, but she couldn't think of anything that didn't sound like false hope. The longer she spent with Nash the more she could see just how much he had cared for Joyce—his concern for her safety was intense. But she worried, too, if that meant he shouldn't be here, be involved in the investigation anymore.

"It's a two-alarm fire," Nash said dully. "Big enough that two different agencies are involved."

"It's been dry," Nikki said. "They're probably thinking about containment."

He didn't respond, and they drove the rest of the way in silence. Nikki's heart thundered in her ears. If Sylvia was in danger, it was Nikki's fault. It didn't matter how good of an actress the girl had been or how damaged she was—Nikki had failed her, probably just like everyone else in the poor kid's life.

The house was still a mile away, but they could see the orange glow in the night sky. Nikki was glad the Kendricks didn't live anywhere near Rory or his family.

The Kendricks' location meant they didn't have immediate

neighbors and there wasn't a lot of traffic, but a uniformed officer was still directing traffic. He nodded at Nikki and gestured for her to park off to the side. They were still a hundred feet from the driveway, but she could tell they were getting the fire under control.

All she and the others could do was watch the fire department fight to contain the blaze.

"There's Miller." Nikki spotted the sheriff walking away from a firefighter. "Stay here," she told Nash.

They were probably five hundred feet from the actual fire, but the smoke was still thick. Nikki waved her hands in front of her, but her eyes still stung. "Survivors?"

Miller shook his head. "They think the fire started downstairs. Two bodies, one in the kitchen and one in the living room."

Nikki's nails dug into the palm of her hand. "Deceased?"

Miller nodded. "We've called the ME."

"I want to go in the second it's even remotely safe," Nikki said. "I'll put on the suit and boots if it gets me inside quicker."

The fire chief refused to consider the offer until the blaze was at least eighty percent contained, and even then, they wouldn't be allowed into the house until it was fully extinguished. Parts of the fire would smolder for a while but once the chief was satisfied the threat was eliminated, he relented and allowed Nikki and Miller onto the property.

"Nicole, please let me go with you," Nash begged. "I should be there."

"You aren't an agent right now," she said. "You can't set foot on that property or it could compromise the entire investigation. Do you want these bastards to get away with what they've done?"

"No." He smacked his hand on the dashboard. "God, this is hard. If she's gone—"

"Just wait," Nikki said. "Let Miller and I see what we can find out."

As they approached the house, Nikki caught the scent of burned flesh. Water bodies were worse, but a burned body was a terrible thing to see. The fire chief led them around to the back of the house, where the kitchen had once been. Nikki could see the female body lying in a pugilistic stance—the body had essentially contorted as it burned, but Nikki could still see some of the human features.

"This one's lying face up," the fire chief said. "I can't let you get any closer, but I'll go in and take pictures of the victims. That's the best I can do until the fire's completely out."

Nikki handed him her phone, and she and Miller waited on the periphery while he took the photos. The ground surrounding the house was marshy from water, which made finding physical evidence unlikely. "They only found two bodies?"

Miller nodded. "They used the bucket truck in the back of the house and were able to sweep the upstairs. They didn't see any bodies."

The fire chief strode back, and Nikki's nerves skyrocketed.

"Both of them are white," he said, handing Nikki the phone. Up close, the body was even more destroyed, the muscles on her face twisted in pain, just like the rest of her body. Nikki knew that fire victims usually died from smoke inhalation, so the woman likely hadn't suffered the actual burning.

"How close is she to the origin?"

"Within eight feet or so," he said. "The fire started in either the kitchen or garage. We think the connecting door was doused in an accelerant. It looks like she tried to crawl to the door."

"She might have been wounded," Miller said. "It's going to be nearly impossible for Blanchard to tell, from the looks of her. ID might take longer."

Nikki zoomed in on the face, trying to forget this had once been a human being. "Most of her hair is gone, but look at her ear. Look at the diamond stud."

"You sure that's what it is?" Miller asked.

"Chief Amir, can we bother you again?" Nikki walked over and showed him the phone. "Is this a diamond earring? I've read diamonds turn white and cloudy in fire."

"It's a diamond," he said. "The other ear basically melted, so I can't tell you if she had them both in."

"Thanks," Nikki said, turning back to Miller. "Mae Kendrick wore diamond studs. They were at least a carat. I don't remember Sylvia wearing any." It wasn't an official medical examiner's opinion, but it was enough circumstantial evidence to make her hope—alongside the fact that both bodies were white— that Joyce might be alive.

They just had no idea where she'd been taken.

"Hold on," Chief Amir said. "They found another body in the garage, which is just off the kitchen. It was so badly burned that we walked over it earlier without realizing it."

Nikki had heard of firefighters walking over bodies because the remains were so destroyed, they no longer resembled anything close to human, but she'd never actually witnessed it. "Doesn't that mean she was close to the origin?"

Chief Amir nodded. "Given the extent of the damage, the accelerant may have been poured on the victim. Your experts are going to have a hard time making an identification. And you'll have to wait until tomorrow to get your science people in here, though."

"Were there any vehicles in the garage?" Miller asked.

"A black BMW, and what looks like an old Honda Civic was parked closest to the door."

Nikki swiped to look at the picture of the other body, hoping it would be easier to identify. The person had died face down, and the entire back appeared charred off. "Once they turn this person over, we might be able to identify them. They're far enough from the fire they still have a decent amount of visible skin left."

"That's not going to be for a while," Miller said. "I'm going to see if I can get the license plate numbers from the car. Can you tell Nash we don't know much more than we did before?"

Nikki dreaded giving him the news. She was certain that the body with the diamond earring was Mae Kendrick, and she couldn't tell if the body on the couch was a male or female. It would be days at best before they found out the identity of the person who'd died in the garage, and the fire had been so intense it was impossible to even guess at the victim's size.

The media had started to gather across the street. Nikki ducked her head, hoping they wouldn't notice her.

"Agent Hunt, are you back? Is this your case?"

"No comment." Nikki was relieved to see the deputies keeping the reporters back. Nash paced like a hungry lion in front of the jeep.

"Is it her?"

"We don't know," she said. "There are three, and it will be a few days before we know who they are. We might as well go back to the sheriff's office and regroup."

Nash shook his head. "I'm not leaving. You go ahead."

"I can't just leave you here," Nikki said. "You aren't going to be any help to these guys. They know what they're doing. All we can do is wait." She walked around to the other side of the jeep, trying to clear her head. Even with the incredibly high heat and the water damage, she'd still been able to smell the victims' burned flesh. She could still taste the smoke odor on her tongue. Fatigue settled over Nikki, and she rested her head against the side of the vehicle. What did they do now?

She retrieved her vibrating phone from her pocket. "Hello?"

"Baby, it's me," Rory slurred. "I got arrested. Can you come bail me out?"

Rory sat alone in the cell, his head down, his dark, wavy hair blocking his face. Nikki could see that his right knuckle was split, and he had blood on his gray shirt and old blue jeans. "Did you at least win the fight?" she asked him through the bars.

Rory looked up at her, shocked. "How did you find out?"

"How do you think?" Nikki leaned her head on the bars. "Please tell me why you beat the hell out of Jay Briggs. Do you think he had something to do with Becky's death?"

"Probably, but I can't prove it."

"That's not your job," she said, her patience thin. "Have you told Miller this?"

Rory rolled his eyes. "Are you kidding? Jay's his star witness."

"What are you talking about?"

"Ask him." He crossed his arms over his broad chest and leaned back, glaring at the ceiling. "Since you have so much trust in the guy."

"Grow up for Christ's sake," Nikki exploded. "If you were in the city—or any other county, for that matter—you would have been arrested and charged with something by now, simply because you won't cooperate."

"They don't want to hear what I have to say," Rory said. "Police never do."

"Just stop it," Nikki said. "No one here has a personal vendetta against your family. Do you realize how serious you are making this? Every action you've taken has made it look like you're trying to hide something."

"Maybe I am."

"Like what? Because I know you didn't hurt her."

"Might as well have." Rory stood and swayed before walking over to the bars. "Do you believe people can really change?" he asked quietly, glancing at the camera mounted in the hall.

"If they want to, yes."

"But certain people are just bad seeds, right?"

"Unfortunately, but most people are the product of how they were raised and their environment. You are not a bad seed."

"According to some people, it runs in my family."

"Mark has been cleared."

"I'm not talking about now."

"Then what are you talking about?"

He wrapped his hands over Nikki's. "I love you, but everything that's going on... I'm no good for you. Or Lacey."

Nikki froze, their gazes locked. "You have been one of the reasons Lacey made it through the last few months." Her voice started to shake. "For the love of God, if you walk out on my daughter after all she's been through, there won't be a second chance. Do you understand what I'm saying?"

"I'm not walking out on her," he snapped. "I just need you to back off and let me take care of things. You really think I'd do something like that?"

"I don't know anymore," Nikki said. "It's like you want to be punished because you blame yourself for Becky's death. You know something, maybe you knew something then and didn't do anything about it because you didn't realize how much trouble she was in. That doesn't mean you're responsible for killing her."

Rory's eyes darkened. "I disagree." He reached through the bars and wiped the hair out of her face. "Where have you been, anyway? You're covered with black stuff."

"Smoke," she said. "Three people dead in a house fire, and we have no idea yet if the woman we're looking for is one of the victims. One of them is probably a child that I spent time alone with and didn't realize she was a trafficking victim. I'm trained in body language and linguistics. I know how to break down a person's micro expressions. Yet I failed that child."

Rory immediately came to her defense, just as she knew he would. "You can't blame yourself. Wasn't Liam there? He didn't notice, either. I know you're damn good at what you do, but you're not infallible. You aren't expected to be."

"And neither are you." Nikki stepped away from the bars. "I could bail you out, but then I'd have to worry that you were running around, doing something stupid."

He raised his eyebrows. "You're really going to let me spend the night in jail? Come on, I'm sorry for taking things out on you." Rory reached through the bars and grabbed her hands. "Take me home and let me make it up to you." He winked, the smell of beer practically seeping out of his pores.

"I have to work."

"Haven't you been working for like, two days straight? Let's go home."

"I can't rest until I know if Joyce and Sylvia are alive. And you need to sober up."

"You're serious? You're going to let me sit in a cell the rest of the night? Don't you think that's going to set you back with my parents?"

"After today, I think they will thank me. Call me later when you're sober, and hopefully you've removed your head from your ass."

She left him standing in the cell, stunned. What did he expect her to do? She knew that they had a stronger lead to follow, that he was no longer the only suspect Miller had. But still, he was coming unhinged, and she didn't know how to fix him.

TWENTY-FOUR

Nikki woke up with her face sticking to the leather couch in the break room of the sheriff's office. She'd crashed somewhere around four, exhausted from worry and guilt. She rolled her neck back and forth, trying to work out the kink.

"Morning." Nash's voice came out of nowhere. She hadn't noticed him sitting at the small table, drinking coffee.

"Jesus." Nikki put her hand over her heart. "You scared the hell out of me. What were you doing, watching me sleep?"

He snorted. "You wish." Like her, he was still in the same sooty-smelling clothes from last night. "No word yet."

Nikki rubbed the sleep out of her eyes. She swung her legs around so she could face Nash. "There won't be for a while, I'm sorry."

"I know." He stared into his coffee mug. "I think she's still alive. You said he wanted to punish her, that he wanted to keep her, right? So why would he kill her now when he just got her back?"

"Self-preservation," Nikki said. "Has anyone found Kendrick?"

"Not that I know of," Nash said. "Liam called the New York bureau office this morning and put a fire under their butts. He told them to do what the NYPD apparently isn't capable of doing."

Nikki had already checked with the airlines and confirmed that Kendrick departed a couple of hours after having lunch with Nash and Nikki. "Did Liam get their financials frozen?"

"I think so," Nash said. "But Kendrick hasn't used his credit cards since he left, and there's no sign of him taking another flight."

Nikki stood and stretched. "Have they checked the morgues?"

"I don't know."

"I think that needs to be the next step," she said. "Kendrick might have become more of a liability than an asset."

She found Liam and Miller in the conference room. They both stopped talking when she walked in.

"Wow," she said. "I guess my ears should have been burning."

"Rory was released about an hour ago. Mark picked him up," Miller said.

"Good." Nikki pulled out a chair and sat down across from them. "He said I should talk to you about why he went after Jay Briggs."

Liam and Miller looked at each other, but Nikki kept going before they could respond. "I know he's innocent. But he's not making himself look very innocent, and I can't help him if I don't know everything. And I don't mean help him not get arrested." She looked between the two men. "I truly believe you will find the killer, and I know you won't make any arrest until you're certain you have the right person. That person isn't Rory, so I'm not worried about him getting in trouble for killing her. I'm worried about him doing something stupid trying to find out who really killed Becky." She leaned forward, hoping they would both trust her as much as she trusted them. "I think it's time we shared all of our information."

"We were just discussing that," Miller said. "Rory said he and Becky didn't talk that much that night, but we have two credible eyewitnesses who dispute that. These same eyewitnesses saw him follow her from the bar to her vehicle. They argued, and then she left. He followed her. That was likely the last night anyone saw Becky, and he could be one of the last people who saw her alive."

"He's denied this?" Nikki asked, trying not to let any emotion leak into her voice.

"He hasn't had the chance," Liam answered. "We haven't been able to talk to him since he came in to make his statement."

"Rory seems to think Jay Briggs might know something about Becky's murder," Nikki said. "He said Jay's also your star witness."

Miller chuckled. "I wouldn't call him a star anything. He corroborated the other eyewitness. Look, I don't know how much Rory has told you about his high school experience, and it's not really my place to divulge details. But he had a hard time, and he had a lot of anger back then."

"He also worked at the McFarlands'," Liam said quietly. "Your faith in me to handle this case means a lot. But I have to be transparent, boss. I'm not as positive about Rory's innocence as Sheriff Miller."

Nikki's first instinct was to defend Rory, but she managed to stay calm. "Why?"

"Innocent people don't usually avoid the police and refuse to answer questions."

"Fair enough," Nikki said. "But I have to disagree, and not just because of Rory." Liam wasn't thirty yet, and he had a good psychological foundation and great instincts when it came to reading and understanding people, but he also had a lot to learn. "And I don't think it's because of bias. You have to look at the person's environment and background, right? Rory learned from a young age not to trust police. He's traumatized and angry, and completely out of his element."

"How so?" Miller asked, genuinely curious.

"He's used to being the one in charge, making the decisions. Not being able to work makes him restless, and, frankly, he's gone through a lot the past three months too. He's watched Lacey and I suffer, and I know it's been hard for him because he can't fix it. And he's a fixer." She looked between the two men. "And Ruth and Larry weren't in a good place during those days. Rory had to go through a lot of things on his own. I guess what I'm trying to say is that I think he's got a lot more demons from growing up than I realized, and all of them are affecting his choices now."

"We talked to three of Becky's friends from high school," Liam said. "He and Becky had a volatile relationship. There was never any talk of violence, but they were known for public screaming matches and make-out sessions. Rory apparently got jealous easily, and Becky was a natural flirt."

"Was she, though?" Nikki explained what Rory's father had told her yesterday. "That's textbook behavior of abuse victims. She was a foster kid too. We all know the statistics there. Did she have any other known foster siblings? What about Jay? Was he fostered as well?"

Miller shook his head. "No, he's Martin Briggs's only biological child. Briggs has a genetic issue that prevented them from having more kids. That's why they started fostering." He flipped through his yellow notepad. "I tracked down a couple of the foster kids who went through their house. Both said it was the best foster home they'd been in."

"Were they both boys?" Nikki asked.

Miller nodded. "And remember, Nash said he couldn't find any connections in the foster record."

"That doesn't mean there isn't one." Nikki decided to take her chances and tell them her theory. "Becky was pregnant, killed in '97. What if she was taken by our traffickers and quickly killed once they realized she was pregnant? It fits a pattern. Two years later, the first of two known Washington County girls disappears. Last year, both were found within miles of where Becky was buried, both pregnant. And we know that Joyce's captor used the foster system as an excuse to take her at the very least."

"Those girls weren't as far along as she was," Miller said. "I checked, and both were less than ten weeks. Becky was five months; she must have been showing more than these other girls were. Why take her?"

"Some women can get away with just wearing baggy clothes right up to their last trimester. Did Becky's friends know she was pregnant?" Nikki asked. "Did she talk about anything to them?"

"Unfortunately not," Miller said. "Rory was about the only person Becky confided in. Her friends said she was a hard nut to crack. None of them knew she was pregnant."

But Rory had, and he'd known the baby's sex, Nikki thought. Becky had to have told him.

"Rory quit working for McFarland about a week after Becky's visit," Liam said. "Not long after that, he enrolled in community college, started trying to get his life together."

"That doesn't mean he killed her," Nikki said, her chest aching from the stress and worrying about Rory. "But I agree, he knows more than he said. And given everything we've just discussed, I think we've got to look at the Briggs family a lot closer."

"Rory has got to tell us the truth," Miller insisted. "The mayor is already demanding an arrest asap because of the publicity. This subdivision is his legacy." Miller rolled his eyes. "I'll make an arrest when I'm damned good and ready, but the longer this drags on, the more chance Rory could lose the contract. If the mayor gets wind that he's a suspect, I promise you he'll drop Rory's company in a heartbeat, even if that means a lawsuit."

"I'll talk to him about it the next time we speak," Nikki said. "He's avoiding me too."

"Why didn't Rory say anything about his suspicions about Briggs to me?" Miller asked.

"He's being stubborn and stupid," Nikki said. "Does Briggs's alibi for the night Becky disappeared check out?"

"He and his dad were both home that night, expecting a visit from her since they'd heard she was back in town. She never showed up," Miller said.

"Why didn't they go to the cops, then?" Nikki asked.

"Because they got those postcards from her," Liam said.

"In her handwriting?" Nikki asked.

"Handwriting good enough to fool them," Miller said. "But I

will dig into Jay Briggs, see what I can find out. Tell Rory that. Maybe he'll finally trust us."

"Thank you," Nikki said. "Have you spoken to the medical examiner's office this morning?" Liam chewed the corner of his lower lip, which meant he had news Nikki wasn't going to like. "Did they identify the remains in the house?"

"No, but the Honda Civic in the garage belongs to Cat," Liam said. "She was the woman on the couch. Blanchard didn't find any soot in her lungs, and X-rays showed a bullet buried in her brain. Blanchard is working on finding out the caliber and make of the gun."

"You're certain Cat's the woman lying on the couch?" Nikki asked, thinking of how badly charred the back of the woman's body had been.

Liam opened his phone. "You know how it works with fire. Since she was away from the origin and face down, some of her features were preserved."

"Let me see the photo," Nikki said.

He slid his phone over to her. "This is from the morgue, after they got her cleaned up as best they could."

Nikki nodded, her empty stomach sour. Part of her face was gone, but it was Cat's body. The girls from the shelter were going to be devastated. "We need to notify the vet's office. Does Cat have any family?"

Liam shook his head. "Our computer guys are combing her driver's license photos with some of the missing kids, trying to locate family. If Joyce knew her when they were young, then Cat was likely kidnapped too. They're still working on the other two victims, but the body in the kitchen had a diamond ring on its engagement finger. Blanchard said it's too badly burned for her to guess age, but the forensic anthropologist should be able to determine that. She's hoping they will have that answer today. The other victim..." Liam made a face. "DNA is the only chance of identifying that one. Even the teeth and jaw are destroyed."

"Nash said you called the New York bureau," Nikki said.

"They need to start checking the morgues. What about flight manifests? The airlines can tell us if Kendrick flew out of the city."

"They're working on it," Liam said. "Problem is, there's also dozens of private charter companies in New York. Kendrick could have used one of them to flee the city."

"We'll need warrants to see their flight manifests," Nikki said. "We'll never get one unless we have strong evidence Kendrick isn't in the city."

"I started going through the missing persons database earlier," Liam said. "Our techs haven't matched any of the pictures, but I'm only looking for the police report from Joyce's kidnapping."

"Good," Nikki said. "We need to find Joyce's older sister. Have you found out who owned the house where we found the remains?" she asked Miller.

"No, but the neighbors were happy to talk about how they'd been trying to get the house torn down, but the city council is fighting it. Apparently, the house is old enough to be on the historical register, and a couple city council members want to save it."

"Maybe they know the house's background," Nash said. "If it's torn down for a new development, the bones would have been found, just like your victim from the construction site."

"He's right." Nikki stood, hoping the energy surge would last for a while. "We need to get those council members in here right away."

"Good idea," Liam said. "Kent, can you think of a ruse to get them here?"

"The city council? Hell, they're on my ass almost as much as the mayor. I can get them in here."

"Do it," Nikki said. "I'm going to get cleaned up. Let me know when the council members arrive."

Nikki went to the break room to get her overnight bag so she could brush her teeth and change clothes. She couldn't stop thinking about what Miller and Liam had told her about Rory and Becky, and now that she'd planted the seed to Miller and Liam, she couldn't stop thinking that Becky was tied to the traffickers.

The hatred in Rory's eyes when he spoke about Briggs haunted her.

Nikki peeked in the hallway to make sure no one was around and then called Hernandez. She explained her theory about Becky possibly being tied to the ring and her gut instincts about Briggs. Her boss didn't need to know those instincts were fueled by Rory, but she owed it to him to be honest about the police considering him a suspect. "I'm obviously biased, and I'm going to try to get him to talk to Miller again, and I don't want to overstep, but we can find out things so much faster than regular police departments, especially if a high-level agent is involved."

"What do you need me to do?" Hernandez asked. "It sounds like the connection between the two cases is circumstantial at best."

"I know," Nikki said. "Miller said he'd look further into Briggs, but his people are having trouble finding out who's behind the dummy corporation that owns the abandoned house we think Joyce was kept in when she was first taken. The corporation's tax status is defunct; they haven't been listed on any public or private list in at least ten years, and the house has been empty longer than that. He probably moved operations when Joyce escaped. We might be able to get the IRS to help us out, but we need a warrant, and Joyce can't wait for that to happen."

"You think she's still alive?" Hernandez asked. "Liam didn't sound confident this morning."

"Until Blanchard identifies her as one of the fire victims, then yes, I think she could still be alive. He wants to possess her, forever. Even if he's no longer interested in her physically, he only just got Joyce back."

"What's the name of this corporation?"

"DM Holdings, LLC. Registered as a corporation in Minnesota in the late nineties."

"Let me see what I can find out," he said. "You get anything from those pictures Joyce drew?"

"Not yet," she answered. "I told the media liaison to focus on the one of the two younger girls. We're getting ready to speak to the city council members who are fighting to keep that old house from being torn down. Their argument to restore it seems really thin given its state."

"Good idea," Hernandez said. "By the way, Patrick came home today."

"That's good news," Nikki said. "How are they doing?"

"All right, considering. Still devastated about Joyce. I haven't told them we think the Kendricks are definitely implicated, and I'm not going to mention the fire unless they ask. But I can't keep the news from them forever."

TWENTY-FIVE

Nikki knocked on Miller's open office door. He'd called the council members in under the guise of talking about their complaints about traffic control downtown. Nikki had suggested bringing them into his office, so they felt important and would hopefully have their guards down.

"Agent Hunt, please come in. Meet Stillwater city council members Angela Stone and Harry Chambers. They're both on the historical preservation board. Council members, this is Agent Nikki Hunt with the FBI."

The council members looked at one another in surprise. "I thought this was about the traffic issues downtown," Angela said.

"We'll get to that," Miller said pleasantly. "Agent Hunt actually had some questions for you about that abandoned house in the Cottage Grove area. The one you both are fighting so hard to save."

Angela looked irritated, but Harry stayed calm. Nikki had already done her research on both and knew they were each in their forties. Angela had children; Harry did not. As much as Nikki wanted to focus her attention on Harry, whose balding head had started to sweat, she knew Angela had to be questioned too. They had no indication that a female assailant was the kidnapper, but at every turn they'd lost women who could have helped with the investigation.

"Thank you for coming in on such short notice." Nikki leaned against the corner of Miller's desk. She'd changed yesterday's smoky-smelling clothes for jeans and an FBI polo shirt. Dry shampoo had taken most of the smoke smell out of her hair, but she still felt grimy. "I'm really curious about your interest in saving this house."

"I would save every historical home," Angela said. "Verbal history states the home in question was built somewhere around the 1850s, possibly at the direction of the Northrups. They were among Stillwater's first settlers."

"But we haven't been able to confirm the story," Harry said, brushing the moisture off his forehead. "The house was slated for demolition three years ago when its heritage was brought to our attention. We've established the house was built in 1853, per historical record. But it's unclear who commissioned the house to be built."

"How is that possible?" Nikki asked. "Isn't that all kept on record by the city?"

"Yes, but in the early days, some places slipped through the cracks," Angela said, a hint of irritation in her voice.

"I have to imagine this has cost the city some serious money," Miller said.

Angela shook her head. "We have an anonymous donor essentially footing the bill."

Nikki knew experience had made her jaded, but did these people even question anyone's motives, or did they just take the money and run? "In three years, this money hasn't helped to establish who built the house? Seems like you haven't tried very hard."

"It's not as easy as you think," Harry insisted, sitting up straight. "Records have been lost in floods and fires; they've been lost because of poor historical bookkeeping. Every town in this country has homes in a similar situation, I assure you."

"Tell us about this anonymous donor," Miller said. "Did he contact one of you personally?"

"Of course not," Harry said. He adjusted his bow tie. "The petition was sent to the entire council, with the offer of financial assistance. We are the only members who actually give a damn."

Nikki couldn't imagine many worse careers than politics, especially city politics. "How did you receive the money? How did you communicate with this person?"

"Through his lawyer." Angela looked at Harry in confusion. He shrugged and gestured for her to take the lead. "What's this all about?" Angela demanded. "The FBI doesn't care about preserving houses."

"We found the remains of at least three females and two sets of fetal remains in the cellar yesterday." Nikki watched as the council members' faces went ashen. "We need to know who owned that house." She didn't normally share so much information, but she needed the shock factor. Even if they hadn't committed any crimes, Angela or Harry might know a lot more about this anonymous donor than they were letting on.

"You're joking," Angela said.

"Unfortunately, I'm not. It's suspicious to me that the council doesn't want to reveal details of ownership," Nikki said.

Harry looked stunned. "Are you saying the council is being used to help protect a predator?"

"Possibly so," Nikki said. "Do you have the lawyer's contact information?"

Angela reached into her bag, pulling out a business card. "It's one of the largest firms in town. Could they be involved?" She looked pale and overwhelmed, and Nikki wondered if she'd faint if she stood up soon.

"We have no way of knowing," Nikki said. "I'm sure it goes without saying that if either of you knows anything else, it's in your best interest to tell me now."

"If it goes without saying, then why did you say it?" Harry asked. He gathered his briefcase and adjusted his bow tie. "I assure you we have no affiliation with any of this. We're just trying to do our job of making Stillwater a nice place to live."

"That's all we're doing too," Miller said. "But I second Agent Hunt's sentiments."

Angela stood as well. "I appreciate what you're trying to do, and I sincerely hope you get to the bottom of this. Please keep us informed."

Both council members left without saying another word.

"I've said this a hundred times, and I'll keep saying it." Miller scowled as he and Nikki stood alone. "City council is worse than just about any form of government."

Nikki was studying the business card she'd been handed. As one of the largest firms in the area, Craig & Associates had a stable of lawyers who specialized in several different types of law, including taxes. She'd seen the name somewhere recently. The company advertised on television, but Nikki hadn't even looked at a TV in days. "I think Craig and Associates are the Kendricks' lawyers. Or they were at some point, anyway. I'm almost positive I saw the name in Tyler's file."

"It will take days to get a client list from them," Miller said. "And if this anonymous donor has money, they'll fight tooth and nail to protect their identity."

"I know," Nikki said. "Angela and Harry both seemed genuinely shocked at the discovery of the bones, but that doesn't mean one of them isn't getting money on the side to keep the house from being torn down. What do you know about their financial situations?"

"Not a lot, but I'll see if I can find out more. Angela is a vice principal at the elementary school. Harry's an accountant, and he's got a waiting list, so he seems very successful."

"See if there are red flags, like medical debt or credit cards," Nikki said, checking her vibrating phone. She tried not to gasp as she read Liam's text.

I found the sister. Calling now.

"I've got to get back to the team." Nikki gave Miller a pointed look. "Sheriff, please join us as soon as you can." She hurried out of his office and sprinted back to the conference room. Liam pointed to the speaker sitting in the middle of the table.

"I just sent you the drawing over text," Liam said. "Our lead investigator is also joining us."

"This is Agent Hunt," Nikki said, collapsing into the nearest chair. "I'm sorry, I didn't get your name?"

"It's Petunia," a shaky, female voice said. "Agent Wilson, I don't have the photo yet."

"Give it a second," Liam said kindly, turning his laptop around so that Nikki could see the missing persons report he'd finally dredged up. She leaned over his shoulder, looking at the photo Liam had found, shocked to see how accurate Joyce had drawn herself at such a young age.

Liam cleared his throat. "Agent Hunt, Petunia's sister disappeared—"

A guttural sob filtered through the speaker. "This is her," Petunia gasped. "And me, the minute we realized something very bad was going to happen."

Nash leaned forward, his fists resting on the table. Nikki squeezed his arm, trying to get him to relax. "Can you tell us what happened when your sister disappeared?"

"My little sister and I were on vacation on Lake Superior with our parents in 1995," Petunia choked out. "She and I wandered off to an area away from our parents and a man showed up. He took my sister. I tried to fight him off, but he shoved me. I hit my head against a log, and when I woke up, they were both gone," Petunia blurted. "My parents thought I made it up, that my sister must have drowned, and I didn't want to tell them because it was my job to keep her safe. But that's not true, and that picture looks exactly like the area she was taken from." Petunia started to cry again. "She loved to draw, even then."

"Where on Lake Superior?" Nash's voice mirrored Nikki's internal thoughts.

"Around Duluth," she said. "It wasn't a public beach area. That's where we were supposed to be, but our parents started bickering and sent us off to keep busy. We went too far," Petunia said softly.

"On the Minnesota or Wisconsin side?" Nikki asked.

"Minnesota," Petunia said.

"Why did your parents believe that she'd drowned?" Nikki asked, jotting down notes she hoped were legible.

"Because her shorts were found tangled in debris a couple of days later, but I knew he'd done that to make it look like Daisy was dead."

"Daisy?" Nash choked out. "Is that her real name?"

"Yes," Petunia said. "My parents named us both after flowers. My sister's full name is Daisy Marie Williams."

"I've seen that name." Liam shoved his laptop out of the way and started shuffling through the missing persons list. "Right here, she's on the missing persons list."

"How did you get these drawings? Did she draw them? Is she still alive?" Petunia begged.

"She did draw them," Nikki said. "We aren't sure if she's alive. Petunia, where do you live now?"

"Madison," she said. "I can be there in less than four hours."

"Are your parents—"

"They're gone."

"I'm sorry," Nikki said. "Do you have family pictures, anything we can use to confirm that we're talking about the same person?"

"Of course," Petunia said. "I'll bring them with me."

"Perfect," Nikki said. "Do you remember anything about what the man looked like?"

"Are you kidding? I remember him like it happened yesterday. I made sure I didn't forget his face."

Petunia's words seemed to jolt everyone's system into overdrive, the energy in the room shifting. Nikki looked around the table at her colleagues and knew they felt it too. Nikki tried to temper her expectations, but the thought of reuniting Joyce with a family member was exhilarating. "Did the man say anything to you?"

"Not a single word," Petunia said. "He just watched us. I remember thinking that he was mentally slow, that maybe he was lost. I asked him if he was okay, and he smiled." Petunia's voice shook. "I've had nightmares about that smile ever since. We tried to run, but he was strong and fast."

"Would you be willing to sit with a sketch artist?"

"Absolutely."

Adrenaline brought Nikki to her feet. She rested her hands against the table, trying to keep the excitement out of her voice. The last thing she wanted to do was give Petunia false hope. "I need you to go to the Madison bureau office. I'll call them and tell them to expect you. They have a very good sketch artist."

"Why can't I come there?" Petunia asked. "If Daisy is in that area, I want to be there."

"You can come here, but if you sit down with the Madison guys, we can have a composite to put out to the media much sooner."

"Then I'll do it," Petunia said.

As soon as the call ended, Nikki went into attack mode. "By this time tomorrow, we'll have a composite sketch of this bastard. The image might be twenty years old, but someone's got to recognize a younger version of him." This was the break they'd been waiting for—she felt it in her bones. "DM Holdings. What a bastard."

"She must have told him her name after he took her," Nash said. "Unless he already knew it."

"He probably did," Liam said. "Stranger abduction is still rare, and if he didn't know her, my bet is that he'd been watching the family. He could have been there on vacation too."

"I'll call the Madison guys and get them on board."

"Tell them to email the sketch the second it's done," Nikki said. "We'll need to run the photo through VICAP. It's possible he has a record, even if it's just misdemeanors."

Liam grabbed his notes and went into the adjacent empty office to call the Madison office.

"I have to do something," Nash said. "Just sitting around here is making me crazy."

"We need to be ready to move quickly," Nikki said. "Once the composite comes in, we'll get it to the media." She was still thinking about the criminal database. Before Petunia's call, they hadn't known enough about the kidnapper to narrow down the search parameters. "Miller, can you go through the Washington County criminal records between 1995 and 2000?"

"We just finished digitizing everything a couple of months ago," he said.

"Look for any reports or arrests about peeping Toms, inappropriate contact with a minor." They'd scoured the sex offender registry, but now that they had a location for Joyce's initial kidnapping along with more details, they could look at county and state arrest records, as well as complaints filed but never charged.

"My gut tells me that he watches girls before he takes them," Nikki said. "If he took all of our victims, then he knew if they were foster kids and vulnerable. From the way Petunia described it, he wasn't afraid of getting caught. He knew they'd wandered away from their parents, and he knew which one of the sisters he wanted." She logged into her computer and pulled up the FBI's criminal database. "Joyce might not be the first child he took, either. We need to look at attempted abductions prior to 1995 too. Justin, why don't you call the Duluth police and tell them we're looking for someone who kidnapped a child from the area in 1995? Ask them to send you copies of the case file, including the missing person's report for Daisy Williams, Joyce's real name. Ask them to go back through the year prior and see if there are any reports of a man watching kids near a school, park, that sort of thing. Can you do that?"

Nash already had his phone out, looking for the Duluth police's phone number. Finding anything helpful from the records was unlikely, but it was worth checking and it would keep Nash occupied for a while. Nikki knew how miserable it was to sit around, feeling helpless.

"Where are you with the council members' financials?" she asked Miller.

"Working on the warrant," he said. "It might be hard to get a judge to sign off without more evidence against the council members. Is that your phone ringing?"

"Shit." Nikki grabbed her phone, hoping she hadn't missed Courtney's call. "Hey, Court, sorry. I had the volume down. You're on speaker with Nikki, Nash, and Miller."

"Rory isn't the father of Becky's baby," Courtney blurted out.

Nikki's body seemed to turn to jelly. "You're certain?" Maybe the news would be enough to get Rory to talk to Miller and come clean about whatever he knew.

"As a heart attack," Courtney said. "There's more too. I was able to get DNA from one of the fetal remains in that cellar you guys found yesterday. Becky's baby and at least one of the remains from the cellar have the same genetic abnormality. Both infants appear to be carriers of Down's syndrome, and they each have the same chromosome translocation, meaning the same parent passed down the genetic mutation."

"What does that mean?" Miller asked. "Becky's baby had Down's syndrome?"

"No, only a carrier," Courtney said. "This sort of thing usually runs in families. The other fetal remains weren't as developed, so it's impossible to tell if they were simply carriers or would have been born with Down's syndrome."

"Just to clarify," Nikki said, her eyes on Miller, "you are telling us that Becky Anderson's baby has the same genetic footprint as one of the fetuses in the abandoned cellar."

"Not the entire genetic footprint, but Becky doesn't have the translocation. Neither do any of the three females found in the cellar, but at least one infant does."

"How frequently does this translocation happen?" Nash asked.

"It's responsible for around three percent of Down's syndrome babies," Courtney said. "So, if you're asking whether or not this could be a coincidence, I'd say it's highly unlikely. Whoever fathered Becky's baby also fathered the ones in the cellar."

Nikki couldn't believe it. She was right: all the cases were connected to the same kidnapper. This twisted killer had been doing this for years. Her heart started to pound as her brain went into overdrive. "Thanks, Court. We'll check back in with you tonight."

She put the phone down and then realized something.

She looked across the table at Miller.

"Didn't you tell me that a genetic mutation ran in the Briggs family, and that's why they only had one biological child?"

Miller nodded, his expression grim. "I did background checks on both Jay Briggs and his father. Jay had a DUI a few years back, but other than that, there's nothing. And the other foster kid I spoke to—"

"Was a boy," Nikki cut him off. "Briggs's preference seems to be for girls. Look, I wasn't there for your interviews and I know you don't suspect them, but I bet if we get a full list of foster kids that went through that home, we'll see complaints here and there that probably weren't taken seriously by the social worker."

"We checked him out. The social worker didn't flag anything. Why would they ignore complaints?" Nash asked. "Their job is to protect kids."

Had he ever really worked in the field? Or did he just not pay enough attention? "The system is overwhelmed. Social workers do the best they can, but kids fall through the cracks. They don't have enough help." She glanced at Miller. "Where do the Briggses live?"

"South Washington County," Miller said. "Near Afton. He's got a few acres, but the satellite pictures don't show any outbuildings." He turned his laptop so she could see it. Miller pointed to the L-shaped ranch house sitting in the middle of several acres of trees.

Nikki tapped the screen to make the image bigger. She didn't see any other structures near the house, but that didn't mean much.

Satellite images and Google Earth weren't always up to date. Every cell in her body wanted to take over and tell Miller to get ready to raid the Briggses' place, but she had to remember this was his county, and he knew the residents better than her.

"How do you want to approach this?" she asked him. "We'll follow your lead, but we need to pay them a visit."

Miller drummed his fingers on the table, lost in thought. "The elder Briggs is in a wheelchair. He's paralyzed from the waist down, so he won't get far. But the Briggses are hunters... which means they're likely armed to the teeth. If it is them, we'll have a fight on our hands."

"Jay Briggs is cocky," Nikki said. "He doesn't think he'll get caught, and that makes him even more dangerous."

"He could be innocent," Nash interjected. "It could just be his dad."

"But he's in a wheelchair now," Nikki said. "Someone has to have helped him. Rory seems certain he had something to do with Becky's disappearance—"

A sudden, terrible thought occurred to Nikki. Rory seemed determined to make sure Jay Briggs was held accountable for Becky's murder. His reaction when she'd mentioned finding remains in the abandoned house near Cottage Grove had been strange, but she'd chalked it up to anger and alcohol. She unlocked her phone and called Rory, praying he answered. Her anxiety went up with every unanswered ring. "Voicemail," she muttered, looking at Miller. "I can't reach Rory. He's hell-bent on getting justice against Jay Briggs. He might be there already."

Miller cursed, shoving his chair away from the table. "I'll drive."

TWENTY-SIX

Miller wanted to keep a low profile, so they crammed into his SUV. "I've got deputies en route." He whipped around a tight curve. "They're going to stay out of sight and set up a perimeter."

Liam nodded, but Nash simply stared out the window, endlessly tapping his foot.

Nikki wiped her sweating palms on her jeans. The Kevlar they wore made her body heat ratchet up several degrees. Given the others' sweating faces, Nikki wasn't the only one.

"How close are we to the Briggses' place?" Nikki had tried Rory twice more, but he still wasn't answering. She'd told him where they were headed and why. If Rory had been able to receive the message, he would have called and argued with her. Instead she'd had radio silence. Nikki couldn't stop thinking about the look in his eyes when he talked about Briggs. If he'd decided on vigilante justice, Nikki wasn't sure how she would be able to help him.

"Ten minutes at most," Miller said. "If Rory figured it out when you told him about the abandoned house, why didn't he say something? He knows Jay's got a temper."

"Because he's blindsided by anger and the need for revenge," Nikki said. She'd texted Mark, knowing the brothers were in constant contact throughout the day, and he hadn't heard from him either. If he planned on doing something to Briggs, Rory wouldn't have involved any member of his family.

"Briggs never said Rory did anything," Miller said. "He only corroborated what Becky's friends saw. He was at the bowling alley with other friends that night."

"He showed us the postcards from Becky," Liam said in disgust. "Two from Minneapolis, with the downtown skyline, a third one saying she'd moved to Wisconsin, and it was postmarked in Madison. If it is them then they must have written those themselves in case anyone ever came looking for her."

"Did Jay Briggs work for McFarland back then too?" Nikki asked, thinking of the construction site where Becky's body had been found.

"No," Miller said. "But he knew Rory did, and he knew how much Rory and Becky fought."

"Something's still bugging me," Nikki said. "Let's say this is Briggs, and his home has been the epicenter of this trafficking ring for years—how did nobody notice? How did they keep all those girls so out of sight that even Becky's boyfriend didn't see them? If Joyce was taken in '95, then Briggs had her while Becky lived with them. But Rory hasn't mentioned anything like that..."

Miller shook his head. "None of our witnesses did. None of Becky's friends mentioned anyone else living with them at that time. Maybe that old house is big enough he could have kept Joyce hidden. Or maybe he kept her in Cottage Grove, where he buried the girls who got pregnant in the cellar."

"When did Mr. Briggs become paralyzed?" Nikki asked.

"Four, five years ago," Miller said. "He told Liam and I that he was fixing shingles and fell."

"That might be the truth," Nikki said. But she wondered about Jay's violence. Could he have been behind things from the beginning? "What happened to the wife?" Nikki asked.

"Cancer, I think," Miller said.

"She either knew and didn't care, or she kept her head in the sand."

Nikki kept thinking about her conversation with Rory in the jail. A terrible realization had started to sink in: Becky must have told Rory about the baby that night. He hadn't trusted Nikki enough to tell her, even if it meant clearing his name. She brushed the thought aside, feeling ridiculous for making it so personal. Rory trusted her, but she was a part of a system that had wronged his family.

Nikki could feel her adrenaline rising, and she knew she wasn't the only one. She twisted around to look at Nash. "I know this is a tough pill to swallow, but we need to follow Miller's lead. He knows these people, and we don't."

Nash's chin jutted out. "If Joyce is in that house, I'm going in after her."

Miller glared at him in the rearview mirror. "No, you won't. If she's still alive, you'll wind up getting her killed."

The radio came to life. "We have a 10-13 on 151 Lang Road," the dispatcher said, using the code for shots fired. Nikki's mouth had gone dry.

Miller grabbed his mic and accelerated. "We're en route."

"Is that Briggs's place?" Nash asked.

Miller nodded. "We're two miles out."

The two miles seemed to take an eternity, despite Miller driving at ninety miles an hour. Nikki readied her Glock, double-checking that she had extra ammunition. She couldn't shake the feeling that something was terribly wrong. She was rusty, Nikki reminded herself, and running on little sleep or food.

Miller turned sharply into a gravel driveway. A wooden wheel-chair ramp stretched the entire length of the ranch house.

"Whose truck is that?" Liam asked.

Nikki couldn't breathe. "It's Rory's."

Miller hit the brakes, and the vehicle skidded to a stop several feet from the house. Nikki grabbed the door handle, but she realized Miller had put the child locks on. "Unlock my door," she demanded.

"You really think that's a good idea?" Miller said. "Rory might be hurt. Or he could have done something really, really bad."

"I know." She kept her voice low and calm. "It's your show, I promise." She'd promised Hernandez on her first day back that she would be able to compartmentalize things and that she would not push the envelope if she was too close to a case. She owed it to him to keep that promise.

"Nash, stay back and listen to Agent Hunt." Miller released the locks and opened the door. "You all have vests on, right?"

Nikki and the others confirmed they'd put on the Kevlar. Her heart beat hard against her chest as she opened her door and slipped out of the vehicle, making sure to stay behind the safety of the metal. "We'll cover you."

Her heart stuck in her throat as Miller slowly approached the house. Even with the vest, he was a sitting duck. A lousy marksman still had a good chance at a successful head shot. Miller had two daughters and a loving wife. Nikki couldn't imagine having to tell them that Miller had been killed in the line of duty. She said a silent plea for him to stay safe.

Brandishing his revolver, Miller reached the end of the ramp. "Jay Briggs, we need to talk to you and your father. I know shots have been fired. Come on out here."

Long seconds passed, the heat beating down on Nikki's back. Sweat stung her eyes. Behind her, Nash stepped out of the SUV, staying behind his door as well. Liam had done the same, and all three had their guns pointed at the house.

"Jay, get out here," Miller called again, inching closer to the ramp. "You don't want me to involve SWAT." He crouched beneath the front window and started inching up the ramp.

The front door swung open. Nikki waited for the hail of bullets. Instead, Jay Briggs sauntered out onto the deck, shirtless and barefoot, a beer in one hand and a sandwich in the other. "What's this about, Sheriff?"

Even at a distance, Nikki could tell he was under the influence of something. He seemed to have trouble standing still, and his face was red and sweaty. Nikki looked him up and down for any sign of blood spatter, but she only saw dirt on his jeans.

"Where's Rory Todd?" Miller asked. "We know that's his truck."

"Rory's an old friend. He's visiting." Jay looked at Nikki and smirked. "Agent Hunt, nice to see you again. Guess you really are a mind reader." Jay burst out laughing at his pathetic joke. "You knew poor old Rory needed you."

Nikki eased out from behind the door. "What did you do to him?"

"I didn't do anything," Jay said.

"Shots were fired. Who did you shoot?" Miller demanded.

"My father," Jay said simply. "I've had enough of the old bastard."

Nikki wasn't sure if she believed him or not. She kept scanning the windows, trying to see if anyone else with a weapon was inside.

"Is he the father of Becky's baby?" Miller asked.

Jay spit a chunk of half-chewed sandwich onto the ramp. "You'd have to ask him. Too bad he's dead."

"Jay, you do understand that I have to arrest you for shooting your father. Is he still alive?" Miller asked.

Jay sneered at him. "Why don't you come in and find out?"

"Where's Joyce?" Nash demanded, abandoning his cover. "We know your father kidnapped her when she was a kid. Did you bring her back as some kind of warped prize for Daddy?"

Jay stilled. "Don't talk about my father like that."

"Like what? The truth?"

"Justin, be careful," Nikki hissed. "We don't know if he's telling the truth. His father could have a gun on us right now."

"Agent Hunt," Jay said. "Why don't you come inside and see your boyfriend? I'm sure you have lots of questions for him."

Nikki glanced at Miller. He nodded.

"If that's what you want." Nikki started walking slowly toward the house. She knew it could be a mistake, but she didn't have any option if she wanted to find Joyce and Rory alive.

"Leave the gun."

She set the Glock on the ground, never breaking eye contact with Jay. She'd stuffed her utility knife into her boot. Hopefully Jay wasn't smart or sober enough to search her for other weapons.

He crooked his finger at her. Nikki eased closer, slipping past Miller at the end of the ramp. "Careful," he whispered.

Nikki held up her hands and walked up the ramp. Jay looked her up and down, licking his lips. "You are a beautiful woman," he said. He tossed the remainder of the sandwich into the trash can next to the door. "I might be persuaded to let your boyfriend leave if you stay."

Nikki's knees felt weak, but she couldn't let Jay know how afraid she was for Rory. He stepped out of her path and motioned for her to go inside. "Ladies first."

Nikki had already caught the whiff of decay. How long had Mr. Briggs been dead, and who else had Jay taken out? She hesitated, thinking of Lacey. She only had one parent now, and Nikki should have thought about that before she accepted Jay's invitation to come inside. But it was too late to turn back now. She glanced back at the team. Nash white-knuckled, his gun still braced against the back passenger door. Liam stood in front of the vehicle, calm and collected. Nikki took a deep breath and stepped inside.

Mr. Briggs's wheelchair sat next to an old easy chair. The old man's head slumped forward, his chin on his chest. A chunk of his brain was stuck to the wall behind him.

"Dear old Dad." Jay laughed manically.

Nikki tried to put the dead man out of her mind and get a sense of her surroundings. The living room opened into the kitchen, and Nikki assumed the single hallway led to the bathroom and bedrooms. The house hadn't been well taken care of, with the carpet ripped up in places and several cabinet doors missing. Her heart lodged in her chest at the sight of Rory sitting in a plastic chair, slumped over like Mr. Briggs. "Rory," Nikki screamed. "Look at me."

His head shot up at the sound of her voice, and he stared at her in confusion. His hands were bound, and he had a cut on the top on his forehead. "What are you doing here?"

Nikki's legs went weak with relief. "My job, you fool. What are you doing here?"

"Getting his ass kicked," Jay said gleefully.

"Did he hit an artery?" Nikki moved toward him, but Jay caught her arm and yanked her against him.

"He'd be dead by now if I did," Jay snapped.

Rory started to get up, but Nikki shook her head. "Just stay there and rest. Jay and I need to talk, anyway."

Grinning, Jay retrieved a .357 from behind a raggedy pillow at the end of the couch and then sat down. He patted the cushion next to him. "Sit."

Nikki obeyed, the smell of death and body odor almost gagging her. The only chance they had was for her to convince Jay that she was here to help him. She positioned herself so that Mr. Briggs's body was out of her eyeline.

"I know I'm going to jail," Jay said. "I just want my story told. I want it to be accurate. I've seen things you couldn't imagine."

Nikki doubted that, but she nodded. "You can still be the hero, Jay."

He snorted, spittle landing on his chin. "You think I'm going to fall for that?"

"I'm serious," she said. "If your father is the abusive one, if he kidnapped Joyce and not you. You were still a kid yourself, growing up in a home with a dangerous pedophile." She put her hand on his sweating arm and tried not to grimace from the touch. "You're a victim too."

His gaze bored into hers. "More than you know."

"Then tell us," Nikki said. "Let Rory go and tell us where Joyce is. I know your father made you take her," she lied.

"He never got over that bitch," Jay said, spittle at the corners of his mouth. "I knew when he brought her home she'd be trouble."

Nikki wanted to ask where Jay's mother had been during all this, but she had to stay focused on him. "And he didn't listen to you," she said. "Even though you were a kid, you knew better than him. I'm sure you didn't want to hurt anyone."

"No jury's going to believe that," Jay said. "He was a cripple, and I killed him."

"Your father subjected you to this horrible lifestyle, and if he's mentally abused you for your entire life and you never had a choice, I think they'll listen to that," Nikki said. "I'll help you."

Jay's eyes glazed over. "You'd do that for me?"

"If it's the truth," she said. "If your father made you take Joyce, made you kill the Kendricks and Cat."

"I didn't kill Mr. Kendrick," Jay said, almost in a trance. "Mae did that. Set the poor bastard on fire in the garage. She thought we'd leave together."

His tone shifted just enough for Nikki to hear the anguish in his voice. "You cared about Mae?"

"I loved her," Jay said. "I always have."

"Did your father introduce you to her too?"

Jay nodded. "He let me keep one for my own. Mae was everything to me. She only married that old pig Kendrick for access to his company. Worked great until the tax audit. She wasn't good with the money." He glared at the gun in his hand. "Dad said the only way for us to stay out of prison was to kill her. He made me do it."

"I believe you." Nikki needed to keep him talking and distract him from whatever the others were doing outside. She knew they weren't sitting around, waiting for her to come out. She just hoped Jay was too high to figure that out too.

"Makes me sick to have to replace her," Jay mumbled. "And that girl's going to need to be cleaned thoroughly before I touch her. God knows where else she's been."

Was he talking about Sylvia? Joyce? Or did he have another child locked up?

Rory's hands clenched into fists. "Like you did to Becky?"

"No, no." Jay wagged his finger. "That was Dad, not me."

"Jay, how many girls did your father kidnap over the years?" Nikki asked. "Do you know what happened to them?"

"Dozens," Jay said. "Joyce was the only one who stayed more than a couple of weeks."

"What happened to the others?" Nikki asked, trying to ignore the horrified expression in Rory's eyes.

"He never said." Jay started laughing, bouncing the .357 around. Nikki could tell the safety wasn't on. She debated trying to wrest it from him, but Jay was big and high on something. She might not be able to overpower him and she couldn't take that chance. "God, my bitch of a mother could have stopped it all. But she'd always wanted a girl, so she was thrilled to bits when he brought that kid home. She was trouble from the very beginning."

"Is she still alive?" Nikki asked.

He shrugged. "Last I checked."

"Where is she?"

Jay didn't answer.

"What about the girl Mae said was her daughter?"

"Don't worry about her," he said, his eyes heavy. "She'll be just fine."

Disgust rolled through Nikki, but she realized that meant that Sylvia could be alive too. She could be somewhere in the house. "Now, that's the attitude that won't help you, Jay. If your father—"

But Nikki didn't have a chance to say another word. Without warning, Jay's fingers met the trigger of the revolver, and all Nikki heard was the immense sound of the gunshot.

TWENTY-SEVEN

When Nikki heard the gunshot, it took everything she had to stay present. She thought of her father teaching her how to shoot, of going to the range with Tyler and taking so much joy in being a better shot than him. Every drill, every suspect, every assailant she had confronted in a situation like this flashed through her mind. She could smell the nitroglycerin, the bullet—hot, metallic, overwhelming. Her eyes had closed involuntarily, but as she opened them, she realized she felt no pain. She hadn't been hit. And neither had Rory.

Jay had put the end of the revolver in his mouth and pulled the trigger. His neck had snapped back from the force of the bullet. It shattered his skull and came through the back, embedding into the couch frame. Jay stared up at the ceiling, blood trickling down his mouth.

The sound of the gunshot seemed to ricochet between Nikki's eardrums. Vomit rose in her throat. She heard Rory calling her name, sounding like he was trapped inside an echo chamber.

The front door broke off its hinges. Liam rushed inside, followed by Nash and Miller.

"I'm okay," Nikki said, her ears still clogged. "He was talking one minute and eating a bullet the next."

"Where's Joyce?" Nash barreled into the house, frantic. "Are they both dead? Did he tell you where he'd hidden Joycie?"

"No." Nikki broke away from her shock and went to Rory, who sat motionless in the kitchen. He hadn't moved since Jay's head snapped back. "Don't look," she told him as she used her pocketknife in her boot to cut the zip ties. "Where's Joyce and the other little girl?"

"I... I don't know."

"What were you thinking?" Miller demanded. "He could have killed you." The words smacked Nikki in the chest, and she leaned against the chair. "Lacey would have been devastated, but I couldn't do anything once you started walking in."

She looked at Rory. "Exactly what did he tell you?"

Rory closed his eyes. "I don't know if I can even say it out loud."

"You'd better, because Joyce is still out there," Nash snapped.

"Becky came here after the bowling alley that night to tell them she was pregnant. She told me it was someone else's, that she didn't even know his name. I had no idea what they were doing to her." Tears rolled down his face. "I knew she had issues with the both of them, but until now, I never dreamed they were raping her. If she would have told me—"

"You and Jay lost touch sometime after the breakup," Miller said. "Were you still friends with him at that point? Didn't you ask him if he'd talked to his foster sister?"

Rory wiped the moisture off his face. "She wasn't real family, and I knew they'd never bonded. I asked if they'd heard from her a couple of weeks later, and they said she'd sent a postcard telling them she was going to give the baby up for adoption. He told me that she was supposed to come by that night and pack up the rest of her stuff, but she didn't. That's why they had called the police initially, but then they got the postcard."

"Did Jay tell you why they killed her?" Liam asked.

"Jay said that she still had a key and walked in on them with the little girl." Rory shuddered. "They had to get rid of her. Those were his exact words."

"Joyce?" Nash's voice cracked.

Rory nodded. "Becky tried to help her instead of running and calling the police. She never had a chance."

"I've got deputies on the way, plus two search and rescue volunteers," Miller said. "We'll dig up the entire property if we have to."

Nikki took Rory by the shoulders. "I need you to think about every second of your conversation with Jay. Did he say anything about a garage or shed? Other property?"

"I didn't get a chance to ask. I tried to get Jay to come outside, but his dad tricked me. Jay snuck up behind me and hit me with something." He rubbed the back of his head. "Then he pulled out that gun and shot his father."

"Try not to think about that right now," Nikki said soothingly. "You didn't see Joyce or anyone else in the house?"

"No, but there's a padlocked door in the basement."

"Miller, you have bolt cutters?" Nikki asked.

"I'll get them," he said.

"I'll go," Nikki said. "You guys check out the rest of the house and the door. Did you call an ambulance?"

Miller nodded. "They can't be too far out now. The cutters are in the utility box in the back of my SUV."

Nikki held out her hand to Rory. His pale, sweaty skin and clammy hand told her that he was still in shock, but he let her pull him up and guide him outside.

Nikki gulped clean air. Her ears were still ringing from the sound of the gunshot, but she was starting to hear better. "Sit down on the ramp and don't move," Nikki told Rory.

She stumbled off the porch toward the SUV. Her hands trembled as she sifted through Miller's supplies. She finally found the sharp cutters and started back toward the house, trying to work out what Jay had said about his replacement for Mae.

He'd said she would have to be cleaned. At the time, Nikki

assumed he meant because other men had already forced themselves on her, but now she wondered if it had meant that he stashed her somewhere dirty. Jay hadn't acted suicidal, and Nikki was fairly certain he'd acted on impulse, which meant the girl and possibly Joyce could still be alive. She knelt in front of Rory. "I need to give these bolt cutters to Miller. Stay here and wait for the ambulance, okay?"

He nodded, leaning his forehead against Nikki's. "I'm sorry," he whispered.

"I know. Stay here." She hurried back into the house. Liam was carefully searching Jay's pockets. He looked at Nikki and shook his head. "Nothing. I checked the old man too."

Nikki handed Miller the bolt cutters. "See if you can use these to get the basement door open. I'm going to look out back."

The sliding door to the deck stuck, but Nikki wrestled it open. Jay took even less care of the yard than the house. Dead grass and junk were everywhere. Nikki scanned the area, uncertain of exactly what she expected to see. She'd been afraid that Jay had buried Sylvia or stashed her somewhere as awful as the old, abandoned cellar, but there hadn't been any digging in the yard. She didn't see any other structures for him to hide them.

She turned to head back and help search the basement, nearly slamming into a white-faced Liam. "They're dead, aren't they?"

"No one's down there. But it's clearly the place Jay takes his victims."

The last of Nikki's hopes sank. "They're probably already dead."

"What a pigsty." Liam leaned against the deck rail, the back of his shirt damp with sweat. "Except for this wheelchair ramp. This thing looks even sturdier than the one up front. Too bad Jay's life was ruined by his dad. He had some talent as a carpenter."

"He said his dad groomed him," Nikki said. "He got Mae for him, supposedly." Nikki walked down the ramp, admiring the detail work. Unlike the one up front, this was made from high-end wood, and Jay had even put some kind of faux exterior on the base so that the ramp looked like it was a part of the house. "Why would he spend so much time making this ramp blend with the house? I've never seen one enclosed like this."

She walked to the far end of the ramp. Wood had been piled all the way to the top of the ramp. Nikki removed the first couple of logs, revealing a crudely cut door on hinges. A pair of blue eyes suddenly appeared in the gap between the door and the deck. Nikki reared back in shock, nearly falling. Delicate fingers rested on either side of the terrified eyes. She could see Sylvia peering through the hole.

Nikki crept forward, trying to find her voice. "I'm going to get you out of there. Is Joyce with you?"

"Yes, but she's not awake. I think she's really hurt."

"Okay, Sylvia—"

"That's not my name. It's Carly, and I want to go home."

EPILOGUE

"Mommy." Twenty-five pounds of happiness bounced up and down on the bed. "Come on. We're going to be late. You can't be late for your own party."

Nikki laughed. She hadn't celebrated her birthday in a few years, but now had seemed like a good time to start. The last six months had been a harsh reminder to celebrate life instead of grumbling about being another year older.

"Uncle Mark said I can jump in the pool first though." Lacey wagged her finger. "Don't be getting any big ideas about upstaging me."

Rory watched from the doorway, smiling. He'd refused medical attention when the ambulance had arrived at the Briggses' house, telling Nikki that Sylvia and Joyce needed it more than he did.

Joyce had been touch and go for a while, the infection caused from the lack of care after she went into early labor eating away at her system. Nash hadn't left her side, but it had been her older sister's voice that made Joyce keep fighting. Petunia's face had been the first one she saw when she woke up the next day. Nikki had been lucky enough to witness the reunion, and she was still trying to process everything.

Joyce had been through a kind of hell most people only heard about, but the sight of her sister and the support of Nash had been all Joyce needed to recover.

After the initial sobbing fest, Joyce had asked about the Briggs men.

"They're both dead, baby," Nash had said, smoothing her hair back. "You're really free."

Two of the women's remains in the cellar in Wisconsin had been identified but little was known about their cause of death. Neither had been pregnant, and both had been unidentified for more than ten years. And Nikki and Liam were still trying to figure out exactly how far Jay's reach stretched: who his clients and friends were. His lair in the basement had been set up with a bed and video camera, along with his computer, which contained hundreds of thousands of images of minors—many he'd taken himself.

Joyce had told them that Mr. Briggs took her and molested her for a long time before he told Jay that he needed to be a part of the family business. She'd screamed and cried, begging Mrs. Briggs for help, but she either couldn't help or didn't care. Joyce had also confirmed what Jay had told Rory about the night Becky died. They were still waiting on the paternity tests to find out which one had fathered the child. Joyce hadn't seen Becky die, but she knew that Mr. Briggs had gone after her with a gun.

"Hey, Lace," Rory said. "I'm pretty sure that Mark said I could jump in the new pool first."

Lacey stopped jumping, her hands on her hips. "We'll see about that."

Nikki checked her reflection in the bathroom mirror one final time. Her skin was clear for the first time in days, her eyes beginning to look less tired. Rory came into the bathroom and wrapped his arm around her waist, burying his head in her neck. She'd convinced him to start therapy, and even though he hadn't had any sessions yet, the thought alone had helped him come to terms with

Becky's death, even though Nikki knew he'd have to work hard to get to a point where he didn't blame himself.

"Have I told you how good you look tonight?" he whispered into the shell of her ear.

"Yes, but you can say it again," she teased, turning around so she could kiss him. They both had a lot of issues to work through, but Nikki didn't care about any of that right now. Rory deepened the kiss, pulling her tightly against him. Nikki almost forgot her daughter was a mere few feet away until Lacey started yelling for them to hurry up.

Rory broke the kiss. "Guess the boss has spoken."

A LETTER FROM STACY

Thank you so much for reading *The Girl in the Ground* and the Nikki Hunt series.

If you enjoyed reading *The Girl in the Ground* and want to keep up to date with all my latest releases, just sign up at the following link. Your email address will never be shared and you can unsubscribe at any time.

www.bookouture.com/Stacy-Green

If you loved *The Girl in the Ground*, I would be very grateful if you could write a review. I'd love to hear what you think, and it makes such a difference helping new readers to discover one of my books for the first time.

I love hearing from my readers—you can get in touch on Facebook, Instagram or my website.

Thanks,

Stacy

stacygreenauthor.com

facebook.com/StacyGreenAuthor

twitter.com/StacyGreen26

instagram.com/authorstacygreen

ACKNOWLEDGMENTS

This book went through many trials and tribulations, and I want to thank my editor, Jennifer Hunt, for her patience and guidance. Research is one of my favorite parts about writing, and this book was no exception. The stunning rowhouse at 599 Summit Avenue in St. Paul is listed as a historical landmark, and F. Scott Fitzgerald did write *This Side of Paradise* during his time there. Summit Avenue is more majestic than I could describe, and I am so grateful to John Kelly for his help in making the locations in the book as accurate as possible.

Thank you to Rob and Grace for their tireless support and patience. Special thank you to Kristine Kelly for her honesty and friendship. To Jan Barton, thanks for being my second mom. It's helped more than you know.

The amazing Lisa Regan has been a fan of the series from day one, and I am so grateful for her support and encouragement. Special thanks to Maureen Downey and Teresa Russ for taking care of social media and other tasks that I just can't seem to get organized. I would be a mess without you both!

Made in the USA
Las Vegas, NV
24 December 2024

15283447R00142